COPYRIGHT

DEDICATION

To J. Moore: Thank you for caring enough to track this book. There is no bigger honor than a spreadsheet.

To Reggie T-S: Are you reading this on a flight somewhere exciting?

CHAPTER 1

With the worn-to-hell baseball cap pulled low over his face, Jeremy Jameson walked into the bar. At least he assumed it was a bar, based on the lopsided sign out front that simply said "Bar" in peeling red paint and the stench of beer and cigarette smoke that permeated the air. The interior space wasn't any cleaner or hipper than the parking lot.

Jeremy tried to remember the last time he had been in a club or bar or restaurant that wasn't sleek with carefully positioned lighting and well-maintained fixtures. Never. The answer to that question was never. Even musicians who started on the bottom and worked their way up probably wouldn't have come to a dive like this; it was too small, too out of the way, and it didn't have a stage or any room to set up equipment.

Internally lecturing himself for thinking about work when he was supposed to be taking time for himself, he forced himself to stop focusing on music and start focusing on beer. A place like this probably wouldn't have imports or microbrews. Maybe he'd ask for whatever they had on tap and call it done. Easier to blend in that way.

"What can I get you?" the whiskey-voiced bartender

asked the second Jeremy slid his butt onto the stool.

"A pint of whatever you have on tap."

"Coming right up."

Tugging the hat lower to make sure his famous green eyes were shadowed, Jeremy glanced around. It was early—seven o'clock on a Tuesday night—so the place was empty save for a table in back where a couple seemed to be arguing. Although for all he knew, the bar could be that empty every night. He'd never find out, because he had no plans to return to Munds Park, Arizona. The town didn't have a concert arena, and Jeremy couldn't think of any other reason to be there.

"Here you go, man." The bartender slid the cool glass in front of him and then wiped his hands on the towel he had tucked into his baggy Levi's. "So what brings you in tonight? Passing through town or looking to hide from the world?"

Both, actually, and the fact that the stranger knew that sent Jeremy's stomach dropping. He jerked his head up, which meant the man could see his eyes, and then he darted his gaze around the bar, fully expecting to find a gang of paparazzi equipped with cameras and microphones. Instead he saw the same grungy brown walls, scratched wood tables, and sticky concrete floor.

"Hey, I didn't mean anything by it," the bartender said good-naturedly. He patted Jeremy's shoulder. "Just shootin' the shit, you know?" He waved his hand around the bar slowly. "It's pretty dead in here."

Realizing his overreaction to the innocuous comment

was obvious, Jeremy felt his cheeks heat. His attempt at being normal had pretty much consisted of hiding in less glamorous locations than his usual haunts and sitting in the driver's seat of a rented sedan instead of the back of a luxury car or tour bus or private plane. Same life, different scenery.

Drawing in a deep breath, he met the bartender's gaze, figuring he had either already blown his attempt at going incognito, or the dim light in the space combined with his well-placed hat were offering sufficient cover to keep his face hidden. "Sorry. I, uh, didn't mean to..." He had no idea how to finish his sentence without admitting the reason for his strange behavior.

"No sweat, man," the bartender said easily. He rubbed his hand over the back of his closely shorn brown hair and grinned. "Everyone needs space once in a while." He started walking toward the other end of the bar, presumably to give Jeremy exactly that. "Holler when you're ready for another drink."

The booted feet had taken only two steps before Jeremy inexplicably said, "Both."

His eyebrows arched in question, the guy looked back over his broad shoulder, his brown eyes focused on Jeremy.

Usually he didn't like having people stare at him, but the bartender had seemed genuinely interested in chatting with him. He didn't know who Jeremy was, so that meant his interest wasn't in selling information to the magazines or gathering facts like a scientist examining a bug. He just wanted to talk. It was refreshing.

"You asked if I was passing through town or if I was looking to hide from the world." Lowering his gaze, Jeremy swallowed hard and said, "I'm doing both."

"Yeah?" The man turned on his heel and returned. "Cool. Where're you from?"

A simple question. Relaxing at the novelty of it, he kept looking the guy in the face. "California."

"Northern or Southern?" the bartender asked. "I was in a frat in college, and we had a bunch of guys from Cali." He shrugged. "Guess our out-of-state tuition's lower than your in-state. Anyway, the NoCal-SoCal rivalry was legendary."

Jeremy could have gone to college—he'd had the option even though his grades in high school hadn't been great—but he'd never had any desire or seen the point. Music was his life, had always been his life, and he had figured no professor could teach him as much about it as he already knew or could learn from his father's friends. Fourteen years recording albums, touring the world, and winning awards had proven him right. At thirty-one, he was at the top of his game. No degree needed.

"All right, so listen to this," the bartender said, smoothly moving on when Jeremy didn't answer his question. "This one semester, the guy in charge of the pledge class—" He paused and furrowed his brow in concentration. "Feltus was his name, I think. Anyway, he was from Palo Alto, and there were like five dudes in the pledge class from OC." He chuckled. "So one night, during hell week, Feltus takes the pledges out to the desert—this was in Tempe; I went to

ASU—and he has them dig holes in the ground. Then he tells the SoCal guys to get in, has the other pledges bury them up to their necks, and makes everyone pile into their cars and drive back to campus." The bartender shook his head. "Fuckin' crazy rivalry, man. I tell you."

People said rock stars were wild, but Jeremy hadn't ever seen anybody get buried alive. Oddly fascinated by the story, he rested his forearms on the bar, leaned forward, and said, "Then what happened? Did anybody get hurt?"

"Nah." The bartender shook his head. "It sounds worse than it was. It's not like the dirt was packed or anything. The guys were able to get themselves out, and right after, a few of the other pledges drove back and picked them up."

"They must have been terrified," Jeremy said, shaking his head.

"It was hell week," he said with a snort. "They were too fucked up to be terrified."

Jeremy chuckled, took a drink of his beer, and sighed contentedly, feeling relaxed for the first time in a long time. It was nice to sit and chat with someone about nothing for no reason.

"I'm Reggie, by the way." The bartender wiped his hand on the towel and then extended it over the bar. "Reggie Moore. But everyone calls me Reg."

After sliding his palm on his gray skinny jeans, Jeremy held it out and shook Reg's hand. "Nice to meet you, Reg. I'm—" He paused, trying to decide if he should stop there, give a fake name, or be honest. He landed on something in between. "Jeremy."

"What brings you to Munds Park on this fine Tuesday evening, Jeremy?" Reg snagged the almost-empty glass, held it under the tap, and refilled it. "You on your way to Flag?"

"Uh…"

Jeremy's confused expression must have given Reg his answer.

"All right, that's a negative on the journey to Flagstaff." He leaned over the bar and perused Jeremy, or at least as much of Jeremy as he could see considering the lighting was crap and Jeremy was seated. "No dirt all over your clothes, so you can't be on your way back from the canyon—"

"I am, actually," Jeremy corrected him.

"Oh really? Cool. Did you hike the south rim? I do that trail a few times a year. Did you go to 'Supai Falls?"

"No, I didn't hike. Didn't have time. I just wanted to see it. I've lived one state over most of my life, and I've never been." Raising his hand to drag it through his hair, Jeremy hit the baseball cap, which reminded him to be careful sharing too much information, no matter how minor, with a stranger. People had a way of twisting things around when they sold them to the highest bidder looking for a catchy headline: "Jeremy Jameson Jumps into Grand Canyon in Drunken Craze."

"You look like you're in good shape, man. You've got to hike it next time," Reg said excitedly. "The falls are amazing."

Hopping around on stage night after night required a hell of lot of energy and stamina, which wasn't as easy in his thirties as it had been in his twenties. Jeremy had a concert tour starting in just over a week, so he had upped his normal exercise routine. It seemed the results were evident, which made him puff up.

"I'll do that," he said, more to be polite than because he meant it. The reality was, he didn't know when he'd next have free time, and scheduling a hiking trip would probably give his manager a coronary.

"Cool." Reg beamed. "Let me go check on those guys"— he nudged his chin in the direction of the only other people in the bar—"and then I'll tell you the best spot to camp."

Stopping in for one drink turned into spending the entire evening at the bar, sipping mediocre beer and having a great conversation. People came in and out, having a drink, bending Reg's ear about their concern with the state of politics or what team stood a chance that season or whatever issue they were having with their girlfriend or wife. And in between those conversations, Reg always returned to Jeremy, smiling and chatting, sharing funny stories and asking questions that didn't seem designed to do anything but get to know him. Jeremy was having a better time than he could ever remember.

After a mutual laughing fit about yet another of Reg's college tales, Reg put an end to Jeremy's joy by saying, "Hey, Jeremy, man, I don't want to rush you out of here, but we usually close at midnight during the week, and it's almost one."

"Oh." Suddenly feeling sober and tense again, Jeremy

rubbed his hand over his nose and reached for his leather jacket, which he'd tossed over the empty barstool next to him hours earlier. "Sure. Yeah. Sorry about that." He pulled a handful of bills out of his wallet and threw them on the bar, not bothering to count them. "Keep the change."

Keys in hand, Jeremy climbed off his stool, planning to leave the bar. He was surprised when Reg darted his upper body forward and snagged his keys.

"Hold on, man. It's late and you're drunk. Is there someone who can come pick you up?"

Jeremy snorted. "No. I'm in, uh...." He tried to remember the name of the nothing little town. "Whatever Park." He rolled his eyes. "Why would I know anybody *here*?"

"Wow. I've had people turn into violent shitheads when I cut them off, but snobby diva is new." Reg flung his ever-present towel into the bar sink and locked up the register. "I was going to offer you my couch for the night, 'cause there aren't any motels in walking distance, and I have better beer than we serve here, but you can go ahead and sleep it off in your car, superstar. I'll bring you your keys in the morning."

"Oh." Hearing that Reg hadn't been throwing him out but had, instead, been trying to change locations, vanquished Jeremy's resurfacing tension. With that relief came the realization that he had acted like all the stuck-up assholes he couldn't stand. "Crap." Falling into a nervous childhood habit he hadn't been fully able to shake, Jeremy tugged the collar of his salmon-colored T-shirt into his mouth and chewed on it. "I didn't mean to, uh..." He rubbed his palm over his eyes.

"I'm sorry that I..." A thought slammed into him, making him flinch and then gape at Reg. "You called me superstar."

"I also called you a snobby diva." Reg arched his eyebrows. "Are you ready to earn a spot on my couch and a bottle of Kilt Lifter by playing nice?"

"Yeah, I, uh, don't know why I said that. I'm not usually, uh..."

"Stuck up?" Reg grinned while he said the word, somehow making it seem more like friendly banter than an insult. "An entitled prick?" He stepped out from behind the bar, still smiling. With both of them standing, Jeremy realized Reg was at least half a foot taller than him. "Such a douche nozzle?" He playfully bumped his arm against Jeremy's shoulder. "Stop me anytime, man. I'm running out of words here."

"Do you know who I am?" Jeremy asked as they walked side by side to the door.

"Are you being a conceited dick again?"

"No. No." Jeremy held up both hands in protest. "I'm serious. You called me..." He sighed, took his hat off, and wiped it against his brow. "Never mind."

"Purple, huh?" Reg asked, glancing at Jeremy's hair. He flicked off the light and then pushed the door open and held it with an outstretched arm, leaving room for Jeremy to pass. "Looks good. You're into the colored hair, right? I think I remember seeing a picture when it was green."

Standing in the cool night air, Jeremy watched Reg lock up. "So you do know who I am?"

"Man, I don't live under a rock. 'Course I know who you are." He turned around and started walking, twirling the key ring over his finger. "At first I didn't, because it's dark in there, but we've been talking for, what? Six hours straight?" He shook his head. "It's not like I can't see your face."

Following a few steps behind, Jeremy processed the comment. The fact that Reg recognized him wasn't a surprise. In fact, the opposite would have been hard to believe. But he wasn't acting like most—or really any—people did when they met *The Jeremy Jameson*.

"Why aren't you freaking out?"

"Dude." Reg shook his head and laughed. "You sure do think a lot of yourself."

"No, I don't." Jeremy rushed forward so he could catch up to Reg. "It's just that usually people act different when they meet me."

"Oh." Reg was quiet for a beat. "Because you're famous?"

Famous. Rich. Powerful. Attractive. And, he liked to think, extremely talented. "Yes."

"Yup." Reg nodded, as if in understanding, which made no sense because a bartender from Nowhereville couldn't possibly understand the first thing about what it was like to be a multiplatinum, Grammy-winning recording artist. "People are weird."

Well, that was one thing they could both agree on.

"So, uh, you live nearby?" Jeremy asked when they started walking along the side of the road, leaving the parking lot behind.

"Uh-huh. I'm right over there." Reg pointed at a tiny house. "I'm on the right side, and my landlord and his wife are on the left."

At first the description didn't make sense, but when they got closer, Jeremy noticed two front doors and realized the small house was actually a duplex.

"Why'd you move back here after college?" Jeremy asked, hoping the question didn't come off as judgmental but wanting to understand why someone as vibrant and personable as Reg had decided to settle down in a nothing town. "I mean, I know you said your mother and your brother are still here, but Phoenix is close, right? You could live there and see them all the time."

"Yup. But it costs more to live there, and I wanted to save up, so I came home." He unlocked his door and stepped aside, letting Jeremy walk into the house first.

The inside looked like the outside: dated, flat, and nothing to write home about. Reg had told him he'd gotten his degree in accounting. That had to pay more than whatever he made tending bar in an all-but-empty dive.

"But you could probably find a job in your field if you lived in a bigger city. Then you'd make more so you could save more."

"I tried that." Reg followed him inside and kicked the door closed. "I worked at one of the big accounting firms after graduation." He walked over to the fridge wedged into the corner of the room that served as the kitchen. "I didn't last there two years."

"Why not? You seem pretty smart."

"Summa cum laude," Reg said as he pulled out a couple of beers.

"Huh?"

"Never mind." Chuckling, Reg knocked the beer caps off by slamming them against the side of the counter, and then stepped over to Jeremy, holding one out. "I left accounting because I'm not a morning person, and being holed up in an office all day fucking killed me." He tilted his bottle against his lips and took a long swallow. "So I ran back home with my tail between my legs, got a job at the bar, and started saving up so I can go backpacking somewhere. That was a year and a half ago. I figure in another few years I'll have enough to take off for a while and wander." He flopped onto his couch, making the springs squeak.

"Where do you want to go?" Jeremy flicked his gaze around the room, settled it on a brown plaid armchair across from the couch, and stepped over to it.

"I don't know yet," Reg said with a shrug. "Alaska, maybe. I've heard it's cool, lots of great hiking. I've got time to figure it out."

Jeremy sank onto the chair and took a pull of his beer. "This is good."

"Yup. Their IPA's awesome too. I have some in the fridge when you're ready for another bottle."

He looked at the label. "Four Peaks? Haven't heard of it."

"They're local, out of Tempe." Reg ran his thumb over the top of the longneck. "How about you?"

"How about me what?"

"Do you like what you do?"

"Most of it," Jeremy said honestly, settling into the chair and stretching his legs out. "The music part, I love."

"You're a musician," Reg pointed out. "Isn't all of it the music part?"

"Nah." Jeremy shook his head. "I mean, the music comes first, yeah? But there's also all the publicity crap. Interviews, events, photographers everywhere." He took in a deep breath and let it out slowly. "It sucks."

"Not a people person, huh?" Reg said, the sideways grin that was starting to look familiar making a welcome appearance.

There was no denying it. "I'm really, really not."

"I was kidding, man." Reg dropped his head against the back of the couch. "You're totally cool."

"Cool, yes," Jeremy agreed. He held the neck of the bottle between his pointer finger and his thumb and swung it from side to side, watching the remaining liquid slosh. "But as a rule, people piss me off, which is probably a good thing, because then I don't get mad when they take off." Whoa. That was more bitter and more honest than he'd intended on being.

"What do you mean?"

"Nothing."

Reg didn't push. Looking relaxed, he took another swig

of beer.

Suddenly, Jeremy felt like sharing. It was probably all the alcohol, the late hour, and the fact that Reg had one of those bartender personalities that made people want to unburden themselves. "What I mean is that I'm never in one place for long. I'm supposed to be seen at all sorts of events, and I have to meet with photographers and print journalists and TV people. Women enjoy that for a little while, especially if they're trying to get noticed, right? I mean, if they're with me, they figure their pictures will turn up places, and then they'll get their big break. But then they realize it isn't really that cool. Mostly they have to stand around waiting for me to finish what I'm doing, and, unless they're already well known, people ignore them. Or if they do get photographed, it's when they're not expecting it and someone catches them without makeup or on a fat day—whatever that means—and they flip out and blame me."

"You should date another famous person," Reg suggested. "She'd be used to all that already."

"Tried it," Jeremy said. "More than once. I never saw them. I was busy doing my shit; they were busy doing their shit." He shook his head and drained his beer. "It was hopeless." Flinging his forearm over his eyes, he sighed. "It's fine. Whatever. Just gets lonely sometimes, is all. And I'm about to go on a big tour to promote the new album, which is the worst. This one'll be for more than six months."

"You don't like touring?" Reg asked incredulously. "Don't you get to go to a bunch of new places and see new things?"

"Yeah, I guess. I mean, I do."

It was hard to explain. At his level, tours didn't consist of grungy busses and cheap motels. He stayed in great places and flew most of the time, especially for international tours, which was what he was about to launch. And even though there wasn't a lot of downtime, he could take in the sights before a show or between shows. But whatever he did, he had to do alone.

"You're lucky," Reg said wistfully. "That sounds amazing."

"You should come with me," Jeremy joked. "I'll tell everyone I stopped dating starlets, and you're my new arm candy."

"Man, I wish." Reg got up. "Want another beer?"

"Sure." He handed Reg his empty. "It sounds good now, but trust me, you'd hate it." Everyone he'd tried to take with him hated it. Last time he toured, his girlfriend of eight months, who had claimed to love him, had broken up with him after two months and started dating an up-and-coming actor.

"No way. How could anybody hate traveling the world?" Reg handed him his beer and sat back down.

"Going from place to place. Having to sit around while I'm on stage. During the day, there's time to do some sightseeing or whatever, and sometimes we have dead nights in between shows, but most nights I'm performing, and then, after, I'm beat, and all I want to do is veg on a couch, drink a beer, and—"

"Shoot the shit?" Reg offered. "Kind of like we're doing now except in more exotic places?"

"Yeah, but I'm not usually this fun."

Reg laughed.

"It's true. I'm annoying in longer doses." He tried to remember words his exes had used. "Needy. Whiny. Grouchy."

"You're cool, man. And you're dating the wrong girls if they complain about getting to hang out with you and see the world."

"Seriously? You think that sounds fun?"

"Like I said, sign me up." Reg got up, walked over to the window, and wiggled it open. "Sorry, man, no A/C." He grabbed the back of his shirt and yanked it over his head, exposing a sculpted six-pack, cut arms, and a striking tattoo that started on his left shoulder and moved down to just above his wrist. With a body that ripped, a handsome face, and the ever-present smile, Reg could easily be in a magazine. "It usually doesn't get hot like this until June." He tossed his shirt on the couch before collapsing on it with another loud bounce. "Barely into May, and it's already sweltering."

"You ever consider going into modeling?"

Reg rolled his head to the side and gave Jeremy a look that clearly indicated the answer was no.

"Don't look at me like that." He pointed the bottom of his bottle toward Reg. "You have the body for it."

"I have the body for hiking, climbing, spelunking, and spending my free time at the gym."

After taking another appraising look, Jeremy had to agree. Reg wasn't slender like the men who modeled high-end clothing, or wiry like him. He was broad and thickly muscled. Any kind of modeling he did would probably involve a minimum amount of clothing, like some of the swimsuit models Jeremy had dated.

"It isn't a bad idea," Jeremy mumbled, the thought taking root.

"Dude, I don't want to be a model. Let it go."

"No, not that." Jeremy shook his head and straightened his back. "I'm talking about bringing you on tour. You want to travel, and you have no trouble making small talk with anybody, drunks included." Jeremy had witnessed that firsthand at the bar. "I'm sick of going on the road alone and having to take whatever girl my manager sends over to premieres and shit." He beamed. "It's perfect."

"Wait." Reg sat up, his eyes wide. "What are you saying?"

"I'm saying, ehm, Reggie Moore, will you be my pretend boyfriend for the next seven months? The gig pays whatever it is you're making now at that bar, and it comes with free travel, room and board. In exchange, all you have to do is smile pretty if I have a public event, make nice with a bunch of people who think they're really important, and, in our downtime, get drunk with me or teach me how to rock climb or cave dive or whatever other cool stuff you do. What do you say?"

"You're serious?"

"As a heart attack." Feeling light and happy, Jeremy smiled broadly. "And I won't even make you suck my dick."

CHAPTER 2

EVEN without the added bonus of going down on Jeremy, the offer wasn't something Reg could refuse. Going just over the border to Nogales was as far as he'd gotten in his goals; if he went on tour with one of the most successful rock stars of all time, he'd see more of the US and other countries too. Plus, he could do it right away, without spending another two to three years saving. And Reg was sure Jeremy's method of travel would be more plush than his plan of bumming rides or taking Greyhound. Bottom line: what Jeremy was offering was as good as winning the lottery, and just like the lottery, Reg didn't figure it would ever actually happen.

"You're wasted, man." He shook his head and grinned, the initial thrill of possibility being replaced by amusement. Who knew *The Jeremy Jameson* would be such a goofy drunk? "I thought I'd heard it all from guys who've had one too many, but you win the prize for most creative drunkery."

"I'm not drunk," Jeremy huffed.

"Dude. You are totally smashed."

"Am not."

"Fine, then, prove it," Reg said. Dealing with people who didn't realize they were no longer sober was part of his job. "Walk the line."

Jeremy's forehead creased. "What does that mean?"

"You've never been pulled over and given the walk-and-turn test?"

"Uh, no."

"Okay." Reg stood, wiped his hands on his baggy jeans, held one hand out to Jeremy, and yanked him to his feet. "See the line where the linoleum changes colors?" He pointed toward his kitchen. "Start on one end and walk it, heel to toe. Then keep one foot on it, turn around, and go back to the beginning the same way."

"Pft!" Jeremy waved his hand dismissively. "My trainer's big on using steps. I do that for hours when we're working out. And all you want me to do is walk across a room on one level? Done."

Swaggering over to the starting point, Jeremy shook his head and said, "We should bet on something because I'm *so* going to win."

"All right."

Snapping his gaze toward Reg, Jeremy stopped with one foot above the decided line. Immediately, he tipped to the right and had to plant both feet on the ground and hold his arms out to the side to get his balance. "You want to bet?"

"Sure." Reg arched his eyebrows in amusement. "Why? Did you already change your mind?" He crossed his arms over his chest and started squawking like a chicken.

"You are *not* making chicken noises right now."

"Hey, if the poultry fits."

"Fine." Jeremy rolled his eyes. "What's the bet?"

"If you can walk the line both ways, heel to toe, without stopping and without using your arms to balance, I'll accept your offer."

"And if I can't?"

"Then you're too drunk to know what you're saying, and you'll have to ask again after you sleep it off."

"That's it? That's all I lose?" He scoffed. "You need to learn how to place a wager. That's—"

"There's more," Reg said.

"Oh. What?"

"I want a year instead of seven months."

Jeremy's face crumpled, reminding Reg of his nephew's expression when he had to take a nap. "I would, but I can't. The concerts are already scheduled. All the arenas are booked. Does that mean you won't do it?"

Keeping himself from ruffling the purple hair took effort. In magazines, Jeremy's mop was always a different color, styled in intentionally random spikes. But after wearing a cap all night in a stuffy space, the locks were stiff with sweat and matted to his head in spots while sticking out in a very nonartful way in others. The look added to the little-boy image, and it made Reg smile.

"I'll do it," he said, clenching and releasing his fists to keep himself from reaching for the other man to smooth away that disappointed expression. "But when the tour's over, we can keep traveling; only we go where we want when we want. No agenda."

Jeremy widened his eyes and parted his lips. "An adventure?" he gasped.

Sure, they could call it that. Reg nodded.

"Just the two of us?" His eyes took on a dreamy quality, and he lowered his voice. "No manager. No groupies. Nobody who needs me to do anything."

Not sure if Jeremy was talking to himself or asking a question, Reg stayed silent.

"It's a deal," Jeremy said. Looking determinedly at the linoleum, he took the first step, immediately throwing his arms out to the sides to keep his balance. He walked toe to heel after two steps, stumbled off the line after three, and on the fourth step, he fell flat on his butt.

Laughing deeply, Reg hustled over and helped Jeremy get to his feet. "Dude, you are so fucking trashed right now."

"Maybe." Jeremy shrugged and gave Reg a goofy grin. "But tomorrow morning we're getting coffee, and you're agreeing to be all mine for a year."

Having been working most of the time Jeremy had been drinking, Reg was still very much sober, so that comment had him firming up down below. Of course, he knew what Jeremy wanted wasn't a real boyfriend. The poor guy needed a friend, someone to spend time with who wouldn't have ulterior motives or make constant demands. It was sad that he felt he had to essentially hire that function out, but Reg wouldn't complain. Jeremy was cool, his music was amazing, and touring the world would be a dream come true.

"I hope so, man," he said. "That'd be awesome."

"It would." Jeremy nodded. "No more lonely nights. No more boring flights with nobody to talk to. No more girls who say they want to be with me when they don't even like me, and all they really want is a leg up." He sighed. "No more."

Not knowing how to respond, Reg squeezed Jeremy's shoulder in support.

Jeremy yawned.

"All right. You're beat, I'm beat. Let's hit it. I'll grab a pillow for you. You need anything else? Blanket?"

"No." Yanking his shirt off over his head, Jeremy stumbled to the sofa. "I'm good." He flopped onto his back, unbuttoned his slim-cut jeans, and shoved them off his trim hips. "I'm stuck," he said pathetically when the jeans got tangled around his ankles. "Why won't these come off?" He kicked his feet and flailed around, looking absurd but adorable.

"You're a funny drunk." Reg walked over and grabbed his feet. "Stay still."

Jeremy froze.

"Shoes first, then pants," Reg teased as he pulled off Jeremy's sneakers.

"Forgot," Jeremy mumbled, his voice sounding thick, his eyes dropping closed. Seemed like the long day and the abundance of alcohol had caught up with him.

"Hold on, superstar." He tugged Jeremy's jeans off, leaving him wearing a tiny pair of black briefs that left very little to the imagination. From the look of things, the guy had a nice set of nuts, big enough to hold in your hand when you were sucking his dick. Brushing off the thought, Reg grabbed Jeremy's ankle and shook it. "You need to hit the head before you crash." When he got no response, he shook his leg again. "Seriously. Get up. I don't need more piss on this couch."

"*More* piss?" Jeremy asked, struggling to rise to sitting position. "Who do you have over that isn't toilet trained?"

"My niece and nephew, their dog, and anybody who used this couch before I found it."

"You *found* a couch?" Jeremy finally managed to stand up, but he wasn't steady on his feet. "Where do you *find* a couch?"

Looking Jeremy over from head to toe, Reg had only one thought: goddamn, the boy was fine with a capital F.

Though he wasn't big—Reg figured Jeremy for five foot ten, one hundred fifty pounds on a good day—he was all lean, cut muscles and smooth, creamy skin. The pictures Reg had seen in magazines didn't do justice to the live version. Reg had always considered Jeremy Jameson attractive, but his image didn't come up in Reg's head when he was alone in bed at night. No doubt that was about to change. After being with a barely clad Jeremy in person, Reg knew the spank bank was officially well stocked as far as inspirational images were concerned.

"I found it on the side of the road"—Reg wrapped his arm around Jeremy's shoulders and led him to the bathroom—"on bulk trash pickup day."

"Oh."

"Are you going to be okay in there, or do you need

help?" he asked once they were standing outside the door leading to the bathroom.

"I don't need help draining the lizard!" Jeremy said, sounding affronted, and then he walked face-first into the bathroom door. "Ow!" Laughing so hard he had to gasp for air, Reg watched Jeremy weave his way into the bathroom, rubbing his forehead and muttering, "Hurts."

"Try not to piss on my floor. Okay, superstar?"

The door slammed. Reg heard a bumping noise followed by another "Ow!" and then what he was pretty sure was Jeremy crashing to the floor. "I'm okay!" The sound of shuffling filtered through the thin door. "Everything's fine!"

Cracking up all over again, Reg went into his bedroom to get out of his boots and jeans, letting himself imagine how great it would be to have nights like that for a year. He really hoped Jeremy was sincere about his offer and it hadn't been the beer talking.

"Reg!"

"Yes." Reg toed off his boots.

"The toilet won't flush."

"You need to jiggle the handle." He tugged his belt off and pushed his jeans down.

"What does that mean?"

Okay, so maybe not exactly like that. Better plumbing fixtures would be nice.

"Leave it. I'll take care of it in a minute." After tossing his jeans onto his dresser so he could wear them again the next morning, he grabbed a pillow off the bed and walked back into the main room.

"'Kay!" The bathroom door opened, and Jeremy came out. "It was just number one."

Reg froze midstep. "Number one?"

Jeremy bobbed his head.

"How old are you?"

"Thirty-one. Why? How old are you?"

"I'm twenty-six, and I stopped saying 'number one' more than ten years ago. Take note of that, dude."

"Huh?"

"Never mind." Reg shook his head and looked at Jeremy fondly. "You're too sloshed to remember this conversation anyway." He shoved the pillow at Jeremy's chest. "Here. Go to sleep."

"I'm not drunk," Jeremy argued, but it was halfhearted; he sounded too tired to really debate the point. He returned to the couch, lay down, and, based on his even breathing, was asleep in seconds.

"You're a cool dude, Jeremy Jameson," Reg said, looking at his gorgeous guest. "You shouldn't have to pretend about anything, least of all having someone in your life who actually wants to be with you." With a sigh, he turned away and went to get ready for bed.

A couple of beers was enough to help him sleep well

but not so much that he wanted to crawl under a rock and die instead of getting up. Knowing Jeremy wouldn't be as lucky, Reg tried to keep quiet the next morning as he used the bathroom, brushed his teeth, and got the coffee going. He wasn't much of a cook, so he didn't keep a lot of food in the house, but he had some bagels in the freezer and his always present stockpile of bananas on the counter. He got those out for Jeremy and made himself his usual protein shake breakfast, leaving the ingredients in the blender but waiting to turn it on so he wouldn't wake his houseguest.

"Ungh."

The pathetic moan from his couch had him turning around.

"Feels like I got hit by a truck," Jeremy whined. Or at least Reg thought that was what he'd said. It came out in an almost unintelligible mumble.

"You did." He filled a glass with water and shook a couple of aspirin out of the bottle he kept next to the coffee. "A beer truck." Walking over to Jeremy, he said, "Sit up."

"Don't wanna." Jeremy fumbled for the pillow and then covered his face with it.

Laughing, Reg picked up the pillow, exposing a gorgeous face, even if it was puckered up in a frown and covered with creases from the sofa. "Drink this."

"Ungh."

"Don't make me tickle your sorry ass to get you up, superstar."

"If you tickle me, I'll pee."

"I'm not into that, so sit up and drink your water like a good boy."

That earned Reg a scowl.

"Oh-ho, look who's pissed. You'll need to get your limbs working if you want to punch me." He pointed to the couch. "Sit."

"I'm not a dog." Grumbling, Jeremy got vertical and then immediately put his hand on his forehead and moaned. "I need coffee."

"Water first." Reg grabbed his hand, held it up, and put the glass in it. "Take the aspirin too." He put the pills in Jeremy's empty hand. "I'll get you a banana and bagel."

"And after that I can have coffee?" Jeremy asked, looking miserable.

Unable to resist the sleepy, morning version of the already adorable guy, Reg did what he'd been itching to do since the previous night and ruffled his hair. "Yes, then you can have coffee."

Leaving Jeremy to drink his water, Reg retrieved the banana and bagel. He had taken one step toward the couch, items in hand, when Jeremy said, "Oh, and about last night."

Giving himself an internal pat on the back for barely stumbling, Reg reined in his disappointment about what he knew would be Jeremy rescinding his offer and said, "Uh-huh?"

"If I survive this hangover, the offer holds." He rubbed his eyes. "What do you say?"

Reg traded the empty glass for the banana and set the

bagel on the table. "You want to tell the world you're gay so you have someone to keep you company on tour?"

"Don't make it sound so desperate, yeah?" He peeled the banana. "You have no idea what it's like living your whole life having people use you for shit." He sighed. "It's exhausting."

Kneeling down in front of Jeremy so they'd be at eye level, Reg pointed out what he thought was obvious, "But you'd be paying me to go with you. Isn't that the same thing?"

"No." Jeremy started shaking his head, and then he moaned and dropped the banana in favor of holding on to both temples.

With a chuckle, Reg picked up the banana and handed it back.

"Thanks." Jeremy cleared his throat, which still sounded raspy from sleep. It was sexy. "Tell me why you'd be willing to go on tour with me."

"Uh, because I'd get to listen to music, see the world, drink good beer, and hang out." Reg paused, tried to think of what he was missing, and, coming up with nothing, said, "Why *wouldn't* I go?"

"See? That's what I mean." Jeremy took a bite of his banana and kept talking while he chewed. "Everybody I've dated says they want to come on tour so they can be with me, but you know what? They don't. What they want is to do the things they enjoy. The red-carpet stuff they're all over, but the rest of it bores them, and being with me alone bugs them, and then they get pissy and resentful, and I don't need to deal with that while I'm working. It's hard enough being on stage night after night, yeah? When I have to do the stuff I hate, I need someone to help me, not someone I have to watch or apologize to or whatever. And I need downtime on my downtime." He took another bite. "You know what I mean?"

"Uh-huh." Reg chewed on his upper lip. "I guess."

"With you, it's different. You're not coming so you can get something else. The thing you want is to be there. Plus, you'll smile pretty for the cameras, but you won't get mad when you're not the one they're focused on. You'll bullshit with the journalist people, who, by the way, will eat your whole tattooed-muscle-boy thing up with a spoon, but you won't get pissy when they don't write anything about you in the article." He grinned, the banana smeared on his teeth. "It's perfect."

Reg nodded and considered what Jeremy said. "You do realize I'm not a woman, right?"

Looking him up and down, Jeremy arched his eyebrows and said, "Uh, yeah."

"And you're okay with the world thinking Jeremy Jameson is gay just so we can drink a few beers and I can run interference for you with annoying press people?"

"Sure. Why should I care what they think about that?"

"Some people care about that kind of thing."

"I'm a musician, not a, uh, I don't know..." He grabbed the bagel and bit off a big piece. "What jobs give a shit who someone's fucking? Politician? Whatever." He shook his head. "You know who my parents are. If my mother can be divorcing husband number seven—that's still on the DL, by the way, so keep it to yourself—and my father spent most of his life high, then got so coked up he died in a hotel room with a bed full of women, and my stepmother *still* showed up at his funeral red-eyed and depressed, getting condolences—I can be gay."

"All right." Reg got up and went to the kitchen. "If you're good with it, I'm in, man. Tell me when we're leaving, and I'll pack my duffel and hit the road." He grabbed his least chipped mug, filled it with liquid heaven, and then brought it to Jeremy.

"First show's a week from tomorrow in Minneapolis, but you should probably come to LA first so we can go together." He took another bite of the bagel and a big gulp of coffee. "Mmm, that's good." Wiping the back of his hand across his mouth, he said, "So you're in?"

A week wasn't a lot of time, but then again, the only things Reg had to do were stuff his clothes in a bag, tell his boss to find someone to cover his shifts, and let his landlord, mother, and brother know he was leaving. A week was plenty long enough to do that.

Holding his fist out, Reg grinned and said, "I'm in, man." Jeremy smiled back and bumped his fist. "It's on."

CHAPTER 3

"JEREMY, you're Hollywood royalty. You can't be gay."

Having grown up around business agents, public-relations experts, and managers, nothing surprised Jeremy anymore. Even so, he thought his manager's latest comment was more absurd than the usual nonsense he heard.

"Does that make sense in your head, Bill? Because out loud it sounds stupid."

"You understand what I'm saying," Bill replied, looking frustrated.

"No, I don't." Jeremy crossed his arms over his chest and leaned his chair back, making it teeter on two legs. He'd seen Reg do it a few times and thought it seemed fun; it was harder than it looked to stay balanced. "Explain it to me."

Flicking his disapproving gaze from the chair to Jeremy's face, Bill gave a long-suffering sigh. "Your grandfather directed three Oscar-winning films. Your mother has the same number of gold statues on her mantle, and at fifty-three, she's still carrying movies. To this day, people say your father was the greatest rock legend of all time, and the anniversary of his overdose is practically a nationwide mourning period." He paused and looked at Jeremy meaningfully. "You are the top-selling musician in the world. You cannot go from dating swimsuit models and whatever starlet the magazines are getting hard-ons over that week to telling the world you're with a guy."

Slamming his chair completely back to the floor, Jeremy said, "I'm the top-selling musician in the world. I can do whatever the fuck I want."

With a roll of his eyes and another sigh, Bill said, "All right. Fine. Any press is good press I guess. I'll figure it out."

Tipping his chair back again, Jeremy rolled his eyes. There was nothing to figure out as far as he was concerned. His personal life should be his business and nobody else's. Even though that wasn't how his life actually played out because of his career, knowing who he was dating and having a say in it were two entirely different things. Besides, once the press got a look at Reggie Moore, they'd wet their pants. The guy had a face and body made for magazines and a smile to match.

"I'll call you tomorrow and let you know what interviews I have lined up."

"Interviews?" Jeremy spat, the chair slamming down as he lost his balance.

"Yes, interviews." Bill rolled his eyes. "You're doing the whole 'coming out of the closet' thing, right? I bet I can get you on *The Tonight Show* and *Today* by tomorrow."

"I'm not going on TV! We have a tour starting in a week."

"Fine." Bill turned his chair to face his computer and

started typing. "A print interview, then. I'll get you the cover of *Rolling Stone*."

"No."

"I'm not arguing with you about this." Bill raised his hand and, without taking his eyes off the screen, shooed Jeremy away. "Go play chess or whatever it is you're actually doing with this new *boyfriend* and let me do my job."

"Why are you saying it like that?"

"Saying what like what?"

"*Boyfriend*," he mimicked Bill's tone. "You're saying it like it's absurd."

"That's because it is absurd."

"It's absurd to be gay?" Jeremy's tone got more high-pitched as his anger rose.

"No." Bill finally turned away from the screen and met his gaze. "It's absurd for *you* to be gay."

"Why? Because I'm Hollywood royalty? That's ridi—"

"How about because you're thirty-one? People don't just magically become gay at thirty-one."

It was a valid point, not that Jeremy would admit to it. "Maybe I've been gay the whole time, and I was hiding it?"

"You? Hiding something?" Bill snorted and shook his head. "I don't think so. And, by the way, nobody else will believe it either. Not with the string of women you've had in and out of your bed and how happy you are to share your, uh, opinions, camera or no camera."

Fine, he might have yelled at a photographer or two hundred over the course of his life, but that was only because they were constantly in his face. "I can be bi. People are bi."

"You're bisexual?"

"I can be."

"Look, Jeremy." Bill rested his forearms on his desk and leaned forward. "I don't know if you're bored or you're trying to pull a stunt or who knows what else, but unless you're attracted to men, you're not gay and you're not bi." He sat up. "Not that I care. You keep making hit music, and I'll make sure our team sells whatever we need to sell about your personal life. It's fine."

"I think men are attractive," Jeremy said defensively but honestly. Hell, he thought Reg was gorgeous. It was one of the things he'd noticed about that man that he knew would make him a good candidate for the job of pretend boyfriend. The camera was going to love him, and the people behind it would too. Good-looking and easy to get along with—a perfect combination.

"You know what I mean."

Like before, Jeremy didn't know what he meant. "No, I don't."

Turning away from the computer again, Bill said, "Thinking someone is handsome in a theoretical way isn't the same thing as being attracted to them. Being gay means you have an emotional connection to another man, you want them physically and mentally." He paused. "Do you understand what I'm saying? You don't feel that way about men, Jeremy. You're not the biggest womanizer around, but you're no monk either."

The most interesting part about that description was that while Jeremy agreed that he hadn't felt that depth of emotion for any man, he also realized he hadn't felt that way for any woman. Not wanting to bare his soul to his manager, he tried to turn the conversation around.

"You sure seem to know a lot about this, Bill."

"As a matter of fact I do." He looked at Jeremy meaningfully.

"What are you saying?" Jeremy asked, worried that instead of regaining control of the conversation, he had lost it entirely.

Crossing his arms over his chest, Bill said, "How long have we been working together?"

"Uh." Math had never been Jeremy's strength. "I don't know. Since Roger retired and you took over his clients. When was that?"

"Eight years ago," Bill supplied helpfully.

"So eight years, then."

"And in all that time, have you ever met my wife?"

Darting his gaze toward Bill's empty ring finger, Jeremy said, "You're married?"

"No."

"Oh."

"But if I ever get married, it'll be to a man."

"You're gay?"

"Yes, I'm gay."

"How is it I didn't know that?" Jeremy asked.

"I also like to ski, and in my free time, which is very

limited because I'm working for you seven days a week, I'm a pretty accomplished chef. You didn't know those things about me either because, like who I date, they have nothing to do with our work."

Feeling guilty for not taking more interest in a person he'd known for so long and who did so much for him, Jeremy opened his mouth to apologize, but Bill held out his hand, stopping him.

"I'm a damn good manager, Jeremy. I get that you were born with family connections and a truckload of talent, but you're not the only person around who comes with that pedigree. Getting where you are didn't happen alone, even though you might not always remember it."

"I know that. There's always a crew of people around me, telling me how to live my life. You think I don't know that?" Well, that was the opposite of apologizing. Crap. Jeremy drew in a deep breath. "Sorry. I didn't mean to—"

"Yes, you did, and it's fine. It's not the first time you've snapped at me, and it won't be the last. Now, if we're done here, get out of my office so I can figure out how to spin the whole 'Jeremy Jameson is gay' thing in a way that lets me unwind it later without offending people on both sides of the fence."

"What does that mean?"

Bill was losing his patience; his stiff posture and pinched expression made that clear. "It means the homophobes are going to be pissed you're gay, and those of us who actually are gay and have dealt with everything that entails are going to be pissed when you change your mind about it as if your sexual orientation is a jacket you can take off and put on whenever you have a whim."

"That's not what I'm doing. I'm not trying to make a statement. I just want..." To have someone to be with while he slept in different cities every night, someone who would keep him company and make him laugh, someone who would remind him that what he was doing was fun, not a chore. "I want Reg with me on this tour." Jeremy stood up, dragged his hands through his hair, and said, "The press can use whatever label they want about that, but I'm not changing my mind. End of story. Make it work."

He had one foot out the door when Bill said, "Make sure you tell your mother about this, okay? We don't need her to get hysterical if she hears about your boyfriend from someone else on camera."

Dammit. He hated when Bill was right about something he didn't want to do. And talking about anything, let alone his personal life, with a woman who spent her life prancing on the corner of vodka and valium most definitely fell into that category.

"All right." Jeremy slumped his shoulders in anticipation of the visit he knew he needed to have. "I'll take care of notifying Paula Radcliffe. You deal with the rest of the world."

"I got the easy part," Bill teased.

"I know."

Standing outside the steep, curving steps leading to his mother's hillside Spanish colonial house, Jeremy struggled to make himself walk toward the front door, his tension rising with every passing minute he remained outside staring at the meticulously trimmed shrubbery. He pulled his shirt collar into his mouth and thought about getting back in his car and handling this with a telephone call or, better yet, telling Bill to send someone else to talk to his mother. When his phone rang, he slumped in relief and answered quickly.

"Hello."

"Hey, superstar, how goes life? You change your mind yet?"

His smile came easily in reaction to Reg's deep, happy voice. "Not changing my mind. In fact, if you could get out here sooner, that'd be great."

"How soon?"

Rubbing his palm over his face, Jeremy glanced at the house again, "Now?" He coughed. "I'm kidding. I just wish you could be here to talk to my mother instead of me, or at least to witness the horror firsthand so we could recover together."

"It can't be that bad. Your mom seems very nice."

"You're basing this on her interviews?" He snorted. "My mother is a very, very good actress. If you saw her on TV, you can pretty much count on the fact that she was playing a role, even if the role was of Paula Radcliffe. In real life, she has a meltdown if she thinks her staff bought sale Diet Coke instead of full-price Diet Coke because she's sure they taste different."

"Man, you rich people are weird."

"It's not me, it's her," Jeremy said defensively. "I'm perfectly nor—"

"Dude, she's your mom. Put on your big-boy drawers, go make small talk, and then take off. Don't make more of it than it is and get all hysterical."

Pursing his lips together in frustration at Reg's lack of compassion and yet fully reasonable assessment of the situation, Jeremy climbed the first step. "Fine. But you need to call me in exactly fifteen minutes so I can pretend there's an emergency and escape."

"When was the last time you hung out with your mom?"

"Hung out?" he scoffed. "People do not *hang out* with Paula Radcliffe."

"Quit being a prissy bitch and answer my question."

Nobody had ever talked to Jeremy that way. Reg treated him like a buddy, an equal, a regular guy. He loved it.

"I don't know." He shrugged, even though Reg couldn't see him. "A few months ago, probably. How should I remember?"

"You both live in LA, and you've gone months without seeing her?" Reg sounded horrified. "Not cool."

"You don't understand."

"I have a mother too, superstar, and I see her a couple of times a week, at least. Get your ass in gear and act like a decent son."

"Fine." His lips pressed into tight lines, Jeremy stomped up the stairs. "But you'll call me in fifteen, right?"

"You haven't seen your mother in months. You're lucky if I call in an hour. Quit bitching and get on with it."

"But—"

"Later."

The phone went dead and Jeremy growled. "Dammit." Though he wanted to turn around, his manager had been right—he needed to talk to his mother and do damage control off camera so she could be her charming self on camera instead of drunk Mommie Dearest. Plus, Reg would never let him live it down if he wimped out of the visit.

"Here we go," he muttered to himself and jogged the rest of the way up the red brick steps to the front door.

After ringing the bell, Jeremy waited while it went through the long string of chimes and then heard the familiar tapping of shoes on Saltillo tile floors before the heavy wood door swung open.

"Jeremy, hi. Paula said you might be stopping by for a visit."

Staring at the well-coifed and somewhat familiar man standing in his mother's doorway, Jeremy tried to place him.

"I'm Harold West." He held out his hand.

Returning the gesture, Jeremy shook Harold West's

hand. The name was vaguely familiar, just like the face.

"Remind me where we've met?" Jeremy said as he stepped into the house, nudging Harold aside as he crossed the threshold.

"Oh." Harold sounded surprised. "I'm not sure we've ever been formally introduced, but you probably know me from my work."

Looking back over his shoulder to where Harold was still standing at the door, Jeremy squinted, crinkled his forehead, and then said, "No. No clue. What work?"

"Jeremy!" His mother came blowing into the room, a colorful wave of fabric, makeup, and perfume. "Of course you remember Harold. A film he worked on showed at Sundance two years ago." She held her arms open and waited for Jeremy to step closer, but not close enough to wrinkle her silk blouse and pashmina. As soon as he did, she leaned forward and gave him an almost-kiss—a real one would no doubt smear her makeup. "And he directed that amazing miniseries they showed on cable."

"Oh." That was all the excitement he could muster about the stranger in his mother's house. "How have you been?"

"Great," she said, drawing the word out, tossing her hair back and smiling in a way a camera would love but real live people found put-on and awkward.

"Paula's going to work with me on a new movie," Harold chimed in. "This one will be with a major studio. Big budget."

Sparing the man another glance, this time Jeremy focused on him a little longer. He was older than Jeremy, but not by much; probably in the neighborhood of forty. And he was good-looking in a way where you wouldn't pick him out of a crowd and pursue him, but if he showed up and asked you to dinner, then fine, whatever, you might as well go. I mean, you have to eat, right?

Now that he paid closer attention, Jeremy realized why Harold looked familiar—it was his eyes. They held an expression of hope mixed with desperation and determination, something Jeremy had seen in plenty of starlets when they were introduced to him. Ten bucks said this was the new guy warming his mother's bed now that his latest stepfather was out of the picture.

"Is that right?" Jeremy said as he slowly returned his focus to his mother. "*Harold* is going to direct your next movie?" Not a chance on earth his mother was going to participate in a project headed by an unknown. People had to have a bank of successful films and respectable accolades under their belts before Paula Radcliffe deemed them worthy of her clout and talent.

"So, sweetheart, tell me what I did to earn this lovely visit." His mother threaded her arm with his and led him through the white-paneled entryway, down the hallway cluttered with photos of her throughout her career, and into the sunroom. Jeremy was never completely sure why she called it that, considering she kept the linen curtains closed all the time. "Have a seat." She gracefully extended her arm toward the white armchairs arranged in a seating group in the center of the room and then slowly lowered herself into one of the chairs, keeping her posture straight and crossing her legs at the ankles.

"Thanks." Jeremy plopped into a chair across from hers and stretched his legs in front of him.

Harold was following behind them, so he was the last to enter the room.

"Oh, how rude of me," Paula said, her eyes going wide. "I forgot to offer you a drink."

"I don't need a—"

"Harold, would you do me a favor and get Jeremy something to drink? I'm sure he must be parched." She waved her hand in front of her face. "It's been unseasonably warm, hasn't it, dear?"

After a moment's hesitation and, Jeremy was sure, frustration, Harold said, "Sure," and he walked out of the room.

"I didn't need a drink," Jeremy said. "I had an iced coffee on my way over."

"Harold doesn't mind. Besides, this way we can have time to talk alone." She leaned forward, her expression going from placid and serene to suspicious and on guard. "I don't think you've ever called me and asked to come over for a visit. What's going on? I know you can't need money."

Which was true, because Jeremy had a trust fund from his grandfather, his father's entire estate, which was still bringing in more than any person could use in a lifetime, and his own income, which his manager said would soon surpass his father's. Money wasn't something he'd ever need from his mother. Apparently, that was a unique quality in her visitors. Uncharacteristic guilt hit him. Reg was right; Jeremy needed to visit her more often.

"No, I don't need money." He took in a deep breath. "I want to let you know I'm seeing someone."

"Oh!" His mother's face lit up. "That's wonderful. Do I know her? Or is she just starting out?"

"*He*'s not in the business, actually."

The statement hung in the air, neither of them moving or speaking.

"I brought you a rum and Coke." Harold stepped into the room and thrust a glass at him. "I hope that's okay."

Moving his gaze up to look the man in the face, Jeremy shook his head, said, "I'm good," and then he turned back to his mother. He needed to assess her reaction so he'd know what measures he'd need to put in place to deal with it.

Seemingly unaware of the almost suffocating tension in the air, Harold shrugged, raised the glass to his lips, and tilted it back, swallowing down the liquid. Once the glass was empty, he shuffled over to one of the chairs and sat down. "So." He looked back and forth between Jeremy and his mother. "What'd I miss?"

Arching his eyebrows, Jeremy waited for his mother to respond. He was almost sure she was going to throw a fit and yell, Lord knew for what reason, but then she surprised him by pulling on a look of contentment and saying, "Jeremy was just starting to tell me about his new boyfriend."

"Jeremy Jameson is gay?" Harold asked, taken off guard.

Not missing a beat, Jeremy's mother turned to him and said, "Sweetheart, what's your preferred terminology? We'll want to make sure we get it right when the press asks." She paused and looked pointedly at Harold. "Isn't that right, Harold?"

"Uh, yes." He bobbed his head. "Right."

"And, please, tell us your boyfriend's name."

Relieved he had his mother's support, unusual though it was, Jeremy relaxed and started telling her about Reg. He was surprised to still be sharing details when Reg called an hour later, as promised. Apparently, he had learned a lot more about the easygoing man in the short time they'd spent together than he'd realized.

CHAPTER 4

"HEY, little dude!" Reg said with a chuckle when his nephew answered the door buck naked and hugged his knees. "Why aren't you wearing clothes?"

"Uncle Reg is here!" four-year-old Presley shouted, clinging to his leg. Reg hobbled into the house. "Uncle Reg is here!"

"Uncle Reg!" Six-year-old Danielle peeled in from around the corner and hopped onto his empty leg, wrapping around him like a monkey and grasping his arm.

"Hey, Dani girl." Reg pushed the door shut and continued his double-limped march through the house, stepping over toys and clothes. "What's on your hands?"

Both kids started talking at once, so it was impossible to know what either one was saying.

"Jules? Ry?" Reg called out. "You home?"

"No," his brother Ryan shouted from the direction of the kitchen. "We left the inmates in charge of the asylum and went out to dinner."

"You're hilarious." With a hand on each child's shoulder to ensure they wouldn't fall, Reg walked through the family room. "Why is Presley naked? And why is Dani sticky?"

When he finally reached the kitchen, he plopped into one of the chairs around the small round table his sister-in-law had painted bright blue. Last month it was red. Before that green. Reg couldn't remember the table's color history beyond that. It made him think of Jeremy's hair, and thinking of Jeremy made him smile.

"What do you mean, sticky?" Jules said, drying her hands on a towel. "I literally just washed her hands." She turned off the faucet and came over to him. "There were large quantities of soap and running water involved. We sang the alphabet together and applied friction." She peeled the girl off Reg's leg and winced when she saw his dirty jeans. "Sorry, Reg. I swear to you, they self-generate mess."

"Don't worry about it. I get shi—uh, stuff on me at work all the time. Old man Thompson barfed on me just last night."

"Lovely," Jules said.

"He's still alive?" Ryan asked without turning away from the stove, where he was stirring something that smelled surprisingly good.

"Barely."

"Dani, how is it possible you're already dirty?" Jules sighed and led Dani to the sink. "Where did this come from? We were washing hands when the doorbell rang, and there is nothing sticky between here and there."

"It's like how they take up the entire bed even though they weigh less than forty pounds," Ryan said.

Nodding, Jules said, "So true."

"You're staying for dinner, right?" Ryan asked.

"Sure. But that's not why I'm here." Reg took in a deep breath. "The, uh, reason I stopped by"—Jules kept washing Dani's hands, Ryan kept stirring, and Presley stayed Velcroed to Reg's leg—"is to let you know I'm moving."

"What?" Ryan swung around, spoon in hand, flinging red sauce onto the wall and counter.

"Why?" Jules looked at him over her shoulder while still balancing Dani on her knee and furiously rubbing soap onto her hands and arms.

"Where're you going, Uncle Reg?" Presley asked, blinking huge hazel eyes at him.

"Everywhere." He smiled at his nephew and then looked at his brother. "I met a great guy. He travels for work and offered to take me with him. You know it's what I've always wanted to do so—" He drew in another breath and let it out. "I said yes. I'm leaving next week."

"Holy fu—"

"Ryan!" Jules warned.

"Holy fungus," Ryan corrected. "You're leaving with a guy you just met? How do you know he isn't going to cut you up into little pieces and store your body in oil barrels on his remote property?"

"Dude!" Reg said. "What the he—heck? You're better off cussing in front of the kids!"

"I don't even want to ask where you came up with that disturbing scenario," Jules said to her husband. "But I may need to add parental controls to the TV to make sure it doesn't happen again." She turned to Reg. "Oil barrels aside, Reg, that's crazy. Nobody takes off with someone they just met."

"He's a good guy, and I get to see the world. I'd be crazy to say no."

After exchanging knowing looks with Jules, Ryan said, "We're going to meet him before you leave, right?"

"Uh, no. He's not here anymore. He lives in LA, and I'm meeting him there before we take off."

"Is he really old or something?" Ryan said. "Is that why you don't want us to see him?"

"No. He's a little older than me. Your age, actually."

Jules set Dani down. Before she had the water turned off, the girl was across the kitchen, climbing onto Reg's lap.

"What's his name?" Jules asked, leaning back against the counter and drying her hands. "Seriously, Reg. Some guy comes in out of nowhere and offers to take you around the world. Who is he?"

"Uh." Reg thought about how to respond. Jeremy said he'd be playing the role of boyfriend in front of the press. That meant Reg could be open about who he was. "Jeremy Jameson."

Ryan dropped the spoon. Jules dropped her jaw. After that, there was a lot of screeching and chaos, but at least his family was no longer worried about him. He stayed for dinner and story time, promised to send lots of pictures, and said good night. The next morning, he planned to have the same conversation with his mother.

"Hey, man, good to see you," Reg said as he tossed his duffel bag onto Jeremy's backseat on Tuesday afternoon. He closed the door, climbed into the front seat, and added, "Looks like you managed to navigate the airport pickup okay."

When Jeremy had told him he'd never picked anyone up at the airport, Reg had laughed and informed him his streak was coming to an end.

"Yeah, yeah." Jeremy wove into the line of traffic and rolled his eyes. "How was your flight?"

"Short." Reg paused. "You didn't need to get me a first-class ticket. I know that must have cost a bundle."

Flicking his gaze toward Reg, Jeremy smiled and said, "Don't worry about it. I make a bundle."

"I guess you do." Reg moved his seat all the way back to make room for his legs and relaxed. "We take off for Minneapolis tomorrow, right?"

"Yeah."

"What do we have on deck until then?"

"If you're hungry, we can grab a late lunch. Other than that, my manager wants to meet you, and then we're done for the day. We can get a pizza and veg." He paused and then in a strained voice said, "Unless you want to go out or whatever."

"The Dodgers game is on. Pizza, beer, and what I assume will be a big-screen TV sound perfect." He leaned across the console and gave Jeremy a soft punch to the arm. "And quit offering to do shit you clearly don't want to do just because you think it's what I want to do. First off, it's doubtful that's going to happen; I think we have the same idea of what makes a good time. And besides, I'm here to make things easier on you, remember? That means if we drag our asses off the couch, it's because we're either doing something we like, something we have to do for your work, or something that can get us killed."

"Uh, you had me until the last one."

"Have you ever gone bungee jumping?"

"No." Jeremy shook his head.

"I've been doing a little research about things we can do on the tour stops where we have free time, and guess what we're doing in Switzerland?"

"Bungee jumping?" Jeremy croaked.

"Yup." Reg bobbed his head. "The Verzasca Dam. Night bungee jumping. I've never done that. It's going to be totally awesome."

"It sounds great, but, uh—" Jeremy gulped. "You can't actually *die* doing it, right? I mean, a company runs it and makes sure it's safe, right?"

"Probably." Reg shrugged. "Either way, you're strapping on and jumping off."

With a deep breath, Jeremy nodded. "Okay. Bungee jumping in Switzerland it is. What else do you have planned for our 'can get us killed' excursions?"

"Umm, let's see. In Italy we're going spelunking at

the Sink of the Mughi, which is supposed to be amazing. In Mexico, we're going scuba diving, but that'll have to be after the tour's over because we'll need to get you certified." He tried to remember all the ideas he'd written down. "Oh! Germany. Autobahn. Rented sports car. We're *so* doing that."

When Jeremy didn't respond, Reg turned to look at him. "You're a little pale, dude. What's the matter? You're not scared, are you?"

"Yeah, I'm scared!" Jeremy chuckled. "I mean, I'll do it, and I'm excited about it, but scared? Yes. Absolutely."

Nodding in agreement, Reg said, "That's what makes it so cool."

"I think maybe you're a little off-balance."

"Could be."

"I like it." Jeremy waggled his eyebrows.

Laughing, Reg gave Jeremy another punch to the arm in thanks.

"All right. I have a serious question."

"What?" Jeremy's forehead crinkled.

"What do you like on your pizza? Because if we're not compatible there, no way can we be pretend compatible anywhere else."

"That's a lot of pressure." Jeremy licked his lips and tried to look serious. "What if I get this wrong? Does that mean we're done pretend fucking?"

"Yup. Which would totally suck for you because I am awesome in pretend bed. So let's hear it: favorite pizza toppings."

Just as Jeremy had opened his mouth to answer, Reg flung his arm out and covered Jeremy's mouth.

"Wait!" he said. "I have a better idea."

"A better idea?" Jeremy asked, though it came out muffled through Reg's hand.

"Yup. Wait until we get to your manager's office, and then you text me your favorite pizza at the same time I text you mine. That way, nobody can cheat." He looked at Jeremy excitedly. "Deal?"

"Yeah." Jeremy nodded. When Reg dropped his hand, he chuckled and said, "You weren't kidding about taking pizza seriously."

"Pizza is the perfect food," Reg said vehemently. "It's the best breakfast-lunch-dinner-fourth-meal food there is."

Quickly glancing over Reg's body, Jeremy said, "You don't look like you eat a lot of pizza."

"Thanks." Reg puffed up a little. "I work it off." He shuffled in his seat. "Are we almost there? I want to see if you're some sort of freak who eats onions and roasted peppers on his pizza."

"How'd you guess?" Jeremy said, his voice overly dramatic.

"Ha-ha. How much longer?"

"It's LA. Nothing here is close, and everything takes forever because traffic sucks." He sighed. "But if we're lucky, we might get caught up in a car chase," he said sarcastically.

"Seriously?"

"Could happen."

"Cool." Reg grinned, looking excited, which made Jeremy laugh.

Though the car chase didn't happen, the rest of the ride was fun, despite the stop-and-go traffic. By the time they pulled into Jeremy's manager's parking lot, they'd caught each other up on the previous few days.

"Did you already tell me why I need to meet your manager?"

"He's a control freak when it comes to every damn thing I do, so he needs to meet you." Jeremy turned off the ignition and pulled out the keys. "Don't worry about it. It's just Bill being Bill."

He was starting to open his car door when Reg said, "Wait. We need to do the pizza thing."

"Oh, right." Jeremy smiled widely, liking how Reg turned the mundane into something fun. He grabbed his phone and started typing. "Tell me when you're ready."

"Now!" Reg stared at his phone, and when the text came in a few seconds later, he gasped. "Ho. Ly. Shit." He stared at Jeremy. "Your favorite is mushrooms and black olives too?" He gulped. "You know what this means, right?"

"Uh, we're going to be eating a lot of pizza?" Jeremy asked.

"Yes!" Reg bobbed his head. "It's like you're reading my mind now." He was quiet for a beat, and then he dropped the dazed expression and laughed. "Kidding, man, but seriously, aces on the pizza. I was worried you were going to say you liked pineapples with Canadian bacon when everyone knows the only time you can put pineapple on pizza is if you add—"

"Jalapeños," they said simultaneously.

"Wow," Reg deadpan. "We are the best pretend couple ever. I think we're going to get pretend married and have two pretend children and a pretend dog named Rover."

"Rover?"

"Definitely."

"Great. We can let Bill know now so he can plan for it. You ready to meet him?"

"Sure. Let's go."

The meeting with Bill had ended up lasting only long enough for names to be exchanged. Then Bill had taken Jeremy somewhere to discuss some allegedly major issue related to the tour and left Reg with a man he introduced as Francis, one of Jeremy's publicists. Without so much as looking at Reg, the publicist had opened his laptop and started asking questions.

"Tell me what I need to know," Francis said.

"Sure." Reg paused. "What does that mean?"

Flicking his gaze toward Reg, he said, "Anything that can come up in an interview and blindside Jeremy or end up on TMZ or the front page of *People*." He refocused on his computer, fingers at the ready. "Basically, anything the press might find out about your past."

His past had consisted of being a decent athlete, a more than decent student, a stressed-out accountant, and, most recently, a pretty happy bartender. "I'm not that interesting."

"I have no doubt," Francis said snidely. "But that's not what I'm asking." He looked at Reg and started counting things off on his fingers. "Criminal record that didn't come up on our background check?"

"You did a background check on me?" Reg asked incredulously.

"This isn't amateur hour. You think we'd let you go on the road with our biggest client without running a background check?"

"No, I guess not. I don't have a criminal record."

"What about anything else?" He held up another finger. "Owe people money?"

Reg shook his head.

"Some ex-girlfriend going to pop out of the woodwork and claim you fathered her kid or beat her up?" Two fingers went up in short order.

"Ex-boyfriend and fuck no!"

"Boyfriend?" Francis said. "Really?"

"Yes. Why is that a surprise?"

Looking away from Reg, Francis started typing. "I didn't figure you for gay."

"I'm sitting here being interrogated because I'm dating your biggest client, remember?" Reg reminded him. "You do realize Jeremy Jameson has a dick, right?"

"Very funny," Francis said without a single indication

in his tone or expression that he found that comment or anything else humorous. "All I'm saying is you don't look gay."

"Dude, you would *so* not say that if you had a camera in my bedroom."

The sound of someone snorting had both of them jerking their heads toward the office door, where Jeremy's manager was standing.

"Why are you laughing, Bill?"

"Because your comment was stupid, and Reggie is funny." He ambled over to his desk, started typing on his computer, and said, "You can take off, Francis. I've got this."

Without an argument or a goodbye, Francis got up and walked out of the office. After a few seconds, Bill went over to the door, closed and locked it, and then leaned against it, staring at Reg.

"So." Bill's expression suddenly turned sultry. "Reggie."

Being hit on by Jeremy's manager was so far outside of Reg's expectations it took him longer than usual to realize it was happening.

"I can see why Jeremy's so taken by you." He strutted over to Reg's chair. "Even with this shirt on"—he reached forward and slowly dragged his finger down Reg's chest— "your muscles are evident. Big." He looked Reg in the eyes. "Are you big everywhere?" Dropping to his knees, he cupped Reg's cock through his pants. "I bet you are."

"Dude! What the fuck?" Reg scrambled backward, trying to squeeze out of his seat without knocking Bill on his ass.

"Relax." Bill leaned down, his mouth inches from Reg's dick. "I just want to have a little fun."

"Look, man, I don't want to hurt you, but I'm not interested. You move fucking now, or I'll make you move."

Slowly rising to his feet, Bill pointed to Reg's groin. "That says you're interested."

The second he had space to get out of his seat, Reg jumped up and backed away. "The only thing a hard dick says is I'm human. A good-looking guy gets on his knees and practically mouths my cock, and I'm going to spring wood. Doesn't mean I'm interested."

"Why not?"

"Because I have a boyfriend!" Reg was starting to understand why Jeremy was so desperate to have him around. Everyone else in the man's life was insane.

"Jeremy Jameson is your boyfriend?"

"Yes!"

"Interesting." Bill rubbed his nose, nonchalantly stepped over to his desk, pressed a few keys on his keyboard, and then turned his monitor around.

"What is that?" Reg asked when he saw a video of the past couple of minutes start playing on the screen. "You recorded us?"

"Yes."

"Why would you do that?" There was only one reason he could think of. "You're trying to set me up?"

"Set you up. Teach you a lesson." He shrugged. "Call it whatever you want. If you're going to *date* Jeremy Jameson, you need to understand that nothing, absolutely nothing, you say or do will be private. There are people out there who would love to catch Jeremy in an embarrassing situation, and if they can't do it directly through him, they'll use you."

"I'm not going to embarrass Jeremy."

"Not intentionally. I agree. You don't strike me as the type." He walked back to the chair Jeremy had vacated. "But getting some on the side from someone you think won't tell can't happen. Jeremy is a rock star. He can screw as many people as he wants, and the world will roll their eyes and laugh. You're supposed to be his boyfriend. You cheat on him, and he looks bad. It's a double standard and it sucks, but if you want to be with him, deal with it."

"I'm not going to fuck around on him. Like I told you when you had your mouth on my dick, dude, I'm not interested." He paused when Bill crouched down again. They were too far apart for the man to be trying the same move, but Reg still tensed. "And Jeremy won't fuck around on me either."

"Whatever arrangement you have with him—and I don't need to know what that is—it's very unlikely he's going to go any length of time without sex, which means he won't keep it in his pants. Doesn't matter." He picked up a phone from the ground and held it up. "You need to keep yourself in check either way." Yet another video of Bill coming on to Reg started playing. "People will do anything, say anything, record anything to earn their fifteen minutes of fame or a few bucks. Nobody cares about you. If you mess up, Jeremy is the one who gets hurt."

"*I* care about him." Jeremy was standing at the door, a key in his hand. "And why are you locking yourself in your office with my, uh, boyfriend?" He jerked his gaze toward the monitor, apparently noticing the footage. "What the hell are you doing, Bill?"

Reg shook his head and sighed. "He was pretending to come on to me to teach me a valuable lesson about not being a total slut and screwing anything with two legs." He walked over to Jeremy. "Don't worry. I passed the test." He rubbed the back of his head. "Can we go home and watch the game now, or are there more rich-people hoops I need to jump through?"

"We're done." Jeremy glared at Bill. "That wasn't necessary."

Bill shrugged, looking completely unperturbed, and returned to his desk.

After taking Reg's elbow in his hand, Jeremy led him out of the office. Once they were alone in the parking lot, he said, "So Bill seriously came on to you?"

"Yes! Man, he practically started sucking my dick. What the hell?"

"And you turned him down?"

"Of course I turned him down! I don't fuck around on people I'm seeing."

"Even the someone you're pretend seeing?" Jeremy asked, smiling softly.

"Especially the someone I'm pretend seeing," Reg

confirmed. "Because my pretend boyfriend is going to buy me dinner and rub my feet during the baseball game."

"I'm not rubbing your feet." Jeremy bumped his shoulder against Reg.

"Well, it was worth a shot."

They reached the car, but before they got inside, Jeremy said, "Reg?"

"Uh-huh?"

Fingering his shirt collar, Jeremy pulled it into his mouth and then released it. "Thanks for, uh, not taking what he offered back there. Most people would have." He pointed back and forth between them. "Even if this wasn't pretend."

"No, they wouldn't. There are lots of good-looking guys offering blow jobs. Most people wouldn't—"

"Bill Hughes is the most powerful manager in the business, yeah? Most people, male or female, gay or straight, would have dropped to their knees and gone down on him just in the hope that he'd help them get a connection." He sighed. "Trust me. Your saying no to him is a big deal."

"Huh." Reg nodded thoughtfully and rubbed his chin. "Well, then, in that case, it sounds like maybe you need to reconsider that foot rub."

"Dream on." Jeremy climbed into the car.

"Fine." Reg joined him. "But you're at least buying me garlic sticks."

"Deal."

CHAPTER 5

"You were great!"

"That was amazing!"

"Everyone is going to be talking about this show!"

Opening night had gone well. Really well. And as Jeremy walked off stage, he saw happy faces and heard accolade after accolade, so he knew the people involved with his concert had noticed too.

"You looked really relaxed out there tonight," Francis said as he stepped up to Jeremy.

Jeremy's manager had too much going on to be able to fly to Minnesota for the opening show—"*Your career doesn't just run itself*"—so he sent one of his PR guys in his place. Because Jeremy considered each and every one of those people to be the first step on the path to things he hated doing, it made no difference to him which of them was there, or if none of them were there. Well, none would be better.

"I feel good," Jeremy confirmed brusquely as he headed to his dressing room, where Reg was waiting for him. He wanted a beer, a shower, and something to prop his tired feet on. In that order. All of it mixed with lighthearted conversation with his new friend.

"Well, it showed." Francis was about the same height as Jeremy, but for some reason he walked much slower, so it always seemed like he was running alongside Jeremy instead of keeping pace. "Keep doing whatever you've been doing and—"

"Hey, superstar. You looked good out there!" Reg's whiskey voice boomed the second Jeremy flung his dressing room door open. With a smile on his face, the big man strode over, his long-legged, limber gait already familiar, and thrust a cold bottle of beer toward Jeremy. "Ready to unwind, or is there more on your plate tonight?" He clamped his beefy hand on Jeremy's shoulder and squeezed it.

Taking the beer, Jeremy said, "Thanks." Then he glanced at Francis. "The answer to Reg's question needs to be no. Say it's no. It's midnight, and we have plans."

Appearing distracted, Francis looked back and forth between Jeremy and Reg, ultimately landing on Reg's hand, which was still on Jeremy's shoulder. After a few moments, he mumbled, "I guess this answers my question about what you've been doing to relax."

Reg snorted, said, "Touché," and he tipped his beer up.

"Francis," Jeremy snapped. "We're done, right?"

"Uh, no." Francis fumbled for his phone and then started scrolling through it. "Bill said you wouldn't mind doing an interview after the show. Something about the only thing you had planned was playing chess anyway... Let's see... Okay, here we go. The *Times*. The reporter and camera person were in the audience." He glanced up at Jeremy, inconceivably seeming to be unaware of how much that information was not welcome. "You can do the interview in here. I'll bring them up now, okay?"

Growling, Jeremy turned on his heel, stomped into the bathroom, and slammed the door shut.

"Nice tantrum, diva!" Reg shouted after him. "Now that you have it out of your system, drink your beer, take a leak, and get your ass out here to meet the press."

"I don't want to!" Jeremy called out, his arms crossed. That position brought the lip of the bottle near his nose. The scent of the beer was appealing, so he took a swallow.

"Oh, come on, now," Reg's amused voice filtered in through the door. "All the other rock stars are doing it." When Jeremy didn't respond, he continued. "It's good for you."

Jeremy chuckled despite himself. After gulping the rest of the beer, he tossed the empty in the trash can, walked over to the toilet, and started doing his business.

"It only hurts at first."

Laughing out loud, Jeremy flushed, washed his hands, splashed cold water on his face, and came out of the bathroom. Ignoring the shocked Francis, he focused on Reg. "Anything else?"

"Umm." Reg's eyebrows knitted in concentration. "I'll be your best friend after?"

"Oooh, that's the best reason yet." He bumped his shoulder against Reg's arm and grinned up at him. "You talked me into it." Turning his head to look at Francis, he dropped the smile and said, "Get the damn reporter and photographer in here. And tell them they've got ten minutes. After that, I'm out of here whether they're done or not."

"That's right." Reg draped his arm over Jeremy's shoulder. "I heard something about chess." He dipped his chin and met Jeremy's gaze. "Did I ever tell you I'm a kick-ass chess player?"

"Shut up."

"No. For reals. I'm awesome."

"I smell a bet coming on." Seeing movement from the corner of his eye, Jeremy glanced away from Reg and glared at Francis. "Why are you still here? The clock is running, and if these people complain about not having enough time to ask me all their questions, I'll tell Bill you were too busy staring at us to do your job, and he'll fire your ass."

Without another word, Francis rushed out of the room.

"You could be nicer, you know?" Reg pointed out. "I think you scared him."

Shrugging, Jeremy walked over to the armchair in the corner and collapsed. "Whatever. I'm one of the nice ones. You should hear how other people talk to their staff."

"Keep telling yourself that, superstar," Reg said, shaking his head disapprovingly.

"No. Seriously. What'd I do? Raise my voice? Explain the facts about his tenuous job security?" He scoffed. "Phil Spector used to point guns at people and shoot them off in the studio."

"Awesome." Reg opened the minifridge and grabbed a bottle of water. "I think you just made your nice-guy mantra,

'Eh, fuck 'em, at least I'm not committing criminal assault.'"

"All I'm saying is it could be worse. Francis shouldn't be in this business if telling him to do his job scares him."

"And this makes you nice?" Reg twisted off the cap and handed Jeremy the bottle.

Being with Reg made Jeremy aware that he wasn't as immune to behaving like a famous person as he'd liked to think. Always having prided himself on being a regular guy, the realization stung.

"Quit pouting. It wasn't that big a deal," Reg said, his voice more gentle. "You'll be nicer to him when he comes back, and that'll be the end of it." He tapped the bottle in Jeremy's hand. "Drink your water."

"You're a bartender. I think that means you're supposed to ply me with alcohol, not water." Jeremy looked up at Reg beseechingly.

"You've been on stage for hours, singing, dancing." Reg crossed his arms, making his shirt pull tightly across his broad chest. "Those lights have to be hot, and you're soaked with sweat."

"I know." Jeremy blinked and raised his gaze to meet Reg's. "That's why I need to relax."

"First you need to hydrate. Then you need to do your interview sober. After that, if you want, we can play chess."

Forehead creased, Jeremy said, "I missed the part of the plan where we're drinking."

"Oh." Reg waggled his eyebrows. "Didn't I mention we'd be playing shot-glass chess?"

"Shot-glass chess?"

"Yup. We'll use shot glasses for the game pieces. Every time you capture one of my pieces, you drink the glass. Same thing when I capture yours."

Sitting up straight, Jeremy beamed. "That sounds fun."

"It is." Reg tilted his chin toward the full water bottle. "Drink your water. Do your interview, and then we can go to the hotel room and play."

"Deal."

"I won," Reg said.

"Yeah, you did." Jeremy lay on the hotel-room floor, staring up at the ceiling. "How come you won even though you drank way more shots?"

"Um. That's why I won, dude." Reg lolled his head to the side and lowered his bleary-eyed gaze from the couch to where Jeremy was laying. "Drinks happen when pieces get captured, remember? I captured more of your pieces, plus your queen and your king, and those were double shots, so I totally outdrank you."

That was way too much logic for three in the morning and a bottle of whiskey. "Shouldn't you be more drunk? Or is it drunker? Less sober? Soberer?" Raising his hand to rub his eye, Jeremy punched himself in the nose instead. "Ow."

"You hit yourself," Reg pointed out unnecessarily. "That

was hilarious."

"Ha-ha." Crumpling his forehead and squinting, Jeremy examined the ceiling. "I think we're having an earthquake."

"Nuh-uh."

"Then why is the ceiling moving?"

Reg flicked his gaze up. "It's not moving."

"I'm looking at it right now and it's moving!" Jeremy insisted.

"You're smashed."

"Yeah." He giggled. "It's great."

"You're a cute drunk, you know that? Some people, you mix them with liquor, and they turn into major dicks."

"Yeah." Jeremy nodded solemnly, then widened his eyes and pointed up. "Do you see that? It's moving again."

Throwing his forearm over his eyes, Reg chuckled softly. "Nothing's moving up there, JJ. It looks that way to you because your head's sloshed, so things are moving on the inside."

"Are you sure?" he asked disbelievingly.

"Positive."

"Did you just call me JJ?"

"Huh?"

"You like nicknames. Superstar. JJ."

Raising his arm off his face, Reg glanced down at Jeremy. "Does it bug you?"

"No." Jeremy moved his head from side to side. Deciding he liked the motion, he kept doing it.

"Cool," Reg said.

After a few minutes of silence, during which Jeremy rolled his head and stretched his neck, he said, "You want to know something?"

"What?"

"I've never had a nickname."

"No way." Reg rolled onto his side, folded his arm, and propped his head on his hand.

"Swear." Jeremy crossed his fingers over his chest as he spoke. Well, he tried to cross his fingers over his chest. Mostly he bumped his chin and tickled himself.

"Why not?"

"Dunno." Jeremy shrugged. "I'm always"—he raised his arm and pointed at a spot above him—"The"—he moved his hand over a few inches—"Jeremy"—he moved it a bit further—"Jameson." He flopped his arm down.

"Huh." Reg furrowed his brow in thought. "What about before that?"

"What do you mean?"

"Well, you weren't recording albums when you were a kid."

"No. I would have, but my father said I couldn't." Jeremy sighed deeply. "It was the only rule he ever had for me. He said being a musician was fine, but standing on a stage was no place for a kid."

"He was probably right. Look at all the messed-up former child stars."

"Yeah. Probably."

"So what about back then? Before you started playing

on stage? I bet someone had a nickname for you before you were famous."

Taking his shirt collar in his mouth, Jeremy chewed on it and mumbled, "There is no before I was famous, Reg."

"What do you mean?"

"I was born famous." Jeremy released his shirt and sighed. "Just because I wasn't playing guitar and singing for crowds doesn't mean people didn't know who I was. Before I was *The Jeremy Jameson*, I was Beau Jameson's son or Paula Radcliffe's son or Walter Radcliffe's grandson."

"But you had friends...have friends. Right?"

"Sort of. There're always people around, but I think you have to be real for someone to give you a nickname, yeah?"

"You're real." Reg looked him straight in the face.

Closing his eyes, Jeremy whispered, "Sometimes I don't feel real." He drew his shirt back in and started chewing on it.

"Hey." Though he hadn't heard him get off the couch, suddenly Reg was right there, his arms on either side of Jeremy's face, his legs bent and straddling Jeremy's thighs, and his breath ghosting over Jeremy's face. "You're real, JJ." Reg tugged his shirt out of his mouth. "You're real."

"You think so. I can tell." He opened his eyes and met Reg's gaze. "I feel real when I'm with you." He grinned. "I mean, I know I'm trashed, but I feel real right now."

"That's because you are real." Reg paused. "*Real* bad at chess."

"Hey!"

"A *real* lightweight when it comes to drinking."

"I am n—"

"A *real* pain in the ass when you don't get your way."

"I'm going to punch you."

"I'd love to see you try, superstar." Reg's body tensed, like he was getting ready to move. "Because you're also a *real* pretty boy, and I would totally beat you in a fight."

He was off the ground and at the other end of the room before Jeremy could react.

"I am not a pretty boy!"

"Aww, sure you are. Just look at those delicate features—high cheekbones, plump lips, long eyelashes."

Jeremy scowled and flipped him off.

"Total pretty boy." With a wink, Reg walked over to the minifridge and picked up a couple of bottles of water and a bag of something Jeremy didn't recognize.

"Are you going to make me drink more water?"

"Yup." Reg raised his hand, said, "Catch," and then he tossed the bottle.

Though Jeremy missed the projectile, it landed squarely on his chest, so he told himself it was a successful catch. Unfortunately, Reg didn't agree.

"Dude, that was totally pathetic."

"I wasn't ready."

Reg arched one eyebrow. "Don't make it worse." He twisted the lid on his own bottle, said, "Bottoms up," and he started gulping it down.

Jeremy was still watching him swallow when he lowered the bottle and wiped the back of his hand across his mouth.

"Drink your water, JJ." Reg tore the edge off the bag he was holding.

"What's that?"

"Almonds. Nature's perfect snack." Reg came back to the couch and sat down, his knees spread and his posture relaxed. "I'll share them with you if you drink your water like a good boy."

"When you're sleeping, I'm going to write on your face in permanent marker," Jeremy threatened, trying to sound angry but pretty sure he wasn't pulling it off. He liked Reg way too much, even when he was razzing him. Or maybe it was because he did it.

"Drink."

With a glare, he started swallowing the cool water, realizing halfway through that he was thirsty. Before he could take the next step in the thinking process and get himself another bottle, Reg was off the couch, bringing it to him.

"Thank you." He blinked up at the big man and noticed that Reg's features were anything but delicate. His jawline was strong, his nose pronounced, though not large, and his cheeks had a constant five o'clock shadow.

"You're welcome." Reg handed Jeremy the bag of almonds. "Eat some of those."

Though he couldn't put his finger on the reason for it, when Reg told him to do something, Jeremy had no qualms about complying. Maybe it was because from Reg, the demands felt like they came from a place of caring rather than a desire to strengthen his brand. When Reg talked to him, Jeremy felt like he was addressing the man, not the star. Like he'd said, Reg made him feel real.

Rising to a sitting position, Jeremy watched Reg stretch his long body across the couch. "Reg?"

"Uh-huh?"

"Are you having an okay time so far?" It had only been a few days, so the question was probably premature, but Jeremy wanted to know, so he asked anyway.

"Totally. Hanging out with you is a blast, and the show tonight was awesome."

"Good." Jeremy smiled, relieved. He popped a few almonds into his mouth, realized he was hungry, and stuffed in another handful.

"How about you? Other than the interview you didn't want to do, you feeling good?"

"Yes," Jeremy immediately said through a mouthful of almonds, spitting onto his shirt and the carpet. Wiping the back of his hand across his lips, he thought about the question and realized he couldn't remember the last time he'd felt as happy as he had the past few days. "I'm feeling great."

"Awesome."

Sighing contentedly, Jeremy raised the water bottle to his lips.

"Come up here." Reg patted the sofa with his foot. "I know that carpet's plush, but it can't be as comfortable as this couch."

Looking over Reg's big body, Jeremy shook his head

and said, "I don't think you've got a two-guys-to-a-couch type of build."

"Oh-ho, that is totally not true. Trust me, dude, I've done a lot of two-guy couch time." He dragged his feet up, leaving a cushion empty. "There you go. Plenty of room."

"Okay." Jeremy crawled over to the couch and climbed up.

Immediately, Reg stretched his legs back out and rested his feet on Jeremy's lap. "Well, would you look at that?" He smiled smugly. "My feet are right there, so you might as well give me that foot rub you promised."

"If by 'promised' you mean said 'absolutely not,' then, sure." Jeremy finished off his water and tossed his bottle onto the coffee table.

"So that's a yes, right?" Reg tapped his feet on Jeremy's thigh. "Come on, superstar, don't leave me hanging."

"You seriously want me to rub your feet?"

Moaning, Reg said, "Totally. Man, a good foot rub is almost as good as a blow job."

"I'm not touching your feet, and I'm not going down on you."

"Oh, come on." Reg wiggled back a little, making more room on the sofa. "Be a good pretend boyfriend." He leered exaggeratedly. "I'll do you if you do me."

Narrowing his eyes, Jeremy looked from Reg's feet to his face.

"It'll be totally worth it, JJ. I give a mean"—he waggled his eyebrows—"foot rub."

"You'll massage my feet?"

"Yup." Reg spread his legs and patted his lap. "Stretch out on the other end, land your tootsies here, and I'll do you."

"All right, fine." Jeremy huffed and rolled his eyes, but he rotated until he was reclining against the arm of the couch opposite from Reg. He stretched his legs between Reg's, laying them on the bigger man's lap.

"Bet you get sore with all that jumping around you do on stage." Reg cupped the back of one of Jeremy's feet and rubbed his knuckle up and down the arch, making Jeremy moan. "I know what it's like to spend a long time on your feet. Taking care of them's important if you don't want to find yourself limping." While he talked, he continued the amazing massage, using his thumb to dig into the pads of each foot and his knuckles to press into the arches.

"Yeah." Jeremy's eyes rolled back from the sensation. "Oh God."

"Feel good?"

Nodding, he arched his back, the amazing feeling in his feet making his whole body tremble.

"Good." Reg's deep voice rumbled. "Just relax, JJ. I'll take care of you."

That was exactly what it felt like Reg did—took care of him, and not only with the massage. Everything from making sure he drank and ate enough to calling him on his shortcomings if he wasn't behaving like a decent human being; Reg was watching him, helping him.

"Thank you," Jeremy sighed. "You weren't kidding

about being good at this."

"Happy to do it." Reg moved his big hands up Jeremy's ankles and started in on his calves. "You make sure to tell me if you need me to help you out after your shows."

Jeremy whimpered.

"I can do your back and shoulders later if they're sore too."

"Ungh," Jeremy moaned.

Chuckling in response, Reg said, "I'll take that sound as affirmation that you like my idea." He paused. "Either that, or I just made you cream your pants without touching your dick."

"It's a near thing," Jeremy joked. "Keep touching me like that, and I might give you more than you bargained for."

"Bring it on, superstar. Bring it on."

CHAPTER 6

"JJ!" Reg shouted. "Get your ass out here. You went to bed early, and you've already overslept."

Off days were welcome rarities on the concert schedule, and Reg had made sure to plan excursions for every one of them. Two months into the tour, they had a three-day break before the show in Seattle. It was mid-July and the weather was perfect for white-water rafting, so he had organized a trip down the Deschutes River. After making certain everything they needed and nothing more was packed into a waterproof bag, he glanced at the closed door leading to Jeremy's latest hotel suite bedroom.

"Last warning, JJ, and then I'm coming in there and forcibly dragging your skinny butt out of bed."

He was surprised when Jeremy didn't immediately start telling him off and defending his backside. And he would have been right. The truth was, though Jeremy was compact, he was all muscle, ass included. Living in close quarters meant Reg had seen Jeremy in his skivvies on multiple occasions, and every time, his hands had itched with the urge to caress those muscular globes.

With his first attempt to rile Jeremy up failing, Reg tried

a different tack. "Don't think the whole 'I sleep naked' threat is going to warn me off, either." Hell, that was an incentive.

When no sound came from behind the door, Reg rolled his eyes and started walking toward it, stomping as loudly as he could to signal his approach. A buzzing sound stopped him in his tracks. Both of their phones were charging on the desk in the corner, and Jeremy's was vibrating and lighting up. Reg turned on his heel and retrieved the phone. Though he wouldn't answer it, he'd happily deliver Jeremy's phone to him...while he jumped up and down on his bed being as loud and obnoxious as necessary to get the man up.

"The river is calling and so is your manager," Reg yelled as he walked over to Jeremy's door. Palming the knob, he turned it and slowly pushed the door open. Squinting and blinking, he tried to adjust to the pitch black room. "How many hours sleep can one little guy need?"

When Jeremy once again didn't respond to his mocking, Reg started to worry. No way would Jeremy stand for being called a little guy. Even if, compared to Reg, that was exactly what he was.

"JJ?" He walked over to the drawn curtains and pulled them open a bit so he could see. "Are you okay?"

The lump in the bed moved and moaned. It wasn't the usual "I'm tired" moans, which Reg was used to. Not the "I'm drunk" groans either. This was a new noise, and it sounded pained. Immediately, Reg hurried over to the bed, his plan to tease Jeremy forgotten with the realization that something might be wrong with his friend.

"What's going on? Pull the blanket off your head and look at me." Reg reached the bed just as the sheet and comforter slid off Jeremy's face.

"Don't feel good," Jeremy mumbled. The puffy eyes, pale skin, and weak voice told Reg this wasn't an attempt at sleeping in.

Worried, Reg dropped the phone on the mattress and pushed Jeremy's now-bleached-blond hair off his forehead, letting his palm linger. "Crap. You're burning up."

"I think I'm sick." Grass green eyes blinked up at him. Jeremy always made sure to have eyeliner in place before he went somewhere he might be photographed, but it was morning, so his eyes were liner free.

The corners of Reg's mouth tilted up as he got an image of what Jeremy might have been like as a little boy. "Yeah, you are." He continued gently petting Jeremy's hair, which was soft without all the gel he used to spike it up. "How bad is it?"

Jeremy shrugged and pouted.

Reg's smile got bigger. "Does it feel like a cold, or should I call a doctor?"

Moving his head from side to side, Jeremy said, "Don't need a doctor."

"Okay. You stay here all cuddled up." Reg straightened the sheets and comforter and tucked them under Jeremy's chin. "And I'll go get you some Tylenol and juice." Unable to resist, he brushed his hand over Jeremy's hair again. "Sound good?"

"What about the rafting trip?" Jeremy swallowed hard.

"I know you were looking forward to it. Do you"—he looked down and bit his lower lip—"want to go ahead? I'll be fine here."

"No way. What kind of pretend boyfriend would I be if I abandoned you while you were sick?"

Jeremy shrugged again, this time glancing at Reg from underneath his lashes.

"I'll tell you what kind—a crappy one." Reg straightened up and smoothed out his shirt. "And I am an awesome pretend boyfriend, so you know that isn't happening." He winked. "Sit tight, superstar. I'll be back in a flash."

When Reg returned to the room with a tray of juice, water, and medicine, Jeremy's bed was empty. "JJ?" He set the tray on the edge of the bed and looked around.

"In here," Jeremy's weak voice sounded from the bathroom.

"Everything okay?" He stepped over and stood outside the door. "Can I come in?"

"Yeah, sure."

Slowly, Reg tipped the door open and walked into the huge, opulent bathroom. The size of the space rivaled his old apartment, except it was much fancier.

"JJ?" he said again when a fast glance showed gleaming marble, sparkling chrome fixtures, and fluffy towels, but no

Jeremy. A rustling sound and a moan drew his attention to the corner, where Jeremy's feet were sticking out of the doorway leading to the toilet. "What are you doing?"

"I'm working out."

His brow furrowed, Reg said, "You're what?" and he rushed over to Jeremy.

"You know that exercise where you're hunched over the toilet, getting a second look at your dinner?" Jeremy was sitting on the floor, slumped against the wall, with his head resting on the edge of the toilet. "I did two sets of that one."

"Well, you can't be that bad off if you're cracking jokes."

"You keep doing that," Jeremy mumbled.

"What?"

Jeremy raised his hand and patted Reg's arm, which was right by his face because Reg was, once again, brushing his fingers through Jeremy's hair.

"Touching my hair."

"Oh. Sorry, I—"

Reg started jerking his hand back, but Jeremy tightened the grip on his forearm. "'S okay. Feels good."

Gently, Reg massaged Jeremy's scalp. "It's soft without all that product you normally put in it."

"I need the product to look like a rock star."

"You *are* a rock star." Reg cupped Jeremy's neck and massaged the base of his skull with his thumb. "Your hair has nothing to do with that."

"Yeah," Jeremy sighed, and his eyelids drooped. "That's true."

"Is your stomach empty, or do you have to hurl more?"

"I'm done."

"All right." Reg crouched down, wrapped his arms around Jeremy's chest, and slowly pulled him to his feet. "Let's get your mouth rinsed out and tuck you back in bed."

"You don't have to touch me." Jeremy tried to pull away, but the effort was halfhearted. "I'm gross."

"You're fine. I was a bartender, remember? I'm used to puke." Reg walked backward out of the room, taking Jeremy with him. "Can you hold yourself up?" He leaned Jeremy against the counter.

"Yeah."

"I'm going to find mouthwash."

"Thank you." Jeremy smiled. His mouth was closed and his eyes were glassy, but it was still a smile.

"You're welcome, superstar." Reg ruffled his hair—he really was having trouble keeping his hands off it—and then dug through the basket on the counter for mouthwash and poured it into a sparkling crystal glass. "Bottoms up." He handed the glass to Jeremy. "That was a joke, by the way, don't swallow." He paused and grinned wickedly. "Wow. Never thought I'd say that sentence." He waggled his eyebrows. "Usually, I'd want the opposite."

Jeremy snorted and spit out the mouthwash. "You're mean." He wiped his hand across his chin. "Cut it out."

"All right. All right." Reg raised his arms in defeat. "Want to brush too, or will that gag you?"

Swirling the last of the liquid in his mouth, Jeremy

nodded, so Reg picked up his toothbrush and squeezed paste onto it.

"Here you go."

Jeremy brushed his teeth, only gagging a little, and then flattened his palms on the counter and sighed. "I'm getting light-headed."

With his arm curled around Jeremy's waist, Reg led them back to the bed. "What happened to sleeping naked?" he asked.

"I was cold." He crawled under the blanket. "You should be grateful. At least you didn't have to look at my hairy ass."

Arching his eyebrows, Reg asked, "It's hairy?"

"Well, not like Sasquatch, but...it's an ass. There's hair on it."

"Your chest isn't very hairy."

"Yes, it is!" Jeremy glanced down, but his shirt covered his chest. "Just because I'm not all"—he pointed and grunted—"Tarzan like you doesn't mean I don't have hair on my chest."

"How do you know Tarzan has a hairy chest?" Reg smirked. "Were you one of the kids who checked out Tarzan in the cartoon?" He swallowed down his laugh. "Because I would have sworn you were more of a Jane guy."

"I hate you."

"Aw, no you don't." Reg sat on the edge of the bed. "You love me."

"Hate," Jeremy grumbled.

"I'm the best pretend boyfriend ever."

Jeremy grunted.

"I have drinks and drugs," Reg pointed out as he held up the glass of orange juice and the Tylenol. "That is totally better than flowers and candy."

Rolling his eyes, Jeremy reached for the pills. "This doesn't count as drugs." He tossed them into his mouth and then grabbed the juice. "Or drinks." He gulped it down and thrust the cup back at Jeremy.

"Thanks, wonderful, handsome, perfect pretend boyfriend," Reg said in a high-pitched voice. "It was really nice of you to get those for me. You're the best!"

"Is that supposed to be an impression of me?" Jeremy asked incredulously. "Because I *so* don't sound like a dying, constipated, one-nutted squirrel."

"Uh." Reg's jaw dropped, and he tilted his head to the side. "You got a lot of experience with injured-squirrel sounds?"

Jeremy narrowed his eyes and glared.

"And how do you get them to roll over so you can examine their balls?"

"When I'm feeling better, I'm going to hurt you." He dragged his gaze over Reg's chest. "Well, when I'm feeling better and you're asleep, I'm going to hurt you."

Reg chuckled. "Sounds like a plan. But I'm awake right now, so it'll have to wait. In the meantime do you need an—"

The sound of Jeremy's phone interrupted them and reminded Reg of the call that had come in earlier. "Crap," he said. "Your manager called before, and I forgot to tell you." He started digging through the blankets. "I brought the phone in here, and then"—he tried to follow the sound and poked his head under the sheets—"you were sick, and I got distracted." Finding the phone, he grasped it just as it stopped ringing. "Sorry."

"Whatever." Jeremy shrugged. "Bill can wait."

Immediately, the phone started ringing again.

"Apparently, he disagrees," Reg said.

With a frustrated sigh, Jeremy answered the phone. "What?"

Reg shook his head at yet another display of Jeremy's frustration with the people who worked for him. He still struggled to understand it.

"What do you mean a leak?" Jeremy said. "How can there be a leak? The only two people who know anything about it are right here, and neither of us is leaking anything."

Reg coughed out a laugh. Jeremy glared at him.

"Whatever. Why should I care what they think anyway?" Jeremy was quiet while Bill spoke. Reg couldn't make out what he was saying, but he could hear enough to realize the words were coming fast. "That doesn't make any sense." Another pause from Jeremy, with more fast talking echoing from the phone. "You know what? I can't deal with this right now. I feel like crap. You figure it out." Jeremy hung up the phone, threw it across the bed, and then rolled onto his stomach and covered his head with the pillow.

"What'd Bill sa—" The phone rang. "Do you want to answer it?"

"No," Jeremy said, the word muffled by the pillow.

Reg waited for it to stop ringing and then tried again. "What'd he sa—"

As if on cue, the hotel room phone began to ring.

"I'm not talking to him," Jeremy insisted, peeking out from under the pillow. "I'm sick. Shouldn't people leave me alone when I'm sick?"

On that point, Reg agreed. "I'm sorry, JJ." Reg rubbed circles on his back. "You're right. It's not—"

During that short back and forth, the cell phone started up again. "What do you want to bet he sends someone up here next?" Jeremy sucked his shirt into his mouth and hid his face again. "They'll bang on the door until we open it."

Gaping at the prospect that Bill would do that and then realizing Jeremy was right, Reg snapped, "This is ridiculous," and he lunged for the phone. "Hello."

After a pause, Bill said, "Reggie?"

"Yup."

"I need to talk with Jeremy."

When Jeremy whimpered, Reg ground his teeth and said, "No."

"Pardon me?"

"You heard me. He's sick. I heard him tell you that. He woke up with a fever, and he threw up. No more stress today. He needs to rest."

"I'm not causing him stress," Bill said, and Reg could practically hear his eyes rolling. "I'm having a simple conversation about a developing issue we need to deal with.

It's called being an adult."

"Uh-huh. Stress."

"Look, Reggie, I don't have time to debate this with you. Put Jeremy on the phone."

Reg wasn't looking for a debate either, so he once again said, "No."

"I'm his manager, and I need to talk to him right now."

Really, Reg wasn't clear on what Bill wasn't getting. "No."

"I don't know who you think you are, but—"

"I'm his boyfriend, who cares about him, and there's nothing he can do about whatever it is you need right now anyway, so I'm not letting you talk to him."

"That's what I wanted to talk about, actually."

Suddenly feeling lost, Reg said, "What do you mean?"

"There's been a leak. The boyfriend thing isn't flying, and we're starting to see backlash. I think we need to go in a different direction."

Reg patted Jeremy's back one final time, climbed off the bed, and walked out of the room so he wouldn't disturb him with the conversation. "I have no clue what you're saying, man. Try it again in civilian-speak, okay? I'm new to the whole, uh, industry lingo or whatever."

With a deep sigh, Bill said, "Basically, a source close to Jeremy told the press you're not really his boyfriend. They're saying it's a front."

After being with Jeremy nonstop for two months, Reg was hard-pressed to come up with a single person who he'd consider *close* to Jeremy. Well, other than him. As soon as he had that realization, his chest ached. Jeremy Jameson was a wonderful man. He deserved to have a lot of people in his life who truly cared about him, not only some guy he'd just met.

"Putting aside the fact that *I* didn't speak to the press, so there's no possible source who'd have access to that information, are you seriously saying they think Jeremy is in the closet about being straight?" Shaking his head at the latest example of things he'd never understand about the people in Jeremy's life, Reg said, "That doesn't make any sense. Why would anybody pretend to be gay?"

"You tell me," Bill said pointedly.

"I would if I could, but like I said, it makes no sense."

"And yet…" Bill let the thought trail off, leaving Reg in the same confused state.

"And yet what?"

"Come on. There's no reason to lie to me."

"Dude, I'm gay. That's not a lie. I don't have a clue why someone would lie about that." Well, unless they wanted a friend by their side while they moved from location to location and felt like it was the only way to have it. But that lie had less to do with being gay and more to do with being lonely. "Like Jeremy said, whatever. Their source is bullshit, and I don't see why it matters, anyway."

"It matters," Bill said slowly, like he was talking to someone who had trouble understanding obvious concepts. "Because with everyone in the LGBT-rights community working hard to pass equality laws and win court cases, people don't appreciate being mocked or—"

"Nobody is mocking anyone," Reggie barked.

Ignoring him, Bill continued, his voice louder. "Or having someone send a message that people can suddenly *choose* to be gay." He took in a deep breath. "Think this through, Reggie. The corollary to snapping your fingers and saying 'I'm gay' is doing the opposite—snapping your fingers and saying 'I'm straight' or maybe going to one of those reprogramming places or marrying a person of the opposite sex or whatever else people claim cures homosexuality."

Bill's rant made sense, and Reg was busy processing it, so he didn't respond. The lack of argument seemed to calm Bill down. He lowered his voice and continued.

"If you can choose to be gay, you can choose to be straight, and I'm sure you can understand how problematic that concept is for people who devote their lives to this work. They don't need the world's most well-known musician undermining their cause."

Collapsing onto the couch, Reg rubbed his hand over the back of his head. He understood Bill's point. Realizing you were gay often came with an initial desire to change it. For some people, that lasted longer than for others. And then there were the well-intentioned and not-so-well-intentioned family members who insisted being gay was a curable affliction.

Reg had been lucky. His bouts of confusion and self-doubt over who he was had been short-lived. Though he'd had a grandfather who likely would have had some choice words for him, he had passed several years before Reg came out. The rest of his family—his mother, his brother and sister-in-law, and his grandmother—had never turned their backs on him or belittled him. He'd lost some friends around the time he had come out, but it was the summer after high school ended, which was a time when people drifted apart anyway. So from a young age, Reg had been in the "I didn't choose to be gay, I just got lucky" camp.

But the fact that his life had been relatively pain free didn't mean he wasn't aware that the opposite was true all too often. He had known guys in college whose parents cut them off, financially and in other ways. He had heard stories about teasing, sometimes leading to physical attacks. He had even known of a guy who had hanged himself in his dorm room because, according to his suicide note, his life wasn't worth living if he couldn't be straight.

"I hear you, man," Reg said. "I get what you're saying."

"Good. So you'll give Jeremy the phone, and I can—"

"No."

This time, Bill's sigh was decidedly annoyed. "We just went over this. The gay story isn't going to fly. We need to do damage control, and the first step is me figuring out what Jeremy's trying to accomplish. Then I need to conjure a plausible explanation for how the whole thing with you was misinterpreted. I have some ideas about that, and I need to discuss them with Jeremy."

"No."

"Reggie—"

"Let me finish." Reg held his arm out in a "stop" motion even though Bill couldn't see him. "I understand what you mean. Believe me, I understand. But Jeremy isn't out there screaming from the rooftops about his personal life. Those reporters and photographers want a story, so they ask every question under the sun, including things people wouldn't be bold enough to ask their best friends, and then they print the answers. Do you really think it's fair that he has to change his life to accommodate them? Isn't who he dates his business and nobody else's?"

"I'll answer that with a word you seem to understand well: no."

"No?" Reg asked in surprise.

"Jeremy has chosen to lead a public life. He put himself in the spotlight. Like it or not, that position comes with the fact that people he'll never meet feel entitled to know everything about him and weigh in on it."

"But it's his life."

"Yes, it's his life. But it's also a public life."

"So he can't be gay because he's famous? That's your advice?"

"You know that's not what I'm saying."

"It's exactly what you're—"

"Jeremy Jameson being gay isn't the issue. I've spent the past couple of months managing that concept, and I've done a damn good job of it. The issue is him pretending to be gay."

"And you think he's pretending because of the *source*."

"I think he's pretending because I know him, and, frankly, if he was actually into men, he wouldn't be with you."

"Uh, I'll have you know I'm a pretty good catch, dude."

Chuckling, Bill said, "I have no doubt. But I've met Jeremy's exes, so I know what kind of women he likes. They're smaller than him, softer, more pliant. They're in the industry, so they understand his life. And they don't call him dude."

"Well, you're right: none of those descriptions fit me. But for now, I'm his boyfriend, and I'm not letting anybody, you included, stress him out while he's sick." Reg drew in a deep breath. "You're not talking to him."

Bill was silent for so long, Reg thought he'd hung up, but then he said, "You actually do care about him."

It wasn't a question, but Reg answered anyway. "Yes. I care a lot."

CHAPTER 7

JEREMY woke up disoriented. He rubbed his eyes, sat up, and darted his gaze around the room. Hotel. Tour. And according to the clock on the nightstand, late afternoon. His body felt sore and achy, and he tried to remember what thrill-seeking adventure Reg had dragged him to that caused his pain.

"Reg?" he croaked. He cleared his throat and tried again. "Reggie?"

The door opened seconds later. "Hey." Reg smiled and walked over to the bed. "How're you feeling?"

That's right. The achy feeling was from being sick, not from jumping off something high or climbing up something tall or whatever other shenanigan Reg might have come up with.

Taking stock of his body, Jeremy said, "Not a hundred percent yet, but I definitely feel better than I did earlier."

"Good." Reg sat on the edge of the bed and rested his palm on Jeremy's forehead. "You're not as hot. How about your stomach? You think you might throw up again?"

"God, I hope not."

"I've got some crackers and water. I'll bring them in here."

"That sounds good."

"You need anything else?"

"No." Jeremy shook his head.

"Okay. Hang tight." With a gentle squeeze to Jeremy's shoulder, Reg stood.

"Reg," Jeremy said as he reached out and grasped Reg's wrist.

Darting his gaze from Jeremy's hand to his face, Reg said, "What's up?"

"I'm sorry for ruining the white-water rafting trip. I know you were excited about it."

"It's no big deal." Reg patted Jeremy's arm. "We'll do it some other time."

Jeremy nodded in response, and Reg left the room, then returned almost immediately with a box of crackers and bottles of Vitamin Water. He set them down on the nightstand and went into the bathroom, then came back with a crystal tumbler in his hand.

"Fancy shmancy hotel, and they don't have any plates." He poured some crackers into the glass. "You can use this instead. There's nothing worse than getting crumbs in the bed."

"True." Jeremy popped a cracker into his mouth.

Reg sat next to him, twisted open a cap on one of the water bottles, and held it out. "I talked to Bill while you were sleeping."

"You did?"

"Uh-huh. I had him on the phone, remember? You

were so tired you crashed when I was in the other room." Reg tilted his chin toward the bottle. "Drink."

Jeremy raised the water to his lips.

"He told you about the issue with what he's calling a leak and I'm calling a lie, right?" Reg paused and frowned. "Well, I guess it's not a lie because it's true, so maybe I should say a lucky guess."

"Yeah. Somebody told somebody you're not my boyfriend, and because apparently this is the first time in the history of ever a celebrity has been perceived to be less than honest about a significant other, all hell has broken loose."

"Uh, I think maybe that's overstating it a little."

Jeremy pouted.

"Quit pouting."

"I don't pout!"

"Okay. Quit pressing your lips together and pushing them out in what strongly resembles a pout."

Flipping Reg off, Jeremy started gulping the water.

"What do you want to do?" Reg asked.

"Right now?"

"About the press issue."

"Nothing," Jeremy said stubbornly.

"Nothing?"

"Why? Are you worried what people will think of you if—"

"No."

Tension drained from Jeremy's body. "Are you sure?"

"Nobody knows me, JJ. They don't care about me. Bill

says this whole thing hurts you."

"Do I look hurt?" Jeremy shivered a little and pulled the blanket higher on his waist.

"Well, actually, right now you're not at your healthie—"

"I'm sick, not hurt."

"I know." Reg leaned forward and brushed Jeremy's hair off his forehead. "And you know what your manager means."

"I rarely know what my manager means."

Rolling his eyes and sighing, Reg said, "Your public image is at risk."

"I don't care."

"You don't care about your public image?" Reg asked disbelievingly.

"Well, I care, I guess. But I don't care, yeah?"

"You lost me."

"I want to sell albums, so of course I care. But this is bullshit. How can people say I'm setting a bad example by acting like I flipped a switch and went from straight to gay if they're not in my head? What if I've been gay and struggling with it the whole time? Or what if I'm bi, and this just happens to be the first public relationship I've had with a man?"

"Are you?"

"Well, no." Jeremy crinkled his forehead together. "But they don't know that. Honestly, sex isn't a big deal anyway. I'm not sure it'd matter who was in my bed as long as they stayed in it."

"Uh, you lost me."

"You know what I mean. The best part of sex isn't the sex," Jeremy said, stating what he knew was obvious.

"It isn't?" Reg asked as he jerked back, looking truly surprised.

"No. The act itself is awkward and messy and sticky."

"What's the best part of sex?"

For the first time since he'd met Reg, Jeremy felt sorry for him. With Reg's large size, deep voice, and daring personality, he came across as older than twenty-six. But maybe at his age, he hadn't done much more than tangle between the sheets and walk away.

Trying not to sound condescending, Jeremy said, "The best part is having someone there, touching you. The before, the after—that's what it's all about."

Understanding took over Reg's face. "You have sex to get a human connection?" he said softly.

"Sure. Everyone does," Jeremy said firmly.

Brushing his fingers through Jeremy's hair, Reg smiled. "I don't know if that's true, JJ. At least not based on what I've heard people say."

"People lie." Jeremy waved his hand dismissively. "It's like the guys in high school who bragged about nailing every hot girl. But ask the girls, and you'd know it was crap." When Reg looked at him, his brow crinkled, but he didn't respond, Jeremy clarified. "It's an image thing."

"Uh, I don't think—"

"You'll understand when you get older." He patted Reg's leg. "Anyway, my point is, nobody else is in my head, so how can they know who I want in my bed?"

Reg nodded. "You're right."

"It's not fair. Gay people are people. They're not all the same as each other. Just because I'm really, really masculine doesn't—"

Reg started laughing. Hard.

"Why are you laughing?" Jeremy asked. When Reg didn't answer and kept cackling, Jeremy glared. "Are you laughing at me?"

Nodding, Reg alternated his laughter with gasps for air.

"Why?"

"You," Reg barely spat out. "You think you're..." It seemed he couldn't breathe enough to finish the sentence. Not with as hard as he was laughing.

"What?"

Holding his hand out, Reg said, "Give me a minute." He drew air in and let it out slowly. "Catching my breath."

"Take your time," Jeremy said sarcastically. "I don't mean to rush you away from mocking me."

"Not mocking." Another breath. "But, dude, you can't actually think you're Mr. Butch."

"What do you mean?" Jeremy asked in confusion.

"You wear makeup."

"On stage!" Jeremy shouted defensively. "I'm putting on a show; that's how it works."

Raising his eyebrows, Reg looked at Jeremy meaningfully. "Only on stage?"

"Yes."

"So you don't wear eyeliner, blush, and lipstick when we go to events?"

"It's lip stain, not lipstick," Jeremy grumbled and crossed his arms over his chest.

"That's a yes."

"Those are public appearances. I have a certain image I need to maintain."

"Right. And when we go for a walk to explore a new city or grab a meal?"

The questions were getting more difficult to answer. "We're in public. We could be photographed. I don't want to end up in some magazine looking pasty and washed-out."

"Right." Reg nodded. "So you make sure to sculpt your hair to within an inch of its life, cover yourself with makeup, and wear tight clothes." He paused. "Totally butch."

"I'm not *covered* in makeup, and you don't understand the industry."

His arms flying up in an exaggeratedly defensive motion, Reg said, "No. No. I get it. It's just like when Bruce Springsteen...uh, wait. Nope. The Boss never wore lip *stain*."

"Are you making fun of my appearance?" Jeremy asked, his voice cracking.

"No," Reg said, no longer laughing. "I think you look great." He squeezed Jeremy's shoulder. "Seriously. My only point is that you being some sort of macho man isn't the reason they don't believe you're gay."

"So you think it's all because of the leak?"

Taking in a deep breath, Reg thought about it. "That's a big part of it. But also, you've been famous since forever, right? That's what you told me. And that whole time, you've dated women, and there's been no hint of rumor or scandal."

"Uh, clearly you don't follow the tabloids. I have been the subject of many rumors and scandals. Some real, most imaginary."

"What I'm saying is you've never been photographed with a guy in a compromising position."

"Great. So all we need to do is put out a sex tape, and that'll solve this whole issue?"

Reg choked on nothing and started coughing furiously.

"It was a joke. Don't get all terrified." Jeremy tilted his bottle and finished off the water.

"I wasn't terrified."

"No?" Jeremy asked, his tone indicating his amusement and disbelief.

"No," Reg rasped, reaching out to tuck Jeremy's hair behind his ear.

Enjoying the feeling of being touched so gently, Jeremy leaned into Reg's hand. "Well, if you can claim you didn't just have a heart attack at the prospect of having sex with me, then I can claim I'm ultramacho," he said, trying to joke, but not doing a great job of it because the feeling of Reg's big, rough palm on his face made his words come out slowly.

It seemed he was more under the weather than he realized. His eyes had drifted shut when he felt Reg climb out of the bed.

"I'm getting you more water," Reg said as he walked out of the room, his back to Jeremy and his voice sounding husky. "Do you want anything else?"

"No. I'm good," Jeremy called after him.

It took Reg longer to return that time. "Sorry," he said as he walked into the room. "I had to return one last call about our trip cancelation." He twisted the bottle open and handed it to Jeremy.

Immediately, Jeremy was flooded with guilt and anxiety. "I'll be okay here alone if you want to go out and do something," he said after chewing on his shirt collar. "We don't have many off days, and I know you don't want to be stuck in here with me."

"Are you kidding?" Reg smiled and sat on the bed. "We'll have a blast. We can watch bad TV, ask each other embarrassing questions, and if you can keep food down, we'll order room service." He ruffled Jeremy's hair and shifted his stance until he was leaning against the headboard and sitting cross-legged. "It'll be fun. Promise."

Though being sick had never been fun, the way Reg explained it made Jeremy believe it'd be true.

"Okay," Jeremy said.

"Cool." Reg beamed. "What do you want to do first?" He reached for the remote. "TV?"

"Uh, let's do the embarrassing-questions thing," Jeremy said quietly.

Flicking his gaze toward Jeremy, Reg snickered. "Why do I get the feeling you already have questions lined up?"

Jeremy shrugged and arched his eyebrows, trying to look innocent.

"All right, whatever." Reg rolled his hand in a "get on with it" gesture. "Let's hear it. What's your question?"

"When was the last time you cried?" Jeremy said immediately.

"The last time I cried? That's your embarrassing question?"

Feeling his cheeks heat, Jeremy lowered his gaze. "Well, you're Mr. Tough Guy, yeah?"

"I am not," Reg denied.

"When we went climbing and I grabbed those rocks wrong and rolled one on your foot, you barely flinched."

"We were on a mountainside. Flinching would have been hella dumb."

"Okay. How about the time those drunk guys stormed us after the show? I was sure we were getting taken down, and you stepped right into their path."

"You have a million security people around at those shows. Nobody was getting to you, and if they'd tried, they would have had to get through me first."

"That's what I mean."

Rolling his eyes, Reg said, "Fine. You want to know the last time I cried?" He pursed his lips and crinkled his forehead in thought. "Uh, it was probably a few years ago, when I found out my brother Ryan got one of those illnesses that makes you think buying fake nuts for your truck looks cool."

"You jerk." Jeremy smacked Reg's arm. "I was being serious."

"So was I. We were all worried." Sighing deeply, Reg solemnly said, "For a while there, it was touch and go. Thankfully, my sister-in-law stepped in and told Ryan if he attached any sort of genital reproduction to their vehicle, she'd assume he was crazy and have him committed so he wouldn't be able to frighten the children." Reg drew in a breath and shook his head. "Those were scary times, man. Scary times." In an instant, he wiped the serious expression from his face, grinned, and said, "All right, my turn."

"You're cheating, but fine." Jeremy chuckled. "What's your embarrassing question?"

"Okay." Reg's brown eyes twinkled. He rubbed his hands together conspiratorially and leaned forward. "I've always wondered…"

Jeremy braced himself for what he was sure would be an invasive and humiliating question.

"How did you choose which instrument to play?"

His jaw dropped. "How is that embarrassing?"

"It's not, but neither is crying, and you asked me about it," Reg explained. "Besides, I've always wanted to know."

"For real?"

"Uh-huh."

"Uh, well, let's see." Jeremy held up one finger. "I'm not intellectual enough to be a keyboard player." He crooked one side of his lips up. "Plus, I wanted to have sex sometimes."

"Even though it isn't that great?"

"Someday you'll share a bed with someone, and you'll understand what I mean. Sex will make more sense when you have a warm body close to you all night. Anyway—" With a deep breath, Jeremy raised another finger. "Being a drummer would have been cool, but I fell short on the 'batshit insane and no personal limits' requirements." He shrugged. "Besides, if I had that much sex, my dick would fall off."

Reg snorted.

"That leaves bass." He raised a third finger. "And, really, what's the point? I'm good enough to play guitar. This way people know my name. Plus, I won't end up bitter and stuck in rehab."

"This game isn't working." Reg slid down until he was lying on the bed instead of sitting on it.

Handing him a pillow, Jeremy asked, "What game?"

"The embarrassing-question game. So far, we've asked two not-embarrassing questions and gotten two ridiculous nonanswers."

"Speak for yourself. My answer about which instrument I play was fully aboveboard."

Arching his eyebrows and twisting his lips in amusement, Reg said, "You're saying you chose your musical instrument based on sex, which you don't even like all that much?"

"That's only one part of what I said. And besides, it was more the idea of sex. I started playing guitar when I was in middle school. It's not like I'd done the deed at that point."

"Okay, fine." Reg rolled his eyes. "You chose to play

guitar for a living because of theoretical sex and fame?"

"Yeah." Jeremy nodded. "That's about right."

Sighing, Reg shook his head. "You can hear yourself, right?"

Jeremy wriggled around until he was comfortable and then lay on his side, facing Reg. "It's not a weird answer, believe it or not. I bet most guitar players have the same two reasons, along with, 'Because it looks cool.' The only difference is they won't admit it. I'm not screaming it from the rooftops either; usually I give some spiel about being inspired by my father. But you asked me for the truth, and you're my pretend boyfriend, so I gave it to you."

With a chuckle, Reg said, "Are you always one hundred percent honest in your pretend relationships?"

"This is my first one, so, yeah."

"Fair enough. How about in your real relationships? Are you always completely honest?"

It didn't take long for Jeremy to come up with several examples of situations when he'd been less than honest with his ex-girlfriends. "No. I haven't always been honest."

"Why not?"

After giving it some thought, Jeremy realized the fundamental reason was always the same. "It's easier that way."

"How do you mean?"

"I told you how it is with people in this industry. They're not with me because of me, and even if they are, it's a small part. Mostly, it's the mystique of dating a musician or someone famous, or a hope that they'll elevate their own careers. With people like that, there's inevitable disappointment because what they came into the relationship wanting and what they end up getting aren't the same thing. The last thing I need to do is add to that frustration and resentment and guarantee some tell-all exposé. So instead of being brutally honest, I spew the garbage they want to hear."

Reg cleared his throat and licked his lips. "Uh, JJ, I don't think what you're describing is a *real* relationship."

"What do you mean? Sure they are. Some people stick it out longer than others, but usually we stay together for close to a year at least. That's a decent length of time for a relationship."

"I know. But like with my brother and his wife, they fight and stuff, but they're in it together. It's not about what they can get from each other. Even my parents, before my dad died, they were like a team. Do you get what I'm saying?"

In theory, Jeremy knew, but that wasn't his reality. "It's not like that when you live your life in the spotlight."

"I'm sorry," Reg said, and he looked sad as he said it. "That must be really hard and lonely."

"It's fine." Jeremy shrugged. "It's all I know."

Reg squared his shoulders and narrowed his eyes. It was his determined stance. Jeremy had seen it whenever the man was about to embark on a challenge nobody else would dare try. He had seen Reg dive off a bridge against the advice of the bungee-jump operator because his cord was so long that most of his body dipped into the lake underneath, face included. His expression had looked exactly the same when he had jumped off, and when he had bounced back, he had been smiling from ear to ear.

"Not anymore," Reg said.

"What do you mean?" Jeremy asked.

"You're with me now, so that won't be all you know."

"Uh, I don't under—"

"I'm going to show you what it means to have a real relationship, JJ." Reg paused and grinned. "Even if it is pretend."

CHAPTER 8

REG climbed out of the cab and walked into the building where he was supposed to meet Jeremy after his interview with the local radio station that had been promoting his show in Portland. He'd offered to come along for the interview, but Francis, the publicist, said there wouldn't be enough space in the small recording studio.

The station had been holding a contest for weeks to choose five winners who could come see Jeremy Jameson in person while he answered questions on the air. Between the winners, the radio staff, Jeremy, and Francis, there wasn't room for anybody else. So Reg had taken the free time to call his brother and mother and then do some research about what he and Jeremy could do on their off days once they were on the East coast.

"Good morning," Reg said to the guard at the front desk. "I'm here to meet Jeremy Jameson at K101." When the guard furrowed his brow, Reg assumed he wasn't giving enough information. Thankfully, he remembered the radio personalities' names. "He's with Tim and Tammy."

"I know where he is." The guard reached underneath the raised counter, and the sound of Jeremy's voiced filled the large, open room for a second before the guard turned the radio back down.

"Perfect." Reg pointed at the elevator bank. "So what floor should I go to?"

"The floor is locked this morning because of Mr. Jameson's appearance." The guard picked up a clipboard. "Are you on the list?"

From his tone, Reg gathered the guard assumed the answer was no, but he was going through the motions. His next move likely would be asking Reg to vacate the premises.

"I don't know if I'm on there. My name's Reggie Moore." Reg leaned toward the clipboard.

Jerking away, the guard narrowed his eyes at Reg before raising the clipboard and making a show out of dragging his finger down the page and shaking his head. "You're not one of the contest winners."

"Oh! Sorry. I didn't realize that was what you meant about a list." He smiled, trying to get the man to relax. "I'm not one of the winners."

"You don't have a badge, so you don't work for the station. If you're not on the list of winners, I can't let you up."

Not wanting to cause a scene, Reg said, "I understand. I'll wait over there"—he pointed to a group of armchairs on the other side of the elevator bank—"until Jeremy gets done. Thanks for your help."

He turned around and got his phone out of his pocket, intending to text Jeremy to let him know where he was waiting.

"I can't let you do that," the guard said from behind him. Then he heard a chair rolling followed by footsteps.

"We need to keep the lobby secure. We can't have fans here harassing Mr. Jameson."

Being considered a security risk was new. Reg decided he'd take it as a compliment. Besides, he knew Jeremy would get a kick out of the story, which made the minor hassle worthwhile.

The guard stepped over to Reg's side, put one hand over what looked like pepper spray attached to his belt, and pointed toward the door with his free hand. "I'm not sure how you found out they're recording here today instead of at the normal studio, but I'm going to have to ask you to leave the building."

After considering whether he should tell the guard he wasn't packing a weapon and ultimately deciding that might make him sound more suspicious, Reg said, "I'm not a fan." He paused. "Well, of course I'm a fan, but that's not why I'm here." He stepped away from the guard, not too far, but enough to get some personal space.

The guard looked Reg up and down, as if measuring his chances, and then tensed and reached for his radio, presumably to ask for help dealing with the Jeremy Jameson stalker in the lobby.

"Look, man, I know Jeremy's here because he told me," Reg explained. "I'm supposed to meet him here after his interview."

"Jeremy Jameson told you he was here?" the guard

said disbelievingly. "Why would he do that?"

"Because I'm his boyfriend, and we're having breakfast together." Reg took in a calming breath. Trying to neutralize the hostile situation, he added, "You know any good places around here?"

"His boyfriend?"

Reg nodded.

"Sir," the guard sighed. "Do you have someone I can contact to come get you? A family member, maybe?"

Great. Now the man thought he was delusional. The situation was getting worse, but on the plus side, the story he'd be able to tell Jeremy was getting better.

"I appreciate your concern, but I'm fine." Reg shook his head and smiled at the ridiculousness of the situation. "You know what? I'll get out of your hair and wait outside."

"Loitering outside the building isn't permissible either," the guard insisted. "I'll have to call the police."

"I'm not loitering. I'm here to meet a person currently working in this building." Reg rubbed the back of his head as he tried to figure out how to convince the guard he wasn't a threat. "How about I call Jeremy's manager, and he can tell you who I am?"

"Manager?"

"Yes."

"How would I know who that is? You could call anyone and say he's Jeremy Jameson's manager."

It was a fair point.

"All right. Next time, I'll get a signed note from Jeremy

giving me permission to see him. But for now, what are my options?"

"Like I said, you're not on the list, and you don't work in the building. The only option is for you to leave."

Before Reg could argue again, his phone rang. He glanced down at his hand and saw Jeremy's number. "Saved by the bell," he said as he answered the call. "JJ, hey, sorry I'm not—"

"I'm done doing interviews!" Jeremy ranted. "Done! I don't care what Bill says or how many times he has Francis hound me."

"What happened?" Reg asked, immediately more concerned about Jeremy's agitated state than the impending security battle he was facing.

"They spent maybe two minutes asking about my album and the show and the rest of the time not so subtly trying to trip me up about who I'm dating or doing or whatever. It's been three months. You'd think they'd get sick of this line of questioning, but no!" About halfway through Jeremy's sentence, Reg could hear Francis in the background, talking at a fast clip. "I don't care, Francis! I'm sick of it."

"All right, superstar, calm down," Reg soothed.

Speaking of calm, he wondered why he hadn't yet been bodily removed from the building. A quick glance up answered his question. His good friend, the security guard, was now outside the glass doors holding his arm out to keep what looked like several camera crews out of the building while he yelled into his radio. Bigger fish to fry, apparently.

"Why do *I* always have to be the one to calm down?" Jeremy asked.

"Because you're always the one getting worked up?" Reg suggested with a chuckle. "If it makes you feel any better, I think it's really cute when you have your little tantrums. I just wish you could tone down the rudeness."

"I'm not cute!"

In addition to Francis's voice, Reg heard a dinging sound.

"Sure you are. In fact, there seems to be a gathering of camera people outside the building wanting to film your cuteness for the world to witness."

"What are you talking about?"

"I'm in the lobby of the radio building. They wouldn't let me up because I'm not on the list."

"What list?"

"Doesn't matter. You're on your way down here anyway, right?"

"Yes."

"Good. Brace yourself, though—there's a crowd of people outside."

"Dammit! Francis, why is there press outside? Who leaked my location again? Why can't you ever take care of this so—"

"JJ, stop," Reg said firmly.

Remarkably, he did.

"I know you're pissed, and it was a bad morning, but calm down. I'm here waiting for you. We'll deal with the press when you get downstairs. Until then, just breathe and try to relax. No more yelling."

"Okay," Jeremy mumbled. "Elevator's here."

"I'll be waiting." Reg pocketed his phone and walked over to the elevator bank, keeping his eyes on the growing crowd outside. "Man, JJ is not going to like this," he muttered to himself.

When the elevator doors slid open moments later, he was proven right. Jeremy stepped out, his expression stormy, glanced toward the windows and glass doors, and then rounded on Francis, his arms flying into the air and his posture threatening.

"Hold on there, hotrod," Reg said as he darted forward and circled his arm around Jeremy's chest, tugging him backward.

Francis was typing on his phone, and then he glanced toward the glass doors and started scooting away. Reg followed his gaze and saw the people outside with their cameras raised and focused on them through the windowed wall. He tightened his hold on Jeremy, pressing his chest to Jeremy's back, and dipped his face so his mouth was touching Jeremy's ear.

"What are you doing?" Jeremy asked, his entire body tensing.

"Everyone can see us," Reg explained.

"They can?"

"Uh-huh," Reg whispered into his ear. "Cameras are flashing, and they're hoping to get a picture of you acting like an ass." He took in a deep breath, enjoying the scent of the man in his arms more than he should. "Don't play into it."

Jeremy gulped and said, "Okay."

"I have an idea."

"Wh—" Jeremy cleared his throat. "What idea?"

"You said they were giving you a hard time in the interview again, right?"

"Yeah."

Reg kept one hand around Jeremy's waist and slid the other around his chest. "They still think you're lying about us so you can get press or attention or whatever?"

"Yeah." He gulped. "Or else they're just nosey pervs. Probably both."

"How about we stand here for a minute"—Reg ghosted his lips over the perimeter of Jeremy's ear—"and let them take some pictures of us like this." He dragged his palm across Jeremy's torso, caressing him through his shirt. "Maybe it'll help answer any question and satisfy any curiosity once and for all."

"Okay," Jeremy rasped.

Relishing the opportunity to touch Jeremy freely, Reg lost himself in the moment and felt every inch of Jeremy's chest, stomach, and sides. He inhaled his scent and was about to take a taste of his heated skin when Jeremy spoke again, reminding him where they were.

"How long?"

"Dunno." Reg moved his mouth from Jeremy's ear to his neck, almost but not quite touching. "You in a rush?"

"No."

The way Jeremy trembled, panted, and pushed into his touch should have taken Reg by surprise, but he'd spent enough time with the man over the previous three months to realize that Jeremy's assertion about nobody knowing what he really felt inside was true for more than the press—it applied to Jeremy as well.

"You okay with me touching you this way?" he asked as he slowly slid the hand around Jeremy's waist down his hip.

"They can see?"

"With lenses that big?" Reg spread his fingers so his thumb moved dangerously close to Jeremy's groin. "You can count on it."

"Well, then, you should keep touching, yeah?"

"I should."

"You don't—" Jeremy gasped when Reg dragged his hand up, his thumb even closer to Jeremy's zipper that time. "You don't mind?"

"Mind touching you?" He moved his fingers over Jeremy's nipple. "Mind holding you?"

"Yeah," Jeremy said after a few beats.

"No, JJ, I don't mind." Reg pressed his lips to Jeremy's neck and squeezed him even tighter. "Do you?"

"N...no."

"Is that because of the cameras, or is it because of what you told me about needing to be touched?"

"I don't...what?"

"Because I'll touch you, JJ." Reg moved his palm to

Jeremy's throat and dragged his thumb up and down the side of his neck. "Cameras or no cameras. You ever need to be held, let me know." He kissed Jeremy's nape. "I'm here." Pulling on Jeremy's shoulder, Reg slowly turned him around and then cupped his neck and tipped his chin up until their gazes met. "In whatever way you need me, I'm here."

Between the two hours they spent holed up in the building with frantic security personnel trying to come up with an alternative exit so Jeremy could avoid the paparazzi, and the time Jeremy spent on the phone with Bill going over the morning's events and complaining, once again, about Francis, the day was shot. They barely had time to go to the hotel and get cleaned up before Jeremy had to be at the concert venue for sound check. Reg came along, staying quiet and calm in the hope that Jeremy could unwind and reduce his stress level before the show.

"You doing okay?" Reg asked after pulling Jeremy aside into the closest corner that could pass for private in the busy arena. "You've been really quiet all day."

After looking at him silently for many long seconds, Jeremy said, "Yeah, I'm fine." He fingered his shirt collar and rubbed it against his lips. "Weird day, I guess. Still processing it."

Reg raised his hand to brush it through Jeremy's hair

and, remembering that it was already spiked for the show, dropped it onto his shoulder instead. "Anything you need to talk about?"

"Probably." Jeremy sighed. "Later, though, yeah?"

"Jeremy!" one of the crew members yelled. "We need you over here."

"Have fun out there tonight, and we'll catch up after," Reg said as he massaged Jeremy's shoulder.

Releasing his own shirt, Jeremy fingered Reg's, tugging gently on the fabric as he looked up at Reg from underneath his lashes. "You'll be here?"

"What, are you kidding me? Of course." Reg squeezed his shoulder one last time. "Haven't missed a show yet, dude."

"Thanks."

"Backstage view of the best rock show around, and you're thanking me?" He shook his head and gently pushed Jeremy toward the people watching them and fidgeting, clearly needing Jeremy to focus on the concert that was about to start. "I'm the one who's grateful. Knock 'em dead, superstar."

Following what had become his usual habit, Reg found a place to stand where he wouldn't interfere with the people who seemed to run all around the backstage from the minute the concert started until the equipment was cleared. He'd stay there until the last act, and then he'd make his way to Jeremy's dressing room so he wouldn't be in the way at the end of the show when things were most chaotic and people were vying for Jeremy's attention.

Watching Jeremy play to the crowd, laughing, cheering, and singing in his honey voice, reminded Reg why he was so successful—the man belonged on stage with a guitar in his hand. In fact, other than when they were alone—no press, no fans, no staff—Reg had never seen Jeremy as at ease as he was when he was singing to tens of thousands of fans. Whether he had learned that skill because of the many years he had been performing as part of his successful career, or whether he had been able to so quickly attain that success because he had been born and bred with the skill, Reg didn't know, and he suspected Jeremy didn't either. Not that it mattered. Whatever the reason, Jeremy was an amazing musician with an unparalleled stage presence; his songs reached past the ears and into the heart and soul of everyone who heard them.

Even if he was acting the part of pretend boyfriend, Reg served a real role in Jeremy's life. There was no doubt in his mind that Jeremy was happy with him, trusted him, felt safe in his presence. And he liked to tell himself that his filling that need allowed Jeremy to shine on stage. So Reg felt like he was partially responsible for bringing the audience members to happy tears as they listened to a show they'd surely remember for the rest of their lives. Being important to Jeremy made Reg feel important, and he found he enjoyed both of those feelings.

"Hey."

Reg twisted his head around and saw a man he didn't recognize standing right behind him. "Hi."

"You're the guy dating Jeremy Jameson or whatever,

right?"

"Right."

"I saw you guys on TV earlier." Dragging his gaze from Reg's face to his backside, the man sniffled and said, "It was hot."

Well, it seemed his plan had worked, at least to some extent. That guy didn't have any question about whether Jeremy was faking his interest in Reg. For that matter, neither did Reg, but he was going to be patient while Jeremy made his way to the same realization.

"You guys play or whatever?" the guy asked.

Though he had never considered himself the jealous type, that was exactly how Reg felt at the mere thought of that man touching Jeremy. It was particularly strange because Reg himself didn't have the privilege to touch Jeremy all that much. Oh, sure, they stood close together and Reg was always fast to offer a backrub or foot rub, but until that morning, he'd never had his lips connect with Jeremy's skin or Jeremy's entire body pressed against his. Based on Jeremy's reaction, Reg was hopeful it had been the first time, but not the last. Jeremy craved physical attention, and he hoped he'd be taken up on his offer to give it.

"'Cause I'm interested or whatever," the guy said.

If he used the word "whatever" one more time, Reg was going to throttle him.

Whoa. Violent thoughts were never a good thing.

Turning around so he was facing the stranger, Reg said, "No, man, we don't play."

"Seriously?" the guy scoffed and then sniffled again, making Reg wonder what he'd been snorting and how he'd gotten backstage.

"How'd you get back here?"

Lifting the badge he had draped around his neck, he said, "I work for the arena. I'm helping with security and shit backstage."

Well, that made Reg feel safe. Forcing himself to take in a deep breath, he suddenly had more sympathy for why Jeremy frequently lost his temper. "All right, well, nice to meet you, man." He turned back around, returning his focus to Jeremy on stage.

"Let me know if you change your mind. We can party later. I'll be—"

"I'm not changing my mind," Reg snapped, his gaze unwavering from Jeremy's hands moving over his guitar. "Jeremy and I are exclusive. Completely." He watched Jeremy rock his hips in concert with the music and rasped, "He's mine."

In his most outlandish fantasies, that was a true statement. When Jeremy had offered Reg the chance to go on tour and to see the world, he had seen no downside. Traveling, adventure, music, and a fun guy to hang out with the entire time—all good things. But as the days and weeks and months rolled by, Reg realized there was one hitch he hadn't considered—developing feelings for Jeremy that went beyond being a travel buddy. The way Reg's heart had pounded that morning when he'd gotten to hold Jeremy in his arms and breathe in his scent confirmed what he already knew deep down—for his part, the only pretending he was doing in the relationship was pretending it was pretend. Because the feelings Reg had for Jeremy were very real.

CHAPTER 9

CONFUSION wasn't an emotion Jeremy felt often. Being born into his family meant having innate knowledge of the music industry and engaging in frequent conversations about everyone in it. As a result, he had never had trouble navigating his way through his chosen profession. And while he was quick to get angry at what he considered incompetence on the part of his staff—like Francis—or intrusiveness into his life—which was just about any interaction with the press—those things were necessary parts of being in his industry.

His personal life had been much the same. He had been raised to understand the dangers of saying or doing the wrong thing with the wrong person and ending up as the lead story on TV or in the gossip magazines with less than flattering information. Which was why he dated other celebrities, oftentimes those who were up-and-coming. If they wanted a long-term career, making enemies of Jeremy's family by fabricating lies about him wouldn't serve them well. So long as he didn't give people reasons to despise him, they generally walked away without creating a scene, content with the ability to forever tell the world they'd been with Jeremy Jameson.

At thirty-one, he'd had about a dozen relationships, all of which had been in the public eye and all of which had ended amicably. Remaining friends with his exes had never been an issue for Jeremy because he didn't expect it. After all, he hadn't been friends with any of them before they'd started dating, or even while they'd been dating, so it would make no sense to suddenly strike up a friendship after they broke up. The basis of his relationships had been a need for someone to walk down the proverbial, and sometimes literal, red carpet at his side and keep him company during his rare downtimes. Unfortunately, Jeremy had found that the type of person who enjoyed dressing up and going to premieres and fancy dinners wasn't the same type of person who enjoyed hanging out at home, watching a game on TV, and drinking a beer.

Until he met Reg, who genuinely enjoyed sitting around hotel rooms or airplanes or busses, chatting about nothing or everything, and was equally happy vegging out in front of the TV, being quiet for hours and yet remaining very noticeably present. Reg went to press junkets without complaint, lending quiet support but never vying for the limelight. And when there was time and energy to mingle with the world, Reg was always full of ideas for adventures and new experiences. The man was a great friend and the perfect companion to have on tour, at a dinner function, and probably everywhere else too. And after the unexpected performance Reg had put on for the press at the radio station, Jeremy wondered whether that perfection could be improved even further.

"You were awesome out there tonight," Reg said when they were finally alone in their hotel room.

"You say that every time." Jeremy did his best to muster up a smile, but even his lips felt tired. He tried to kick off his shoes, almost tripped, and gave up, leaning against the wall instead.

After the show, there had been two hours of answering questions from reporters and meeting fans and shaking hands and posing for pictures until Jeremy thought he was going to collapse. And he had three more nights of that to look forward to because he had back-to-back shows in four different states, giving him barely enough time to sleep and travel each day before he had to be on stage again.

The second he had a chance to breathe, he planned to call Bill to tell him something had to change. He wasn't twenty anymore. His shows started late and ran even later, and the last thing he wanted to do when they were over was promotional work.

"That's because it's true every time." Reg wrapped his arm around Jeremy's waist and tugged him close. "Come on, superstar. Bedtime."

Their hotel room was similar to those in every city they'd stayed—a suite with a separate living space and sleeping space. Reg walked Jeremy through the suite and over to the bathroom. "You okay to brush your teeth and drain the lizard solo, or are you going to fall into the toilet if I leave you alone?"

"Ha-ha." Jeremy lightly smacked Reg's muscular chest and stumbled into the bathroom. "I'm fine."

"Good night, JJ." Reg smiled and turned to leave. "Get some sleep."

"Wait."

"You need help?" Reg asked, flipping around right away and stepping toward Jeremy. "What's wrong?"

"Nothing." Jeremy shook his head. "But I was wondering—" He swallowed hard and lowered his gaze, trying to gather the courage to make his unusual request. No matter how many times he'd gone over it in his head, it still sounded weird. But he trusted Reg not to get angry or offended. "Earlier, you said—" He licked his lips and breathed rapidly.

"Hey," Reg said soothingly as he reached out and pushed Jeremy's hair back.

Needing to cool down and wash the sweat off before meeting people, Jeremy had showered after the show, so the makeup and styling products he wore on stage were gone. But he'd put a bit more on after the shower because pictures were being taken. So while Reg was able to move away the locks that had fallen into his eyes, he couldn't run his fingers through it and massage Jeremy's scalp the way he had when Jeremy was sick. That memory at the end of a long day, combined with what Jeremy had been craving since he realized it might be an option, made Jeremy shiver.

"You're shaking. What's wrong?" Reg grasped his chin and lifted it, forcing Jeremy to meet his gaze. "Talk to me, JJ."

"Nothing's wrong. Sorry." Jeremy blinked rapidly. "I'm beat, really beat, and earlier you said you wouldn't mind—"

He closed his eyes and bit his lip, intending to take one more deep breath before finishing his sentence, but Reg beat him to it.

"You want me to hold you?"

Sighing in relief, Jeremy nodded. "You don't have to. I know it's weird and—"

"No, it isn't," Reg assured him. "Everyone needs to be touched." He cupped Jeremy's cheek. "You more than most, I think. But that's a good thing, not a weird thing."

"So you don't mind?"

"I don't mind." Stepping closer, Reg pulled Jeremy into his arms and hugged him tightly. "In fact"—he hunched down and buried his face in Jeremy's neck—"I think I'd enjoy it just as much as you."

"Yeah?" Jeremy could feel a smile forming. "So I'll finish up in here and meet you in bed?"

"I didn't shower at the stadium, so I'm going to grab a quick one after you're done in the bathroom. After that"—Reg squeezed Jeremy's shoulder—"you're on."

"Thanks."

"You've got to quit thanking me for doing things I like." Reg chuckled and backed away, giving Jeremy his privacy in the bathroom. "Getting to share a bed with you might be the one thing I'll enjoy more than listening to you play."

A lot of thoughts bounced through Jeremy's mind as he used the bathroom, washed his face, and brushed his teeth, but he was too tired to process most of them. Front and center was that memory of Reg combing his fingers through Jeremy's hair. Deciding he wanted to relive the experience, Jeremy ducked his head under the sink and rinsed all the product out.

He toweled off his hair and then walked out of the bathroom. "It's all yours," he called to Reg, who was digging through his bag.

"Thanks." Reg grinned as he hurried into the bathroom. "I won't be long."

True to his word, Reg was out of the shower by the time Jeremy had his hair brushed and was dressed in his sleep shorts and long-sleeved T-shirt.

"As tired as you were, I thought you'd be asleep already," Reg said as he walked into the room wearing cutoff sweats and a T-shirt that would have been baggy on anyone else but practically clung to Reg's wide chest.

The shirt sleeves were cut off, and the sides were open to midwaist, so Jeremy could see his whole tattoo. He wondered if Reg would ever consider going shirtless so he could look at it more carefully. Knowing how open Reg was to anything and everything, Jeremy thought he probably would. But he'd wait to raise it. Asking the man to share his bed was probably pushing things enough for one night.

"I just got into bed," Jeremy said. "You take the fastest showers known to man."

"It doesn't take long if all I'm doing is getting clean." Reg climbed onto the right side of the bed and slid under the comforter. "So are you always on the left side, or do you switch around?"

"Oh, uh, I don't think about it." Jeremy shrugged. "Switch around, I guess." When Reg scooted toward the center of the bed, Jeremy started wondering if discussing which side of the bed to sleep on was expected in these situations and he had been rude by making the decision on his own. "Do you want me to move?"

"Nuh-uh." Reg rolled onto his side in the center of the bed. "I'm good here. I usually take the side closest to the bathroom because of how much water I drink."

Chuckling, Jeremy said, "You really do. Never met anybody who takes hydration more seriously."

"Hey, if having your thirst quenched is wrong, I don't want to be right," Reg said while waggling his eyebrows. "Okay, superstar, how do you want to do this?"

"What do you mean?"

"You want to back up, and I can hold you from behind?" He opened his arms wide. "Or do you want me on my back, and you can rest on my chest?" He patted his chest.

"Uh." Jeremy darted his gaze from Reg's body to his face. "I've never done either of those."

"No?"

Shaking his head, Jeremy said, "Uh-uh. You've seen the women I dated. They're small. It wasn't like I could climb on top of them." Jeremy's cheeks heated. "That came out wrong. I already told you about the sex, and after that there was some cuddling, but sleeping on them would have squished them, which would have been bad, and most people don't like being touched when they're sleeping. But sharing the bed is good enough. It's still warmer than sleeping alone, and sometimes I can reach out and—"

"You're rambling." Reg curled his hand over Jeremy's back, and pulled him close. "Which is cute, but it's time for you to go to sleep." He held Jeremy against him, chest to chest, tipped onto his back, and took Jeremy with him. "I'm not easily squished." He wrapped one arm around Jeremy's neck and the other over his waist, holding him tightly, so they were connected from thigh to head. "Is this good?" he asked. "Or is it too much?"

"It's good," Jeremy rasped, amazed at how true that was. Reg's strength and warmth enveloped him. Cuddling closer, he shoved his leg between Reg's thick thighs, used his muscular chest as a pillow, and sighed contentedly. "You're sure you don't mind?"

"I'm sure." Reg kissed the top of his head. "You feel perfect."

"Not perfect." Jeremy shook his head. "I'm needy."

"No, you're not." Reg massaged the back of Jeremy's head and softly rubbed his lower back.

"I made you get in bed with me."

"You didn't make me do anything. I volunteered because I wanted to do it."

"Only because you're the nicest guy ever." Jeremy wiggled a little, trying to burrow closer to the hot, hard body beneath him. "Nobody else would put up with this." He let out a deep breath and mumbled, "You're the perfect one," as he closed his eyes and finally fell asleep.

Jeremy couldn't remember ever having felt warmer, inside and out, than he had the past few nights. Though his travel schedule had been rough and there'd been various hiccups with the venues and he had been forced to smile pretty for too many cameras, he felt happy and at peace deep down. Based on his history, Jeremy knew that at any other time in his life, he would have been yelling and throwing things and probably starting to come down with some ailment. He also knew the change was due to Reg.

His frenetic schedule meant he had barely had time to think, let alone to talk to Reg about what he was thinking, but that hadn't kept him from sharing his bed with Reg every night. It had gotten to the point where Jeremy was so desperate to get to the hotel and feel Reg's heat and strength and safety that he practically vibrated at the end of every day.

The first morning he woke up tangled around Reg's body like a monkey, he worried Reg would be angry or uncomfortable. But when he'd glanced up to see Reg's expression, Jeremy had been met with a sleepy smile. Then Reg rubbed his big hand over Jeremy's back, kissed the top of his head, and said, "Good morning, superstar. You sleep okay?" So Jeremy relaxed and let himself enjoy the feeling of being held and petted.

After that, it was remarkably easy to climb into bed next to Reg every night and crawl over so he could get closer. He had never fallen asleep as easily or slept as soundly as he did when Reg was wrapped around him. Even Reg getting up to use the bathroom in the middle of the night was a good thing, because when he returned, he always pulled Jeremy to him again and caressed his leg or his chest or his back. Sometimes he'd even nuzzle Jeremy's neck, his hot breath ghosting over Jeremy's skin along with his stubbled cheeks. If Jeremy had ever experienced a more perfect moment, he couldn't name it.

Which was why on Saturday morning, Jeremy stayed still and quiet, tucked into Reg's side while he slept. The next show was on Monday night, and they didn't have to leave until Sunday, so other than a couple of phone interviews, they had the whole day off. Knowing how run-down Jeremy was, Reg hadn't planned an adventure, instead saying they'd spend the day in sweats watching TV or playing cards. It sounded perfect.

"How'd you sleep?" Reg rumbled, his voice always extragravelly first thing in the morning.

"Really good." Jeremy had his head on Reg's shoulder, his arm around Reg's chest, and his leg draped over Reg's hip. He didn't want to move.

"Me too." Reg rubbed his hand up and down Jeremy's back. "I better get up to hit the head." He dipped his face forward, pressed it into Jeremy's hair, and inhaled deeply.

"Mmm. You smell good, JJ."

After another breath and a full-body squeeze, Reg climbed out of bed. "Be back in a flash."

After rolling onto his back, Jeremy stared up at the ceiling and started thinking. For the first time in as long as he could remember, he felt well-rested and clear-headed. He knew it was time to talk with Reg.

"You still tired?" Reg asked as he walked back into the room. "Or are you ready to get up?"

"Not tired." Jeremy sat up and slid his feet onto the floor. "But we can stay in bed for a while and talk." He darted his gaze toward Reg and then glanced away. "If you want."

"Sure." Reg hopped onto the bed. "I'm game for whatever. It's a free day, right?"

Smiling, Jeremy said, "Right. But first, it's my turn in the bathroom."

He made quick work of draining his bladder, brushing his teeth, washing his face, and brushing his hair. Then he went back into the bedroom, where Reg was sitting up in bed typing on his phone.

"Sorry," he said. "Just returning a few texts. Be done in a sec."

Deciding to turn that comment into an opening for the conversation he wanted to have, Jeremy said, "No problem." He sat on the other end of the bed. "Who're you texting?"

"Uh, my brother right now. Just finished answering my mom."

Jeremy scooted closer. "If there's anyone else you need

to text or call, that's fine, yeah?" He paused, and when Reg didn't respond, he said, "Is there?"

"Huh?" Reg looked away from his phone.

"Is there anyone else you need to catch up with?"

"Oh." Reg kept typing. "Yup, a couple of buddies, but it's no big. I can do it later."

"Buddies?"

After setting the phone on the nightstand, Reg turned to Jeremy and gave him his attention. "Yup. Guys I know from college. They're still in Phoenix, so I don't see them as much as I used to, but we keep up."

"Oh." Jeremy chewed on the inside of his lip, trying to figure out what to say to get the conversation moving in a way that wasn't pushy or offensive. "What about, uh, your exes?" He lowered his gaze. "You keep up with them?"

"Not really." Reg shook his head. "But I don't have a lot of exes like that. I've dated and hooked up and shit, but as far as relationships, there's only been one, and it was in college, so it's been years."

Whether it was on purpose or unintentional, Jeremy didn't know, but Reg seemed to always phrase things in a way that kept Jeremy from knowing anything about his dating history. Giving up on subtlety, Jeremy finally said, "How come you never talk about your ex and people you've dated?"

"Oh." Reg jerked, looking surprised. "I didn't mean to make you feel like I was keeping secrets, JJ. I'll tell you anything anytime. It's just that there's nobody worth talking about."

"I know you don't keep secrets; you're probably the most honest person I know. But usually people are eager to talk about every person they ever had dinner with, and you never say a word."

"Seriously?" Reg asked in surprise.

"Oh, yeah. In this business, the first rule of dating is you always talk about who you've dated. I mean, if you don't tell every single person you meet that you once had coffee with Brad Pitt or Angelina Jolie, then it doesn't count." Jeremy scoffed. "I've known lots of people who'll go out on a date with someone they know they'll never be interested in just so they can say they've dated in interviews. There are some agents who go so far as to set that up for their clients. A couple of public dinners, a premiere, and then they're through, but the pictures last forever."

"Man, your world is so deeply fucked-up." Reg shook his head in apparent disgust. When he didn't say anything else right away, Jeremy thought he'd have to press harder or give up on knowing anything about Reg's past, but then Reg took in a deep breath and said, "Okay, so you want to know my dating history?"

"Only if you want to, uh…yeah."

"It's boring, but at least it's short." Reg lay down on his side, folded his elbow, and propped his head on his hand. "I didn't date in high school because I wasn't interested in girls, and I wasn't ready to say I was interested in guys, you know? Then in college, I did the whole hookup thing a couple of times—nothing worth mentioning or remembering—but it wasn't my speed."

Even though his reason for forcing the conversation was his suspicion that Reg was gay, Jeremy was still taken off guard by the easy way Reg announced it. Clearly, he assumed Jeremy knew. Forcing himself to focus, Jeremy said, "What do you mean not your speed?"

"Hookups. Getting off is fun, but I was hoping for something more, and then I met this guy—Kirby." For the first time since Jeremy had met him, Reg looked sad.

"That's your ex?"

Reg nodded. "We were together a year and a half."

"That's a long time." Longer than Jeremy had ever dated anyone.

"Yup. Especially in college, because you're together practically nonstop. He lived on my floor freshman year, so it got serious pretty fast. We'd bunk with each other whenever one of our roommates was out." Reg turned his lips up at the corners, like he was remembering something happy, and Jeremy found his stomach rolling, which was a weird reaction. "Sophomore year, I lived in my frat house, and he moved in with some friends." Reg gulped. "That's when it fell apart."

"What happened?"

"He got real big into Tina. Real big."

"Tina?" Jeremy repeated.

"Crystal meth. He played around with it a little when we met, but he was more into pot back then."

"Did he overdose?" Jeremy's voice broke when he

asked the question, the memory of the phone call telling him his father was dead suddenly fresh in his mind.

"No." Reg shook his head. "But he was getting high all the time, especially when we had sex. He was all into booty-bumping." Reg looked at Jeremy and elaborated. "He'd inject it up his ass, and then we fucked."

Though he had what he considered an unusually close and open relationship with Reg, Jeremy was taken aback by that level of frankness.

"You know, you're really sheltered for a guy who's seen the world," Reg said.

The comment could have been offensive, but Reg's tone was soft and kind, so Jeremy wasn't upset.

"What do you mean?"

"I don't know." Reg shrugged and furrowed his brow. "I guess I always thought rock stars were wild and crazy, with parties and drugs and all that." He smiled at Jeremy and, for the first time since they'd started the conversation, reached out and combed his fingers through his hair. Jeremy scooted closer to him. "Here I am, a guy from Munds Park, Arizona, whose most exciting adventure until you came along was a trip across the border to Nogales to get drunk and camp on the beach in Rocky Point, and yet you have no idea what I'm talking about."

Having a father who had abused drugs for as long as Jeremy could remember, and who'd ultimately died as a result, meant he had less interest in them than people expected. And aside from that, he'd always been carefully managed, both in his personal life and his professional one.

"I came up different from a lot of guys in this business," Jeremy explained. "My parents said I could start playing publicly when I turned eighteen, so I had to wait, but everything was lined up: manager, record company, promo. They were all ready for me, watching me. My grandfather too, before he died. My father's people. My mother's people. I wasn't one of those guys who grabbed a guitar and went out on the road solo." Sighing deeply, Jeremy added, "Besides, I never wanted to turn into my dad."

"That's good." Reg massaged Jeremy's nape. "I'd hate to see that happen to you." He swallowed hard. "It's the worst."

"So what happened with that guy, uh, Kirby?"

"I broke up with him. I tried to get him to stop, but I was barely twenty, and I didn't know how. Then I found out he was staying up all night, letting his roommates do him, and other guys who came over to the apartment." Reg cringed. "I couldn't deal; he wouldn't stop, so I walked."

"And you didn't hear from him after that?"

"No. He finished off the semester and then went home to Texas that summer and didn't come back. Word was his parents made him transfer to school out there so he could be closer to home. He didn't keep in touch with anyone I knew." Reg rubbed his palm over his face. "I always hoped he got clean and wanted a fresh start."

"I'm sorry." Jeremy curled his fingers around Reg's and squeezed his hand.

"I'm good. It's been more than five years. I'm over it."

But Jeremy could tell from the sadness in Reg's eyes and the tension in his large frame that while he might be over his ex-boyfriend, the experience still hurt him. Feeling guilty for making Reg talk about something painful merely because he wanted to know if he was gay—the very thing he got angry at the press for constantly obsessing over—Jeremy pushed closer to Reg and hugged him.

"Thank you," he said hoarsely as he cupped the back of Jeremy's head and buried his face in Jeremy's neck.

When he had asked Reg to join him on the road and pretend to be his boyfriend, Jeremy hadn't considered the possibility that he was anything other than straight. Looking back, Jeremy realized he'd had no basis for that assumption. He had been railing for months about how ridiculous it was for people to care and make assumptions about his personal life. He had shrugged off any question about whether dating a guy would be an issue. So no way was Jeremy going to act like a hypocrite and change the rules of his friendship with Reg just because the man was gay. He'd said it didn't matter, and he'd meant it.

He'd shared a room and even a bed with Reg and never felt uncomfortable; no reason to start now. Besides, it wasn't as if Reg had ever come on to him, which was a good thing. Still, Jeremy rubbed his palm over his chest and wondered why.

CHAPTER 10

"HOLY shit!" Jeremy screamed. "Get off!"

Standing over the toilet, Reg wasn't in a position to help right away, but he did his best to finish, shake, tuck, and zip as quickly as possible. "What?" he said as he rushed out of the bathroom and looked around the small hotel room. "What happened?"

With the two of them sharing a bed, they'd stopped getting multiroom suites for short stays. The brief amount of time they spent in the hotel was for sleep, so there was no point. Hotel rooms in New York were smaller than in many of the other cities they toured, so there wasn't a lot of space to hide, but at that moment, Jeremy was doing his level best, wedged into a corner between a desk and a window, his hand held straight out in front of him.

Darting his gaze around the room, Reg tried to find the source of Jeremy's fear. "Was someone here?" he asked as he quickly checked the door. The locks were in place. All four of them. "JJ?"

"Spider," Jeremy said, his voice high-pitched. He was pointing at the bed and seemingly trying to crawl into the wall. "Huge spider!"

"Seriously?" Reg chuckled and shook his head as he walked toward the bed. "I'll get it."

"No!" Jeremy yelled. "It's dangerous! Don't go near it."

"One of us has to go near it, or it'll stay on your suitcase, and you won't be able to get your pants." Reg looked meaningfully at Jeremy's sexy bikini briefs. He was a boxer man himself, but Jeremy always wore skimpy briefs. Damn, did Reg enjoy the moments when he got to see him changing. "I assume you were getting pants."

Forcing himself to look away was difficult, but Reg managed to do it. Lustful leering carried a real risk of making Jeremy uncomfortable, and the last thing Reg wanted to do was push too hard too fast and scare Jeremy away. Especially when he felt like they were making progress.

No straight guy, regardless of how comfortable he was in his sexuality, would sleep with his ass shoved into another man's groin, or his legs and arms wrapped around another man's body. No way. Jeremy was confused about himself and shockingly slow at getting a clue, but he wasn't straight, and Reg planned to be there, arms open wide, when he figured that out.

"Yeah. I was getting my jeans." Jeremy nodded. "But it's not worth it. I'll buy new stuff."

Pausing, Reg twisted his head back. "You want to throw your clothes away because there's a spider on your suitcase?"

"That thing is huge. It might be poisonous." He gulped and looked at the door desperately. "We need to get out of here."

"I'm pretty sure it's a Golden Garden spider. Those aren't poisonous."

"How do you know?" Jeremy's forehead wrinkled. "It could be a black widow or a, uh… It could be a black widow."

"It has stripes, and it's not black," Reg said calmly. "So that is very unlikely."

"What if you're wrong?" Jeremy was panting. "You're closer to the door. You can make a run for it."

Unable to keep his amusement to himself, Reg dryly said, "And leave you here unattended?"

"I think I can scoot around the desk and make it over to you. Either way, you need to go."

Incredibly, Jeremy had missed his attempt at sarcasm.

"You'd better not try that." When Jeremy looked at Reg questioningly, he added, "What if it jumps?"

"They jump?" Jeremy twisted his shirt collar and pulled it into his mouth, exposing his lower belly. "Oh my God. Oh my God. Oh my God."

"JJ, I was kidding."

Smiling at the adorable image Jeremy made—his cheeks flushed, his eyes wide, wearing nothing but underwear and a long-sleeved T-shirt with another T-shirt over it—Reg marched over to the nightstand, tore two pieces of paper off the pad placed there, and then approached the spider.

"What are you doing?" Jeremy asked in a panic. "Reg! What are you doing?"

"I'm going to get the spider off your suitcase." He kept

walking. "Do the windows open?"

"I don't know. Why? Oh my God."

Taking a fast look at the windows, Reg said, "Never mind. Looks like they're painted shut." He slid one piece of paper under the admittedly large spider and used the other to herd it toward the center, keeping it contained. "I'll flush it."

He had just turned toward the bathroom when Jeremy said, "You can't flush it. It'll die."

Freezing midstep, Reg stared at Jeremy. "You're not serious."

"What?"

"You said I can't flush it because it'll die."

"It will." Jeremy bobbed his head unusually fast. "Spiders aren't waterproof."

"Waterproof?"

Another guileless nod.

"Two seconds ago you were ready to burn down the hotel room just to get away from it."

"I wouldn't set a fire," Jeremy said, apparently having lost his sense of humor along with his common sense at the sight of the spider.

"Fine. You said it was dangerous and deadly," Reg pointed out.

"It is." Jeremy nodded quickly.

"Then I'm getting rid of it." Ignoring more protests, Reg walked into the bathroom, shook the spider into the toilet, and flushed. "There," he said. "It's gone."

"Are you sure?" Jeremy asked from the other room.

Reg waited for the toilet to stop running and flushed again for good measure. "Yes, I'm sure."

He could hear Jeremy's sigh of relief all the way in the bathroom. Chuckling, he said, "Get dressed, superstar. You have a few interviews before the show."

"No, I don't."

"Yes, you do," Reg said as he stepped out of the bathroom again. He leaned against the wall and, with Jeremy's attention diverted, let himself have a moment to enjoy the sight of the lithe man wiggling into his tight jeans.

"Bill didn't say anything."

"That's because he called me instead."

Raising his head and furrowing his brow, Jeremy said, "Why?"

"Because he's, and I quote, 'sick of listening to you whine about doing your job.'"

"He said that?" Jeremy asked, sounding equal parts surprised and angry. "I'm going to—"

"You're going to get dressed, put on all your makeup and hair shit, and then we're getting in a cab and going to the show."

Jeremy narrowed his eyes and glared at Reg. Reg arched his eyebrows and stared right back.

"Fine!" Jeremy huffed after several long seconds. He threw his arms in the air. "Just fine."

"Good. And on the way there, you're calling your mother because you haven't spoken with her in two months."

"That's not true!"

Quickly doing the math in his head, Reg said, "You're right. It's closer to three."

"Dammit!"

Reg walked over to Jeremy and waited.

"What?" Jeremy snapped.

"Do you need a hug?"

Looking at Reg's chest longingly, Jeremy said, "I'm not a child."

"I know." Reg reached out and smoothed Jeremy's hair back. "You're a grown man with a lot of responsibilities, and you're worked up because you have a huge televised concert tonight, you saw a spider, which you're scared of, and you loathe interviews but have to do a bunch."

Swallowing hard, Jeremy nodded.

"C'mere."

Letting go of the metal-studded belt he'd been threading through his jeans, Jeremy slowly stepped toward Reg. Reg scooped him up and squeezed him tightly. It only took a moment for Jeremy to sigh and melt against Reg's bigger frame.

"Thank you," he whispered. "I know this whole thing's turned out to be more than what you signed up for."

"What whole thing?"

"Being with me." Jeremy's voice broke on the words.

"In that case, it's turned out to be better than what I signed up for." Reg rubbed his back.

"Yeah, right. You have to deal with my annoying PR

guy, and bugs, and me acting like a needy kid, and—"

"I'll happily be your permanent PR-dealer, hug-giver, and spider-eviscerator."

"Spider-eviscerator." Jeremy snorted. "That's funny." He took in a deep breath and said, "Okay," as he moved out of Reg's embrace and squared his shoulders. "I'm good. Let's go do some interviews."

"That show was your best one yet," Reg said softly. They were back in the hotel room after the Madison Square Garden concert. Reg was leaning against the headboard, and Jeremy was curled around him, his head on Reg's stomach, arm around his waist, and leg shoved between his thighs.

"You always say th—" Jeremy looked up and met Reg's gaze. "*Best* one?"

"Uh-huh." Reg set his phone on the nightstand and buried his fingers in Jeremy's hair, massaging his scalp.

"Mmm," Jeremy moaned and closed his eyes.

"Feel good?"

"Yeah."

Spreading his fingers wide, Reg rubbed his way to the back of Jeremy's head, where he knew he was most sensitive.

"You done answering e-mails?" Jeremy asked, his words coming out slowly.

"Yup."

"Took you longer than usual."

"That's because Francis e-mails five times as often as my family and friends combined," Reg said with a chuckle.

"I can tell him to stop."

"No. I'd rather him e-mail me than you. This way I can screen what needs to be screened, and you only have to deal with the really important stuff. I'm your PR-dealer, remember?"

"That's not a real thing. You're just trying to keep me from yelling at him."

"Partly," Reg admitted. "But mostly I know you hate dealing with it, and it's something I can take off your plate." Reg slid his hand to Jeremy's nape and pressed hard against the tense muscles.

Jeremy groaned.

"I want to make things easier for you, JJ."

"You didn't sign up to be my secretary."

"I prefer the title 'personal assistant.'" Though the personal things he wanted to assist with weren't included in reputable companies' job listings.

"You didn't sign up to be that either."

After weighing the potential risks and benefits of his response, Reg said, "I think this—me being here with you—has turned into something different from what both of us expected." He cleared his throat. "Right?"

"Yeah." Jeremy bobbed his head. "I figured you'd be a good travel companion and we'd have fun, but..."

"Uh-huh?"

"You're, like, the best friend I've ever had," Jeremy confessed in a whisper as he tightened his grip around Reg's waist. "I know that might sound dumb with all the friends you have who text and call all the time, but—"

"It's not dumb."

Jeremy sighed and his body went lax.

"Roll on top of me."

"What?" Jeremy blinked up at him.

Reg spread his legs and scooted down so more of his belly and chest were flat. "Climb on me, facedown, and put your forehead here." He patted his chest. "That way I can get a better grip on your neck and shoulders and work out all your tension."

"You sure?"

"Yup."

Jeremy carefully climbed over Reg's leg, settled himself between his thighs, and lay down. "Like this?" he asked once his upper torso was pressed against Reg from groin to chest.

"That's perfect."

Not as perfect as it'd be if they were naked and Reg could feel Jeremy's dick and balls press against him, but he'd take what he could get. There was nothing he enjoyed more than touching Jeremy's smooth, hot skin. Feeling his lean body in his arms, breathing in the scent of his hair, and hearing his soft moans made Reg so hard he ached. And in their current position, with him wearing nothing but a pair of thin cutoff sweats, he knew Jeremy could feel it. But, as he'd hoped, Jeremy didn't back away.

"Reggie?" Jeremy whispered so quietly Reg almost didn't hear him.

Reg slid his hands over Jeremy's shoulders, working the muscles there before going back to his nape. "Uh-huh?"

"Do you ever, uh." He gulped. "I mean, we've been touring for four months, and you're with me almost all the time, so I don't think you've hooked up with anyone, but—"

Tangling his fingers in the back of Jeremy's hair, Reg tugged, bringing Jeremy's gaze up to meet his. "I haven't been with anyone since before I met you."

Nodding, Jeremy said, "I figured, so, uh"—he rubbed his lips together—"do you ever, um... Of course you do." He dropped his forehead back onto Reg's chest. "Never mind."

"Every day. Usually twice, sometimes more."

Barely raising his head, Jeremy looked up at him from underneath his lashes. From his expression, Reg knew he wasn't sure Reg's answer was to the question he'd been too uncomfortable to articulate.

"Every time I take a shower," Reg elaborated. "Morning, night, sometime in between, whenever. Me plus shower equals jacking off."

Jeremy jerked, seemingly shocked by Reg's frankness. The truth was, Reg wouldn't have been that open with anyone else. He didn't have any shame about sex, but he wasn't interested in sharing details about his personal life with people. With Jeremy, it was different. Partly because Reg felt closer to him, but mostly because he wanted Jeremy to feel comfortable talking to him about sex and to think about him in relation to sexual things. He wanted Jeremy under him, over him, in him. He just plain wanted Jeremy. So he kept talking.

"First thing in the morning too. I wake up with wood, and I need to take care of it. And then at night, if I can't sleep, I go into the bathroom and yank one out." He grinned and waggled his eyebrows. "Once usually does the trick, but if it doesn't, I do it again."

After closing his gaping mouth and swallowing a few times, Jeremy said, "I thought you slept closer to the bathroom because of all the water you drink."

"That too." Reg winked. "But if I'm in there for longer than a minute, you can be pretty sure I'm beating off."

"Seriously?"

Reg nodded.

"Wow." Jeremy looked stunned.

Given Jeremy's self-proclaimed ambivalence toward sex, Reg would have thought he spent a lot of time getting handsy with himself, so he was surprised by that reaction. "What?" he asked. "Don't try to tell me you don't get yourself off."

"I do, but"—Jeremy ducked his face—"that's a, uh, lot, isn't it?"

"Maybe," Reg said with a shrug. He spent every night with a sexy guy he desperately wanted but couldn't have wrapped around him and every day watching that guy move and bend and smile. He was a giant ball of hormones, and the fact that he went into the bathroom to relieve himself instead of dropping trou and painting Jeremy with his ejaculate was a minor miracle. The thought of his seed on Jeremy's skin made him groan. He cleared his throat and forced himself to focus. "How often do you do it?"

"Uh, I don't, uh—" Jeremy blinked rapidly. "Every few days, I guess."

Though he thought he knew Jeremy well, Reg was surprised by that response. He had figured a light sex life with other people meant Jeremy had a really busy sex life with himself. "Really?" he said. "You go three days with nothing?"

The only light in the room came from the partially open bathroom door, so Reg couldn't see Jeremy's face well enough to know if he was blushing, but he'd have bet his last dollar on it.

"Not always, but I get busy and tired and—" Jeremy sighed. "I'm thirty-one. That means I've come into a dirty sock more times than I can count. It gets old. Maybe I should try the shower idea."

"A dirty sock?"

Jeremy immediately lowered his face, resting his forehead against Reg's chest. "I didn't mean, uh… I don't have a kink or anything. It's just that it's already dirty so, uh—"

"That's resourceful," Reg said. "I'm not as environmentally conscious when I masturbate."

"Because of all the showers?"

"That too. At home I had my Fleshlight, so showers were shorter, but I still had to clean up after, so I don't think I saved much water." He shifted and moaned quietly, getting ridiculously turned on by the conversation. "It was more fun, though."

"Your flashlight?" Jeremy glanced back up, meeting his gaze. "What do you do with—"

"Fleshlight. Not flashlight. It's a toy."

Jeremy's expression was blank.

"You've never heard of it?"

"No." Jeremy shook his head.

"Oh, man. Too bad we're traveling light—I didn't bring mine along. It's shaped like a flashlight, but the inside is made of some supersecret material that feels almost like the real deal, and you basically fuck into it." Reg stopped breathing, and his heart rate increased. "Hey, I have a great idea."

"What?"

"I'll buy us a couple, and then we can play around." He vibrated with excitement. "I'll even show you how to use it."

"You're nuts," Jeremy said with a snort and settled himself onto Reg's larger body again, shifting from side to side until he found a comfortable position and then sighing.

Reg immediately got to work, sliding his fingers along Jeremy's shoulders and neck. "I'm serious."

"You're not buying us sex toys."

"Why not? It'll be something fun to do when we're too worn out to go out and we're vegging in a hotel room." And if he was lucky, it meant he'd get to see what Jeremy looked like when he was turned on, when he came. The thought of that was almost enough to make Reg lose it. If he actually got to see it—Jeremy's cheeks flushed, his expression tense with passion and need, his dick hard... Reg was going shopping the next day.

"You mean when *I'm* too worn out to go out and I drag you down with me."

"Cut it out," Reg said, his lustful thoughts abandoned. "I don't like it when you run yourself down."

"I wasn't running myself down. You know it's true. You're never the one who's tired; it's always me."

"I'm not the one sharing his passion on stage and having to talk to strangers about things I don't enjoy and getting my picture taken by a bunch of assholes everywhere I go."

"I'm so sick of that."

"Which part?" Reg knew it couldn't be the performing part. Jeremy glowed when he was on stage.

"The paparazzi." Jeremy's muscles tensed under Reg's hands so he rubbed harder. "They're relentless. I've never had to deal with them this much."

"Really? But this isn't your first tour or big album. You've been in the spotlight forever."

"Right. I'm not saying I've *never* dealt with them, but it was usually only during public events where they knew I'd be, or if I got unlucky and they happened to spot me somewhere. This time it seems like they're everywhere. I might as well have sent them my itinerary and a road map for my colon given how thorough they are at being up my ass all the time."

That comment made Reg laugh hard.

"Quit it." Jeremy lightly smacked his hip. "You're making my pillow shake."

"A road map for your colon?" Reg laughed harder.

"It's true! They figure out every hotel we stay in, every place I have an interview, every coffee shop we stop in."

"You're exaggerating." Reg ruffled Jeremy's hair and smiled at him. "They almost never find us when we're getting coffee."

"I've had pictures taken in at least three Starbucks and four independent coffee shops this week alone," Jeremy reminded him.

"That's because we both have caffeine addictions, and you're nice to your fans. Don't tell me the college girls who squealed and texted their friends after you smiled at them are being hired by magazines."

"Fine," Jeremy grumbled. "That wasn't a good example. But the rest of it's true. Those assholes are coming out of the woodwork, and they're way too aggressive. I think I'll call Bill about it again tomorrow."

"Let me know if there's anything I can do to help."

"Thank you." Jeremy moved his hand up and down the side of Reg's thigh.

Reg wondered whether Jeremy was aware of it or if touching Reg came so naturally now that he no longer noticed he was doing it. "I don't think I had a chance to ask you what your mom said on the phone earlier. By the time you hung up, we were at the Garden."

"Nothing worth knowing. She mostly talked about

a few projects she's considering and how much they want her for them and how perfect she'd be for the roles, but how she can't possibly have time to do them all. Oh." Jeremy paused and then looked up and smiled conspiratorially. "This is interesting. So you know her divorce from my latest stepfather is almost final, and she's been spending time with that new guy—Harold West."

"Uh-huh."

"Well, he wants her in his movie, and even when I was over there visiting before we left LA, I knew she was just stringing him along. So while she was telling me about all these movies she's considering—none of which are his—I could hear him in the background asking about his movie, and she completely ignored him. I mean she didn't say a word to him. She just kept talking to me like she couldn't hear him, which is impossible because I wasn't even in the room, and I could hear him."

"That's no way to treat people. Especially someone you're supposed to care about."

"My mom doesn't care about some barely on the radar indie director," Jeremy scoffed.

"You said she's dating him, right? Has been for several months. Isn't that reason enough to care? What does his career success have to do with it?"

"It doesn't, really. What I meant was that my mother doesn't care about anything or anyone other than her career. She likes to keep a guy around at all times, and Harold West is good-looking and attentive, so he landed the part. But she would never trust him with a role that actually matters to her."

Wanting to make sure he understood the backward logic, Reg said, "So you're saying she cares more about whoever is directing her in a movie than whoever is sharing her home?"

"Oh, absolutely," Jeremy said without hesitation. "She always has."

"I don't understand your world." Reg shook his head. "Jobs come and go. I went to school for five years to be an accountant, ended up as a bartender, and now I'm"—he waggled his eyebrows and grinned—"a personal assistant. What does it matter? The only thing that stays constant is family. My brother and his wife have been together through who knows how many jobs. Shouldn't your mother care more about a man who she might marry and spend the rest of her life with than a job that'll only last for a short time?"

"Uh, I have news for you, Reg," Jeremy said. "My mother doesn't marry for life. In fact, when you consider the prefilming stuff, the actual filming schedule, editing, and then the release promo, a lot of movies last longer than her marriages."

"Wow." Reg shook his head. "I totally can't relate."

"No?"

"My dad's been dead for going on ten years, and my mom won't even consider the idea of dating. She says 'til death do us part isn't long enough, and there's no room in her life for someone else." He sighed and concentrated on massaging Jeremy's shoulders. "That's what marriage is supposed to be."

"That sounds nice," Jeremy said quietly. "I mean, I'm sorry for her loss and for yours. But that kind of commitment, caring about someone so much—" He cleared his throat. "It sounds nice."

Looking down at the man cuddled against him, Reg's heart swelled. "It is," he whispered.

CHAPTER 11

"DID you talk to Bill about it?" Reg asked.

"Quit using that voice on me!" Jeremy yanked his shirt off, balled it up, and threw it at the hotel wall. It barely made a sound, which was disappointing. "It won't work this time."

Once again, Francis had planned interviews on the same day as a concert. Thankfully, they were earlier in the day instead of after the show. Well, at least that was what Jeremy had thought. But it turned out there was a reporter waiting when he got off stage too. Not to mention the photographer who *happened* to be outside the diner where they'd stopped to grab dinner.

"What voice? I'm just asking a question."

"No, you're not. You're using your Calm Jeremy Down voice." He toed off his shoes, picked one up, and threw it against the sliding glass door. There. That made a more satisfying sound. "I will not calm down!"

Reg turned his lips up in his crooked grin, leaned back against the wall, and crossed his arms over his chest. "My Calm Jeremy Down voice?"

"Yeah, you know." Jeremy picked up his other shoe and threw it at the same spot. The glass shook again, but not as hard. "It's lower and has a slower cadence than your regular voice."

"I didn't realize I had another voice."

Looking around for something else he could throw, Jeremy saw the remote control and headed for it. He managed to get it in his grip, but before he could raise his hand, Reg was behind him, curling his large frame around him as he took hold of the remote. The fight immediately started slipping out of him.

"We're not breaking electronics, superstar."

"You're using the voice again," Jeremy warned, but he could no longer muster up the energy to yell.

"You're vibrating, like you're spoiling for a fight." Reg's hot breath ghosted over his ear and neck, making him shiver. "Tell me what Bill said that has you all riled up."

"I haven't told him about the interview after the show yet because I talked to him before I went on stage, but when I called to tell him about all the people I had to meet earlier today, he said it's part of my job and I need to stop complaining." Jeremy frowned and grunted. "I should fire him."

"No, you shouldn't. He's a good guy, and he works hard for you." Reg moved his hands up Jeremy's stomach and brushed his thumbs over Jeremy's nipples, which pebbled up under the attention. Jeremy hadn't known he was sensitive there until Reg first traced his fingers over them; now he found himself subconsciously leaning into the touch, wanting the sensation. "What'd he say about the photographer outside the restaurant?"

"Um." It was hard to concentrate with the adrenaline draining from his body. "I think he's finally getting what I've been saying for months: it isn't normal the way they show up everywhere."

"See? That's good. Sounds like you made progress. Now, let's see what we can do to get you to stop thinking about work." Reg dragged his hands down Jeremy's flank and tugged on his waistband. "You want these off?"

"Yeah." Jeremy nodded.

"You tired?" Reg asked as he unbuttoned and unzipped Jeremy's jeans.

"Yeah, but I'm too worked up to sleep."

"Well, I have an idea to help get your energy out." Reg pushed Jeremy's jeans past his hips, and they fell the rest of the way, pooling on the floor around his feet. "It'll get you nice and relaxed."

"Is it using that voice some more? Because that doesn't calm me down." Except it did. Reg's deep, warm voice, his understanding eyes, his hard, strong body—all those things relaxed Jeremy, helped ease his stress.

"No, it's not the voice." Reg chuckled, dropped to a squat, and started removing Jeremy's socks. "I have something else in mind." When he didn't say anything more, Jeremy twisted his head and looked down. "I was thinking of a, uh, game." Reg smiled wickedly. "Sort of."

"Oh. Like a drinking game?" Jeremy nodded. "Yeah, let's do it."

"Nuh-uh." Reg stood up, rubbing his chest against Jeremy's bare legs and back as he rose.

Things between them had gone beyond any normal friendship boundaries. Jeremy was sure of it. He'd been telling himself it was because Reg was gay, and maybe gay men were touchier with their friends than straight ones. Of course, Reg wasn't touchy with anybody else.

"You need to be sober for this one," Reg said.

Curious, Jeremy turned around and tilted his head up, meeting Reg's gaze. "I don't think they have nighttime bungee jumping or windsurfing in Pittsburgh."

"No, it's nothing like that," Reg said with a laugh. He cupped Jeremy's cheek. "We won't even have to leave the room."

"Okay. I'll bite. Tell me."

"I did some shopping." Reg focused concerned brown eyes on Jeremy. "I bought a few toys."

"What do you me—" Jeremy gulped. "Toys?" he repeated, his voice suddenly hoarse.

"Yes." Reg looked at him intently. "I can give you some privacy, let you try it out on your own and release all that energy, or..."

Jeremy licked his lips. "Or?"

"If you want, I can show you how to use it."

It took Jeremy a few beats to catch his suddenly short breath. "What do you mean 'show me'?"

"Well, I bought two Fleshlights, so I can do myself, and you can follow along." Reg cleared his throat. "I won't have to touch you or anything."

Illogical disappointment flooded him, and knowing how easily Reg could read his expressions, Jeremy ducked his chin to hide it.

"But we don't have to," Reg said quickly. "We can do something else." He paused. "How about cards? I'll even let you cho—"

"No," Jeremy said in a rush as he jerked his head up. "I want to." It wasn't until he'd said the words that he realized they were true.

Given how often Reg talked about masturbating, Jeremy had started imagining it. Other than a few brief attempts to watch porn and totally missing the appeal, Jeremy hadn't ever seen anyone else stroking himself off. The prospect of watching it live was too intriguing to pass up. And with Reg starring in the show... Jeremy felt himself hardening and hoped Reg wouldn't notice.

"You want to?"

"Yeah." Jeremy bit his lip, thought about it, and then again said, "Yeah."

"Awesome." Reg smiled broadly. "I'm going to hop in the shower, and then I'll get everything ready while you have your turn." He grasped Jeremy's arms and briskly rubbed his hands up and down. "Sound good?"

Jeremy nodded, and seconds later, he was alone in the hotel room while Reg was whistling from behind the bathroom door.

By the time Jeremy was done with his shower, he was a ball of nerves. Was he actually going to go out there, get naked, sit on the bed, and use a toy to masturbate while his friend watched and did the same thing? The thought made him simultaneously nauseous and aroused.

"Come on, JJ," Reg called from the other room. "I promise we'll have a good time, and if it isn't fun, we'll stop."

Apparently he'd given himself away. It seemed staying in the bathroom for several minutes after turning off the water was an indicator of anxiety.

"Do you need me to come in there and dry you off?"

Knowing that likely wasn't an idle threat, Jeremy said, "No, I'm good." He grabbed the towel, quickly ran it over his body and hair, and wrapped it around his waist. Then he brushed his teeth and hair, took a few deep breaths, and forced himself to open the bathroom door and step out.

"You look good squeaky clean," Reg said, his tone light and teasing, which relaxed Jeremy a bit. "Ready to play?"

"Yeah, what should I—"

Jeremy stopped midsentence and midjourney to the bed the second he noticed Reg was nude, totally and completely nude. He was sitting cross-legged at the head of the bed, his back leaning against the wall and his package on clear display. Jeremy struggled not to stare, but it wasn't easy.

"Lose the towel and hop on up here." Reg patted the bed. "I have some dry towels spread out already so we don't have to sleep on wet spots."

And that made Jeremy trip over a bundle of nerves.

"You okay?" Reg asked.

"Yeah. I'm good. I'm good." Reminding himself to put one foot in front of the other, Jeremy made it to the side of the bed.

"So how much are you freaking out right now? Scale of one to ten?"

"I'm not freaking out. Why do you think I'm freaking out? I'm not freaking out."

"You're squeaking." When Jeremy started darting his head around, looking for the source of a squeak, Reg clarified. "Your voice. It was getting high-pitched." He laughed and shook his head. "Never mind. Get in here, superstar. This'll feel good."

"Okay," Jeremy said, but he couldn't seem to move.

Sharp as always, Reg crawled to the edge of the bed, climbed to his knees, and covered Jeremy's frozen hands with his larger ones. "You won't need this," he said gently as he pried Jeremy's fingers from the towel.

With Reg right in front of him, everything was on display, and it was impossible for Jeremy to look away. "I'm not, uh, built like you," he confessed, the words coming out fast and panicked as he tightened his grip on the towel. "I'm, uh…and you're, uh…"

"I bet you're just as gorgeous naked as you are wearing clothes." Reg smiled and Jeremy let him pull the towel away. "Besides, I'm not here to judge."

"You think I'm gorgeous?"

"'Course I do. I have eyes, don't I?"

He did have eyes. Warm, kind brown eyes that had yet to look away from Jeremy's face even though he was now just as naked as Reg.

"Come on." Reg threw the towel toward the bathroom and started backing up, returning to his previous spot on the bed. "You'll love this."

"Okay." Jeremy climbed onto the mattress. "Where do you want me?"

"Put your butt on that towel." Reg nudged his chin toward a towel next to him. "You can either lie down or sit up."

Lying down would make it easier to avoid Reg's eyes if Jeremy felt like he needed to hide a little. Plus, he'd be able to look at Reg all over without it being too obvious.

"I'll lie down."

Immediately, Reg tossed a couple of pillows beside himself. "Here you go. Let me know if you need more." He waited for Jeremy to get settled and then sat next to him, his legs spread and stretched out next to Jeremy's shoulders. "I already lubed the Fleshlight, but you'll want to get yourself nice and slick too." Reg poured some lube onto his palm and then put the bottle in Jeremy's hand.

Given how nervous Jeremy was, he found it incredible

that, in comparison, Reg could so easily sit there and start rubbing himself off, spreading shiny liquid across his semihard shaft.

"Go on." Reg tipped his head toward Jeremy's groin, still not looking away from his face. "Unless you want my help."

Blood rushed south in reaction to the suggestion, but Jeremy's heart also started pounding so hard against his ribs he was sure Reg could hear it. "Sorry," he said. "I've, uh, got it." He drizzled the lube onto his hand, and then, focusing on Reg's chest instead of his face so he wouldn't melt from embarrassment, he reached between his legs and took himself in hand.

"Keep going until you're hard." Reg's voice sounded husky and aroused, making Jeremy lower his gaze where he saw confirmation that Reg was in fact getting turned on in the form of an even thicker, longer dick.

"You're huge," he said, before he could stop himself.

"Bigger than some, smaller than others." Reg shrugged. "It isn't a competition." For the first time, Reg looked away from Jeremy's face. Like a caress, he moved his gaze down Jeremy's chest, across his belly, and landed on his now-erect cock. "But if it was," he rasped, "you'd do well, JJ." Reg trembled. "Really well. You're beautiful."

Feeling himself thicken and twitch in reaction to Reg's praise, Jeremy whispered, "What's next?"

"Right." Reg closed his eyes and shook his head, as if to clear it. Then he reached over to the nightstand and handed

Jeremy what looked like a giant flashlight filled with a pink rubbery substance. "See the hole?" He picked up another identical toy and pushed his finger into the slit on the top. "It expands, but holds you tight." Gripping the base of his dick with one hand, he raised the toy, wiggled it on his flared crown, and then pushed it all the way down his thick shaft. "Ungh," he moaned as he pumped it up and down. "Now you, JJ."

Unable to look away from the erotic scene playing out in front of him, Jeremy somehow managed to press the toy against his glans and slide it down. "Oh God."

"Feel good?" Reg asked hoarsely.

"Yeah." He increased his pace, moving his hand up and down quickly. "Really good."

"Keep going." Reg grabbed his balls with his free hand, squeezing and rolling them while he slid the toy over his shaft. "Wanna hear you."

That admission made Jeremy cry out. He thrust his hips up and back in counterpoint to his hand, gasping for air as he felt himself get closer and closer to the end. All the while, he kept his gaze glued to Reg, alternating between his face, tense with pleasure, and his long, hard cock and huge balls.

"I'm close," he said, suddenly realizing he was about to come faster than he ever had in his life. "I never... Oh God. Oh God. I'm close."

"Do it," Reg urged, his hand flying. "Let me see you finish."

With an almost pained moan, Jeremy arched his back and came so hard the world went gray around the edges.

He heard Reg hiss, "Yes, so hot," and glanced up in time to see him throw his head back as his expression turned to bliss.

As if in sympathy, Jeremy's cock pulsed again, releasing another string of seed and making him gasp. "Holy shit," he said breathlessly.

"Good?" Reg asked, sounding similarly strained. He was still moving the toy over his shaft, but the speed of his strokes had slowed. "'Cause it looked fun from here."

"Yeah." Jeremy nodded, his chest heaving as he tried to get air into his lungs. "It was good."

"Told you." Reg smiled and finally pulled the toy off, leaving his dick exposed.

Even with his arousal waning, it was impressive—thick and long with veins running up the sides, which Jeremy had an insane desire to trace with his finger. Or tongue. He was losing his mind.

"The Fleshlight's the bomb," Reg said.

The toy was great. No doubt about it. But Jeremy had the sense that it wouldn't have been as enjoyable if he'd been doing it alone.

"Look at you," Reg said tenderly. "You came, and two seconds later, your eyes are closing."

"No, they're not."

"Uh-huh, right." Without warning, Reg reached over and pulled the toy off Jeremy's softening dick. "Use the towel to wipe yourself off while I clean these up." He held up the Fleshlights. "Then we can go to bed."

Reg was off the bed and walking into the bathroom before Jeremy could be embarrassed.

With his body boneless and sated, Jeremy couldn't bring himself to freak out over what he'd just done. Besides, Reg didn't seem the least bit bothered, so he shouldn't be either. His internal musings must have taken longer than he realized, because suddenly Reg was back.

"You didn't get dressed," Reg said as he stepped over to the bed. Before Jeremy could apologize and get his clothes, Reg pulled up the blanket and slid underneath. "Cool. I like sleeping naked better anyway." He reached for the lamp. "You ready to get under here, or should I leave the light on?"

Whenever Reg shared Jeremy's bed, which had been every single night since the first one over two months earlier, he didn't sleep on the other side and let Jeremy occasionally bump their feet together or touch his hip. No. Unlike any of Jeremy's previous bed partners, Reg scooped him close and wrapped his muscular body around Jeremy, holding him tightly all night. With them both naked, it'd be impossible to avoid contact with each other's private parts, and Jeremy was sure that should revolt him, but for some reason it didn't.

"Stop overthinking things and get under the covers, JJ."

His body was moving before his mind had a chance to refuse, and the next thing Jeremy knew, the light was off and he was being held against Reg's strong chest.

"Get some rest," Reg whispered as he ran his fingers

through Jeremy's hair. "You've had a long day."

"Reg?" Jeremy whispered after a few minutes. "You asleep?"

"Nuh-uh." Reg skimmed his hand down Jeremy's back. "What's up?"

"What we did just now, was it weird?"

Reg shifted, and Jeremy's bare balls slid across his thigh. He hadn't thought their nights together could get more intimate, but they had. "What do you mean weird?" Reg asked.

"I don't know." Jeremy stroked over Reg's bicep and up to his shoulder, where he knew from memory his tattoo started. "But I'm pretty certain most people don't do that with their friends."

"I'm sure you're right."

"So isn't that weird?"

"Did you have a good time?" Reg asked.

"Yeah," Jeremy answered without hesitation.

"Me too. I got off hard. Looked like you did too." He shrugged. "Why does anything else matter?"

It didn't. "It doesn't," Jeremy admitted.

"Good." Reg chuckled. "Because I totally want to do that again."

Feeling his dick fill at the mere prospect of repeating that evening's activity and knowing there was no way to hide it with it pressed against Reg's hip, Jeremy reached for a topic change. "I don't think I've ever asked about your tattoo. Does it mean anything?"

"Nah. I'm not that deep. I wanted a tat, so I sketched this out. It's just lines and shapes, but I thought it looked cool, so I had it inked. Started with my shoulder and then added on a couple more times 'til I got to my wrist."

"It looks good," Jeremy said, tracing his finger over Reg's arm. "Are you going to have more done?"

"Maybe. Depends if the urge strikes."

Jeremy smiled. "That's one of the things that amazes me about you."

"My tattoo amazes you?"

"No." Jeremy hugged Reg. "The way you're so relaxed about everything. You never get angry or hysterical. You just take things as they come."

"There's no other way to take them," Reg said as he petted Jeremy's nape and back. "Getting angry won't change anything."

"I know, but I still get all worked up and upset all the time."

"Yup, you do." Reg chuckled. "It's cute."

"I hate when you call me cute," Jeremy growled.

"You *love* when I say you're cute."

It was true. He did. "No, I don't."

"Okay, JJ. Whatever you say." Reg kissed the top of his head. "Good night."

"Good night, Reggie." Jeremy cuddled close, tucked his head under Reg's chin, and sighed happily. "Thanks for cheering me up tonight."

"Anytime." He paused. "Seriously. Anytime."

CHAPTER 12

"Oh my God, why is he dressed like that?" Jeremy said, sounding petrified. "Reg!"

They were in a club room off the lobby of the hotel where they'd stayed for the Chicago concert the previous night. They were leaving immediately after the interview for the show in Madison the following night, so there was no risk of their location being leaked yet again, and it made things easier to have the reporter come to them.

"It's Halloween," Francis said. "People wear costumes."

Reg followed Jeremy's gaze out the window to the men approaching them. One was carrying a few cameras. The other one... "Dude. What the fuck?"

"It's a costume," Francis snapped. "Would you two calm down?"

"That's the creepiest thing I've ever seen." Jeremy had been pacing back and forth across the room, his usual preinterview nerves evident, but the sight of the reporter had him scrambling to Reg's side on the leather love seat. "Make him change, Francis. I can't talk to him when he's dressed like that."

"He's a clown, for goodness sake. Clowns are happy."

"No, they're not!" Jeremy shouted, seeming more panicked as the reporter got closer.

"Of course they are," Francis argued. "Everyone loves clowns."

"Not me." Jeremy looked up at Reg, his expression pleading. "I'm afraid of clowns. I always have been."

Reg put his arm around him.

"Dude, there isn't a single person alive who thinks a grown man in white face paint with those painted-on eyebrows, a blood red mouth, and that freaky-ass pom-pom costume is happy. That shit is freaky and unprofessional."

"He's here, so stop acting like idiots." Francis stepped toward the door.

"No way." Jeremy scrambled onto Reg's lap. "I can't sit in a small room and have a conversation with a clown. No. Make him go away."

Francis wasn't going to stop; his squared shoulders and haughty expression made that clear.

"I'll take care of it," Reg said, patting Jeremy's knee before he slid him off his lap and got up.

"What're you going to do?"

"I'm sending him home. I'll give them half an hour to get another reporter here if they want to interview you."

"You can't do that," Francis growled.

Reg shouldered his way past him. "Look, man, I don't want to tell you how to do your job, but that shit"—he pointed at the clown, now right outside the door—"isn't appropriate. He's here to interview the biggest rock star of our generation.

He needs to show some respect."

Not having time to wait for a response and continue the argument, Reg tugged the door open and stepped outside.

"Hello. You're Reggie Moore, right? I'm Clifford Crew with the *Post*." The clown reached his white-gloved hand out. "It's an honor to be able to meet Jeremy Jameson."

The man seemed nice and genuinely excited, but it didn't change the fact that Reg wasn't letting him anywhere near Jeremy.

"Good to meet you, Clifford." Reg took his hand. "But I'm afraid we have a problem."

Clifford's forehead crinkled in concern, causing the thick makeup to crack and making him look even more frightening. "What problem?" He darted his gaze around, and the red contacts he was wearing couldn't keep up so it looked like blood was sliding over his pupils. Reg said a silent thanks that Jeremy was too far away to see it. "I'm on time, aren't I?"

"Yes. But your clothes." Reg looked up and down the reporter's body. "And the makeup. Dude, you're here for work, and you show up as a scary clown?" He shook his head. "Tell your paper to send someone else, and we'll wait for a little while, but you're not interviewing Jeremy dressed like that."

"But I was told to wear this." Clifford tugged on the colorful one-piece suit. "They said Jeremy would be dressed up for Halloween, and I was supposed to go along with it."

"Who said that?" Reg narrowed his eyes suspiciously.

"I don't know. One of Jeremy Jameson's people. My boss might know who it was. Do you want me to call? I can call." He reached for what Reg assumed was a pocket, but came up empty when all he encountered was polyester. "Damn it. Give me a sec, I can—"

Flicking his gaze to the club room, Reg saw Francis on the phone and Jeremy curled into the side of the love seat, looking pale. "Did you choose the costume?" he asked as he returned his attention to Clifford.

"Are you kidding?" he said incredulously. "I'm dressed like a clown. Why would I choose this?" Clifford sighed. "My boss said it was part of the deal."

"Uh-huh." After giving the situation a few seconds of thought, Reg said, "All right, dude, here's what's going to happen. We have a suite upstairs. Our stuff is out of it, but technically it's ours until noon. I'll get you a keycard, and you go up there and wash that shit off your face." He paused. "You wearing anything under there?"

Nodding, Clifford said, "Jeans and a T-shirt. Normally I'd wear a suit, but—"

"It's fine. I understand. Go clean up and get out of that clown gear, and then you can interview Jeremy."

"Okay, sure." The reporter was too nervous and frantic to argue. "No problem."

"Cool. Let's go to the reception desk and get you a keycard," Reg said. He looked at Jeremy, waited for him to meet his gaze, and then mouthed, "Be right back." Once Jeremy nodded, Reg led Clifford toward the reception area.

"Thanks, uh..."

"You can call me Reg, man."

"Thanks, Reg." The clown leaned closer to him and whispered, "And off the record, I want to tell you I think it's great what you guys are doing."

Reg immediately went on guard, the comments he'd been hearing for months about Jeremy lying about their relationship front and center in his mind. "What do you mean?"

"The way he's so open with you, so casual about it." He bobbed his head, making his curly orange-red hair bounce. "You have to know what a difference that makes to all of us, especially kids coming out." He paused. "*Jeremy Jameson* is gay." He sighed. "That's huge."

They walked the rest of the way to the desk in silence, and Reg got a keycard for the reporter. "I'll take your photographer with me so he can get the pictures out of the way while you get changed."

"Okay." Reg had just turned around to head back to Jeremy when Clifford gasped. "Hey, I have a great idea." He rushed over to Reg, pom-poms swaying and his big floppy clown shoes slapping against the floor. He looked ridiculous. "Are you guys staying here tonight? Because you should come out to Boystown. It'll be a blast. Everyone will be in costume." He looked down at his clothes. "Good costumes."

The idea had merit. Jeremy never had the opportunity to go out and party like a normal person. But on Halloween, he could dress up, and nobody would recognize him. Reg thought about taking Jeremy to a bar in Boystown where they could dance and rub their bodies together. Maybe if he got lucky, Jeremy's brain would finally catch up with his body, and he could get a kiss. His cock immediately throbbed.

"Nah, man," Reg said, already making plans to book another hotel room for the night. "Thanks for the offer, but we're taking off right after this."

"Explain it to me again," Jeremy said. "What are we doing?"

"Here, put on your hat and sunglasses." Reg handed Jeremy's usual disguise to him. "And wear my jacket."

Pulling the bill of the hat down low, Jeremy said, "Your jacket will be huge on me, Hulk."

"It'll cover you up."

"Fine." With a huff, Jeremy slipped the jacket on. "Now explain."

"I booked us a room at a different hotel." Reg heaved his duffel over his shoulder, put his hand on the small of Jeremy's back, and led him out to the street. "We'll leave first thing tomorrow and make it in plenty of time for your show, but this way we can spend Halloween in Boystown."

"Boystown?" Jeremy asked as he followed along, pulling his suitcase behind him.

"Gay village. Lots of bars. Should be a fun party." They

stepped over to the doorman. It had taken Reg a while to get used to the way things worked at the fancy hotels where they stayed, but after more than five months on the road, he had the hang of it. "We're going to Lakeview," Reg told him. "Can we get a cab, please?"

The man nodded, went over to the line of cabs, and waved one over.

"Reg, you know I can't do that," Jeremy said under his breath, not wanting anyone to hear. "I'll get mobbed."

"Not if they don't know it's you." The cab pulled up, and Reg opened the back door. "Get in. I'll put our bags in the trunk." Jeremy climbed into the cab, and Reg closed his door. "I'll get it," he said to the cabbie as he opened the trunk and put the duffel and suitcase inside. Then he jogged over to the other side of the cab, got in, and gave the cabbie the name of a hotel close to the one he'd booked. On the off chance the man recognized Jeremy or someone was following them, he didn't want to give away their real location. "Okay, here's the plan," he whispered to Jeremy. "We check into the new hotel and then go out and shop for costumes."

"Costumes?"

"Yup." Reg nodded and grinned, already looking forward to a great night. "Something with a mask, so nobody recognizes you. We can grab dinner, hit the bars, mingle, dance." He squeezed Jeremy's knee. "Nobody'll know it's you, so you can unwind, let go, and have a good time. It'll be awesome."

Jeremy pulled his shirt collar into his mouth, a sure

sign he was nervous. But based on his expression, he was hopeful too. "You think it'll work? With the way we've been hounded by photographers…"

"I have a theory about that, and we can talk about it later, but, yes, I know it'll work." Reg twisted sideways so he could look straight into Jeremy's eyes. "Nobody knows we're here. Even if they figure out we didn't leave Chicago, they'll have no idea where we're staying. Not Francis, not Bill. Not anybody."

Jeremy visibly relaxed—his shoulders lowered, the crease in his forehead evened out, and he released his shirt.

"You'll have to wear a mask too, yeah?" Jeremy said. "They've gotten pictures of you. I mean, you're not plastered on the magazines like I am, but you're still there, so somebody might recognize you, and then they'll rec—"

"No problem. We'll both go in masks." Taking a chance, Reg reached for Jeremy's hand and placed it between both of his, smiling when Jeremy clutched him tightly. "So you have anything particular in mind?"

"As far as masked costumes?"

"Yup." Reg dipped his chin.

"Uh, superheroes, I guess." Jeremy shrugged. "They wear masks."

Reg settled in his seat and tugged Jeremy's hand onto his thigh, rubbing his thumb over the back. "Superheroes it is."

An hour later, they were in a costume store, flipping through the racks.

"Have you ever noticed that all the women's costumes start with the word 'sexy'?" Jeremy said.

"What do you mean?"

"Sexy nurse," Jeremy said as he held up a skimpy white dress. He put that one back and said, "Sexy police officer," as he lifted an almost identical dress, except in black. "Sexy Batgirl." He waved the latest costume and then went to put it back on the rack.

"Wait." Reg grasped his wrist. "That one has promise."

"Uh, what kind of promise? Street hustler by day, crime fighter by night?"

"I was thinking more along the lines of your costume for tonight." Reg grinned and waggled his eyebrows.

Looking from the leotard in his hand to Reg's face, Jeremy furrowed his brow in confusion. "This is a girl's costume."

"Doesn't have to be. People go in drag all the time, and you have the build for it."

"Are you saying I have a woman's body?"

"No." Reg dragged his palm down Jeremy's firm chest to his tight belly. "But you're trim. You have this tiny waist and muscular legs." He licked his lips and looked at Jeremy appreciatively.

Flicking his gaze to the costume again, Jeremy said, "You seriously want me to walk around in public in a women's bathing suit?"

"It's not a bathing suit. It's a black leotard."

"It looks like a bathing suit."

"Well, it's not. Besides, there's also a big yellow belt, a cape, and a mask. We'll find a wig and tall boots too. It won't be just the suit."

"See! Even you said it's a bathing suit."

Truth be told, Reg wasn't sure he understood the difference. Didn't change the fact that he wanted to see Jeremy in the skintight, skimpy outfit, and he couldn't imagine a better disguise.

"You'll look superhot in it, and nobody will know it's you."

"Yeah? You really think so?" Jeremy held the costume up in front of his face and examined it.

"Totally sure."

"What will you be?"

"Uh." Reg glanced around. "I can be Batman so we coordinate."

"Batman?"

"Yup. I'll ask the guy up front if they have one."

Jeremy followed behind Reg, staying close and keeping his face ducked. Reg hated that Jeremy felt like he constantly had to hide, but he enjoyed having the smaller man close to him. He reached back and rested his hand on Jeremy's side.

"Do you guys have any Batman costumes?" Reg asked the cashier.

"We do, but"—the man leaned past the counter and looked Reg over—"everything's pretty picked over, and I don't think you'll be able to squeeze all those yummy muscles into what we have left."

Jeremy went rigid behind him. "We'll figure out what he can fit his yummy muscles into," he barked. "Just point us to the costumes!"

"Oh, testy." The guy winked and laughed. "They're right over there, honey." He pointed to the other end of the store.

Jeremy turned on his heel and stomped across the store, his hands balled into fists. Reg followed and tried not to laugh. Did Jeremy even realize he was jealous? And if he did, how was he explaining that to himself?

"Here," Jeremy snapped and flung a costume at Reg. "Batman." He crossed his arms over his chest, hitched his hip to the side, and tapped his foot. "See if you can fit your *yummy muscles* into it."

No way could Reg keep himself from smiling at that display. "You jealous, superstar?" he asked as he reached out and clasped Jeremy's shoulder.

"Don't be ridiculous," Jeremy scoffed. "Why would I be jealous?" He rolled his eyes and sneered. "That's insane."

"Oh-ho, this is your best tantrum yet." Reg yanked him forward and then wrapped his arm around him and forced him to stay close. "Quit wiggling and let me hug you."

"I don't think I'm the one who wanted a hug. Maybe

you should go ask your new friend."

"But I don't want to hug my new friend." Reg hunched down and kissed the side of Jeremy's neck. "I save that for my boyfriend." He paused and then, in a quieter voice, said, "My pretend boyfriend."

Jeremy grunted but stopped trying to move away, instead circling his arms around Reg's waist. "How's the costume?"

"Uh, let's see." Keeping one arm around Jeremy, Reg held the costume at arm's length. "The mask and cape will work fine, but there's not a chance the shirt and pants'll fit."

"Damn. Should we look somewhere else? I was kind of excited about the matching costumes," Jeremy confessed. Then he cleared his throat. "I mean, I was excited because you were excited and, uh, yeah."

"This'll be fine. I have black boots, and I saw three racks of leather pants up front. I'll pick up a pair of those, and I'll be ready to go."

Jeremy stepped back and fingered the foam costume shirt. "What about this shirt with pretend muscles?"

"I think I can cover the muscles on my own." Reg flexed. "Besides, if you're wearing a bathing—I mean leotard, I can skip the shirt altogether."

Jeremy's eyes widened, his nostrils flared, and he gasped. "You're going to wear leather pants and no shirt?"

"Yup." Reg turned around and strutted toward the cash register. Tight leather pants. Low rise so his hips would show. The top of his pubes too. He'd been patient for months.

It was time to speed things along.

"I don't think this is going to work," Jeremy yelled from the hotel bathroom, where he was trying on his costume.

"Come out here and let me see."

"I look ridiculous."

"Let me see, JJ."

The bathroom door swung open, and Jeremy stepped into the doorway, his cheeks red. "See? I look silly."

"Your boobs are a little crooked, but other than that, you look great." Really great. The leotard fit him like a glove, highlighting the V shape of his chest and waist. And with his legs exposed all the way to the tops of his thighs, they looked even longer. "Seriously, JJ. You're hot."

"My legs are hairy, I can't get my breasts to stay in place, and doesn't it look weird to have a bulge, uh"—he glanced down at his groin—"here?"

"I'll tighten your bra and tape the stuffing into it." Reg stepped toward him, cupped the fake breasts in both hands, and adjusted them. "You can tuck your dick, but I think you should leave it showing. Makes the whole thing hotter." Reg was looking at Jeremy's package as he spoke, so he could see the effect his words had on Jeremy's swelling member. "And as far as the hair..." He dropped to a squat, putting himself at eye level with Jeremy's dick and ignoring his gasp and moan.

"How about I shave you down?"

"Sh...sh...shave me?"

"Uh-huh." Reg skimmed his hands over Jeremy's thighs, making sure he scraped his thumbs along his pelvis. "I used to shave my head." He glanced up. "So I'm good with a razor."

"I don't, uh—"

"You go hop in the shower," Reg said as he stood. "And I'll get the shaving gel and razor ready."

"Okay," Jeremy said breathlessly.

With a hand on Jeremy's back, Reg steered him into the bathroom. He turned on the water and adjusted the temperature while Jeremy started peeling his costume off.

"I, uh, don't have anything on under this, so I'd better get—"

"You're good naked," Reg said, trying to keep his tone casual. "That way I won't miss anything." Like Jeremy's furry balls or his slender, pink shaft. "Hop on in, the water's perfect."

Reg busied himself with getting the shaving supplies ready, waiting until Jeremy was under the water before turning around. "Hey, you mind if I come in there with you?" he asked. "That way we won't get water all over the bathroom floor."

"Uh."

"It's big enough for two, right?" Reg asked, even though he already knew the answer.

"Yeah."

"Cool." Reg quickly stripped out of his clothes, slid the

curtain, and stepped into the tub, a bottle of shaving gel in one hand and a razor in the other. "Ready?" he asked Jeremy, trying to keep his voice even and his expression casual so he wouldn't terrify Jeremy more. Jeremy's green eyes were wide, and Reg knew he was tiptoeing on a dangerous line.

"I guess so."

Reg dropped into a squat, held on to Jeremy's ankle and said, "I'll do your left leg first." He carefully shaved both legs up to the top of Jeremy's thighs. Jeremy wasn't particularly hairy, at least not compared to Reg, but he changed out the blade on the razor halfway through anyway, just to make sure it stayed sharp.

Though Jeremy remained quiet throughout the process, Reg knew he was enjoying the attention because his dick had been hard from the first touch, and by the end, it was curving up toward his belly button. With the water flowing around them, it was hard to tell, but Reg was pretty sure the drops seeping from Jeremy's slit were precum, not water, and he longed for a taste.

"Bikini line next," Reg said hoarsely and tried to ignore his own throbbing shaft. "Spread your legs."

Jeremy moved his left leg to the side, exposing himself more fully. "Don't cut me, okay?"

"I won't. Promise." Reg spread the shaving gel over the area, rinsed his hand, and said, "But I'll cup you just to make sure." Without waiting for a reaction, he placed his palm over Jeremy's balls and shaft, covering them.

"Ah!" Jeremy cried out. "Reg, I don't think—"

"Shh, it's okay," Reg cooed. "I have you."

Slowly, methodically, he shaved the area free of hair and then did the same to the other side. By the time Reg was completely done, Jeremy's chest was heaving, his nostrils were flared, and he was clenching and unclenching his fists.

"You should probably go so I can, uh, I need to—" He gulped. "I—"

"You're hard," Reg rasped as he set the shaving supplies on the edge of the tub and rose to his feet. "I can feel." Reg stepped forward until he was close enough that Jeremy had to tip his chin back to meet his gaze. Though he was done doing his job and no longer had an excuse, if anyone could call his flimsy rationale for touching Jeremy an excuse, he took Jeremy's shaft in hand anyway. "I can help you out with this, JJ." He gazed into Jeremy's eyes and hid nothing. "Do you want me to help you?"

Trembling, Jeremy looked at him, his gaze searching, questioning.

"We can talk later, okay? Everything will be fine, I promise. But right now you need to let go." He stroked up Jeremy's shaft. "And I want to give this to you." Bending forward so he could inhale Jeremy's scent, Reg kissed his shoulder. "Let me." He swallowed hard. "Please let me."

"Yes," Jeremy said, the word barely audible. He raised his arms and clutched Reg's waist. "Please."

In no time, Reg was scrambling for the body wash and drizzling it on Jeremy's shaft. Then he gripped it, not too tightly, but not loosely either, and started stroking with one hand while he cupped and fondled Jeremy's balls with the other.

"Reg," Jeremy moaned.

"That's it. Let yourself enjoy it."

"I do." Jeremy's breathing quickened. "I've never liked...not like this, not like with you." He dug his fingers into Reg's sides. "Why is that?"

"Because this is right." Reg twisted his hand at Jeremy's crown, making him cry out. "This is how it's supposed to be."

There wasn't time for more explanations because Jeremy rose onto his tiptoes, threw his head back, and screamed Reg's name as he came.

Excited beyond belief at the sight in front of him and the feel of Jeremy's hot seed spilling over his fingers, Reg breathlessly said, "Will it freak you out if I jack off, JJ?" His entire body shook. "I'm really close."

"Do it," Jeremy said, his gaze glued to Reg's groin. "I want to see."

Making sure not to let the water wash Jeremy's ejaculate off his fingers, Reg smeared it onto his dick. "Using your cum for lube," he explained.

"God," Jeremy gasped. "Yeah."

It didn't take long, not with as turned on as Reg was, not with Jeremy looking at him with heated eyes and running his long-fingered hands up and down Reg's chest. "JJ," Reg said reverently. "Fuck, yes, JJ." With one last pull, he shot hard, coating his hand and stomach.

Jeremy held on to him through it, watching, touching,

and when Reg was finally spent, Jeremy blinked up at him and said, "Reg?"

Reg slid his arms around Jeremy's waist, cupped his backside, and tugged him close. "Yes?"

"I think maybe I'm not straight after all," he said, his expression earnest.

Reg tilted the corners of his mouth up. "I think maybe you're right."

CHAPTER 13

AFTER they'd finished the most erotic shower—most erotic anything—of Jeremy's life, Reg had insisted they table any conversation and go have fun. Though he hadn't thought it would be possible, Jeremy had managed to do just that. Somehow he had shut his brain down and gone along with Reg from bar to bar, laughing, dancing, and drinking.

Remarkably, Reg wasn't the only person who had come up with the idea of a shirtless costume. In fact, there were lots of guys who seemed to think merely taking off their shirts meant they were in costume. No capes or masks or any indications of a character, just seminudity.

New awareness of his feelings made Jeremy wonder whether the fact that he could appreciate those exposed male forms meant he was gay. He assumed if the appreciation gave him tingles below the belt—the thick, yellow, faux-patent-leather belt with a black bat emblem—the answer was probably yes. Regardless, any appreciation he had for the strangers he saw that night was exponentially dwarfed by his appreciation for the man at his side.

Reg was his usual attentive, jovial, touchy self. He dragged Jeremy onto every dance floor and taught him the fine art of grinding. He sang along, loud and off-key, to any song he recognized. He laughed and joked with random people they met, immediately making new friends, but never failed to include Jeremy, even if it was merely with an arm around his waist.

As the night progressed, it seemed as if Reg was monitoring their alcohol intake more than usual. When Jeremy asked about it, Reg said, "I don't want either of us too drunk to make smart decisions tonight, superstar. Besides, we're having a good time, aren't we?"

Unable to argue with that statement, Jeremy let it go and enjoyed himself, feeling liberated and unrecognizable in his costume. Unfortunately, the rush of being free and happy started to fade as they walked into their hotel, and by the time they made it through the lobby, up the elevator, and down the hallway to their room, Jeremy was on the cusp of a meltdown.

"You shower first, then put on your sleep pants and a shirt and get in bed," Reg said as soon as they stepped into the room.

The sentence was like a punch to the gut. Jeremy was hurt and confused that, after what they'd shared earlier that evening, Reg would want them to shower apart and get dressed before going to bed. Did that mean Reg hadn't enjoyed what they'd done in the shower as much as he had? Did it mean Reg no longer wanted their bare bodies to connect during the night? Were the desires slamming through his head and chest and groin one-sided?

His feelings must have shown on his face, because Reg pulled off his mask, drew him into a hug, and gently said, "Earlier tonight you said you wanted to talk, and I can see that you're getting worked up again." He removed Jeremy's wig, tossed it on the bed, and then buried his fingers in Jeremy's sweaty hair, massaging his scalp. "If we get naked together right now, I don't think I'll have the self-restraint necessary to keep from jumping you, and then we'll never get to hash out whatever you've got going on in here." He tapped Jeremy's temple. "That's the only reason I'm not dragging you into the shower and burning all your clothes so you're forced to be nude. I promise." He kissed the tip of Jeremy's nose. "Okay?"

"Yeah." Jeremy's cheeks heated. "Sorry."

"Nothing to apologize for." Reg kissed him again—his cheek that time—and then nudged him toward the bathroom.

Being alone in the shower meant being alone with his thoughts, which meant wondering what was wrong with him and how a guy as charismatic, good-looking, and self-confident as Reggie Moore could stand him.

"I'm putting some clothes in here for you, JJ."

Reg's voice jerked him from his downward spiral. "Uh, what?"

"Clothes. I put them on the counter. Now stop freaking out and finish up in there. I'd drag you out myself, but then I'd see you naked and wet, and the next thing you know, I'd have you pinned to the bathroom floor with my mouth around your dick."

"Oh God."

"The moaning isn't helping," Reg said hoarsely. "Get out of there so I can have my turn in the shower. Then we can talk, and if you're still awake after, I can blow you."

The door closed with a loud thud. Jeremy snapped out of his stupor and scrubbed down as quickly as possible. Once he was dry, dressed, and had his hair and teeth brushed, he walked out of the bathroom.

Reg stood by the bed, wearing his briefs and clutching his sleep clothes. He stared at Jeremy, his gaze hot and full of longing. Then he stepped by him to get to the bathroom and groaned. "Fuck. You smell good."

"So do you," Jeremy whispered. Underneath the odor of beer and bars, there was the scent of Reg's body, which Jeremy realized made his groin tighten. He had gone from having what he'd considered an average sex drive his entire life to constantly feeling like a bundle of hormones ready to explode at the smallest touch.

Leaning toward him, Reg's nostrils flared, and his lips parted. Jeremy was sure he was about to be kissed. Despite how close he was to Reg and how comfortable they were touching each other; despite the fact that they'd played with the Fleshlights many times over the previous couple of weeks; despite the fact that Reg had taken him in hand earlier that night and brought him to the most powerful orgasm of his life...they hadn't ever kissed. As Jeremy stood still, watching Reg's handsome face nearing him, he found himself wondering what it would be like to feel Reg's lips against his, to know his taste.

But just before Reg got close enough to touch or kiss, he shook his head and moved away. "I'll just be a minute," he said and hurried into the bathroom.

True to his word, Reg showered quickly and then came to bed wearing sweats cut off above the knees and a T-shirt with the sleeves removed. It was an outfit Jeremy had seen him in frequently, but for the first time, he gave in to his urge to look at Reg's thick, muscular thighs, his corded arms, decorated with a sexy tattoo, and his broad, hard chest.

"You gotta quit looking at me like that, JJ."

"Like what?" Jeremy asked without moving his gaze from Reg's long cock, clearly visible underneath the thin shorts.

"Like you want to eat me alive," Reg answered as he crawled onto the mattress. "Because I really, really want to let you."

That comment immediately made Jeremy think about what it would be like to go down on Reg. Could he do it? Could he take another man in his mouth? Could he lick Reg's balls and suck his dick? His cock jerked and filled in response to the raw fantasy, giving a clear answer to his question.

"I feel so stupid," Jeremy admitted, squeezing his eyes shut.

"Why?"

The bed dipped and Jeremy knew Reg was right next to him. The fingers that began combing through his hair confirmed it.

"I'm almost thirty-two years old," Jeremy said. "How is it possible I never knew this about myself?"

"This?" Reg repeated questioningly.

"Me and you. The way I feel." Jeremy opened his eyes and met Reg's gaze. He pointed his finger back and forth between them. "*This.*"

Nodding in understanding, Reg said, "Well, I'm not sure anyone except you can answer that question with any degree of accuracy, but if you're asking my opinion, I think it's because you've always had so many people in your life telling you how to act, telling you who you are, that you never had the chance to get to know yourself."

"What kind of person doesn't know himself?" Jeremy said, his voice high-pitched and hysterical. He covered his face with his hands. "God, I'm an idiot."

"You're not an idiot," Reg said firmly. "And you're not the first person in his early thirties who's still learning who he is." He peeled Jeremy's hands off his face. "Look at me, JJ."

Jeremy shook his head and kept his eyes closed. It was childish, he knew, but he couldn't bring himself to see Reg's expression. The man had known who he was since he was a teen, had lived his life openly and honestly. No matter what he said, Jeremy was sure Reg had to think he was pathetic.

"Don't hide from me. I'm your friend, and I won't judge you."

Trusting Reg, Jeremy slowly opened his eyes and lowered his palms. "You're the only person alive who wouldn't judge me for this." He shook his head ruefully. "I can only imagine the headlines and the late-night talk show jokes. Nobody would think *The Jeremy Jameson* is something special if they knew who I really am."

"Jokes are meant to sell commercials, and headlines are meant to sell magazines. None of them mean anything." Reg cupped the side of his neck and massaged his nape. "And quit being so hard on yourself. So you're not perfect. Who is? Hell, even Mick Jagger shits."

"I'm a better singer than Jagger," Jeremy grumbled.

Reg laughed. "And more modest too."

"I wasn't trying to brag, but it's true!"

"See? That's exactly my point. You sit here beating yourself up in every way except your music. That's the one thing you're sure of, the one thing you're quick to defend." Reg gazed at Jeremy with warmth and affection. "You're a musician." He brushed his fingers through Jeremy's hair, something Jeremy loved, which, of course, Reg knew. "It's your calling, and you've spent your entire life focused on it. Nothing else mattered to you except your music, including your personal life." He grinned and shrugged. "So you neglected the small stuff. Lots of people do it. No bigs."

"Small stuff?" Jeremy said incredulously. "Reg, I've spent my entire adult life dating women and thinking I couldn't connect with any of them because I didn't have it in me, that it wasn't something my lifestyle had room for."

Reg stopped moving, his hand frozen in place and his expression serious. "And what do you think now?"

"Well, I guess now I wonder if maybe the reason they

weren't interested in anything except what I could do for their careers was because I wasn't really interested in them. Maybe *that's* why we didn't connect."

"And about the other?" Reg asked, his voice sounding rough.

"Uh, what other?" Jeremy crinkled his brow in confusion.

"Does your lifestyle have room to connect with someone, JJ?" Reg gulped and looked at Jeremy intently. "Do you have it in you?"

It was a fair question given Jeremy's dating history and everything he'd ever said about relationships, and his parents' relationship histories and everything he'd ever said they'd said about relationships, and most rumors about most rock stars' relationship histories and... It was a fair question. But Jeremy would have thought the answer was clear.

They had been on the road for well over five months, spending almost every moment together. They talked about their childhoods, shared their insecurities, ate together, laughed together, even slept together. Jeremy had never felt more connected to another human being in his life; it was as if Reg had burrowed under his skin. But if Reg asked that question, it meant Jeremy wasn't expressing his feelings well.

Having no experience to draw from, no history of successful relationships to use as models, Jeremy reflected back on what he might have said or done to Reg and tried to figure out where he had gone wrong. Almost immediately, he realized that every bit of physical contact he shared with Reg was initiated by Reg, not him, and was aimed at making him feel pleasure, not Reg. Cringing at his own selfishness, Jeremy took in a deep breath, gathered his courage, and pounced.

Taking Reg off guard, he was able to roll the bigger man onto his back and lay on top of him. He slammed his mouth on Reg's, initiating their first kiss. Well, he had aimed for Reg's mouth. In the heat of the moment, he landed closer to his cheek. But that didn't deter Jeremy. He clasped Reg's shoulders and landed kiss after kiss until finally he felt their lips connect. He mashed his mouth against Reg, wanting to make his feelings clear.

"Hey," Reg said softly. He leaned away and put his big hand on Jeremy's chest, keeping him back. "What's going on?"

Being turned down wasn't what Jeremy had been expecting, so it stung. "Oh. I—" He gulped. "Sorry. I didn't—" He tried to wiggle off Reg, but strong hands on his hips kept him in place.

"Where're you going?"

Ducking his head, Jeremy said, "I thought you wanted me to stop."

"No." Reg took Jeremy's chin in his hand and raised it. He looked Jeremy straight in the eyes. "I want to know if you think there's a chance for something between us; something that isn't pretend; something that'll last much longer than this concert tour. I want to know if I can finally make love to you and show you that the sex is just as good as the cuddling afterward." He paused, lowered his gaze, and then looked at

Jeremy from underneath his lashes. "I want to know how you feel about me."

"I'm not pretending," Jeremy assured him. "I want you to touch me. I want to touch you. I want to—" He cleared his throat. "I want you to... And I feel...I feel..." He felt overwhelmed with unfamiliar emotions and desires he didn't recognize and couldn't articulate. "I feel..."

"It's okay," Reg said, cupping both of Jeremy's cheeks. "We can talk more later. I heard what I need to know for now."

In one smooth motion, Reg rolled them over so Jeremy was under his huge, strong body. With his forearms resting on either side of Jeremy's head and his fingers tangled in Jeremy's hair, Reg wedged himself between Jeremy's thighs.

"Have I ever told you how much I like your lips?" he asked with a soft smile.

Jeremy shook his head, his gaze locked on Reg's kind face.

"Well, I do." Reg rubbed his thumb over Jeremy's lips. "I look at them all the time. When you're singing, you part them. Not just when the words are coming out either. If you're on stage, microphone in hand, your lips are almost always parted." He dipped his face and slid his mouth over Jeremy's in a barely there motion, gentler than the kisses Jeremy had initiated and yet infinitely more intimate.

"You squish them together really tight all in the center when you're angry and getting worked up for one of your tantrums." Jeremy scowled in response to that comment. Reg threw his head back and laughed. Then he leaned down for another kiss, this time increasing the pressure slightly. "And when you're really mad, like, about-to-throw-shit mad, you stretch them out until they're super thin and almost white."

Caressing Jeremy's cheek, Reg looked into his eyes as he darted his tongue out and swiped it across Jeremy's lips.

Jeremy found himself breathless.

"And when you're happy and laughing, they tilt up so high on the sides that you get little lines here"—Reg kissed one side of Jeremy's mouth—"and here." He kissed the other side. "But you want to know my favorite one?"

"What?" Jeremy rasped.

"When we're alone and I'm touching you—massaging your feet or giving you a hug or holding you in my arms— you get this expression on your face." Reg shuddered at the memory. "You look peaceful and content, and, to me at least, a little aroused, and your lips—" He swallowed hard. "They get really red and full, and I want more than anything to kiss you."

With his heart racing, his breath coming out in short bursts, and his body tense and primed, Jeremy clutched Reg's shoulders and stared up at him.

"Do you want me to kiss you, JJ?"

Though he opened his mouth to answer, Jeremy couldn't form any words so he nodded instead.

"Eventually, if you'll let me, I'll kiss you all over. Your hip." Reg shifted a little to the side and ground his hard shaft against Jeremy's hip. "The freckles on the inside of your thigh." He moved over, keeping his dick on Jeremy, and then he thrust into the juncture between his thigh and pelvis, where Jeremy didn't realize he had freckles. "Your balls." Reg planted his hands on the mattress and straightened them, lifting himself up. Then he moved his groin down before rolling forward, pressing the head of his fabric-covered cock against Jeremy's balls.

"Oh God!" Jeremy shouted.

Again and again Reg pumped against Jeremy, the defined muscles in his arms bulging, his gaze smoldering.

"Reg, you need to stop." Jeremy grabbed Reg's arms and held on so tightly he was sure to leave bruises. "Oh my God, if you don't stop, I'll…" He spread his legs and tilted his hips up, unable to prevent his body from seeking more friction even when his mind knew that would end things sooner than he wanted.

"You'll what?" He rocked forward. "Am I going to make you come in your shorts?" He nudged forward, putting more pressure on Jeremy where he was most sensitive. "Don't fight it, JJ." He covered Jeremy's mouth with his and slid his tongue inside, tasting, licking, only pulling away when air became a necessity. "Because it's going to happen more than once tonight."

"Can't," Jeremy gasped. "Once is all I'm able to—"

"Oh-ho, a challenge." Reg nipped at Jeremy's chin. "I love a challenge." He lowered his body onto Jeremy's groin, putting weight onto his already sensitive balls, and moved from side to side.

"Reg," Jeremy cried. "Reg!"

"Aches, doesn't it?"

"Yeah."

"But it feels good, right?" He didn't wait for an answer. "Look at you, barely holding on. It's okay. I promise you'll go again." He slotted his dick next to Jeremy's, the thin fabric of their sleep shorts the only thing separating them, and ground back and forth. "Let go, JJ. Enjoy it. And after, I'll lick my way up your shaft and suck you down until you come again."

And that was exactly what Jeremy did, opening his mouth in a soundless cry, arching up against Reg's larger body, and losing his breath as he pulsed his pleasure over and over again.

"Oh my God," he gasped and stared at Reg.

"That looked like a good one." Reg grinned, looking very proud of himself. "Was it?"

"Yeah." So good Jeremy was having trouble breathing. And feeling his legs.

"Let me ask you something, superstar."

In that moment, Reg could've asked him anything and he'd answer. No. Not just in that moment. Reg had earned his complete trust months earlier.

"You came in your shorts, so I know you're messy and sticky."

Jeremy's cheeks heated and he wriggled under Reg.

"But do you feel awkward?"

Stopping to consider the question, Jeremy shook his head. "No. I feel..." He felt undone but in a good way, as if tension he hadn't realized he carried was suddenly gone. "I feel good."

"See that? And your clothes were still on," Reg pointed out as he tugged on Jeremy's T-shirt. "Imagine what I can do when I get you naked." He tucked his hands under Jeremy's shirt and shoved it up his chest. "Sex can be messy and sticky, like you told me once." He eased the shirt over Jeremy's head and pulled it off his arms. "But if it's right, it feels way too good to be awkward." Reg rose to his knees and took hold of Jeremy's shorts.

Jeremy whimpered.

"I'm going to blow your mind, superstar." Reg pulled off his shorts, used them to wipe the seed off his groin, and tossed them across the room, leaving him lying naked and exposed. "But first"—he scooted down and hunched over, his face inches from Jeremy's groin—"I'm going to blow your dick."

CHAPTER 14

THREE. That was how many orgasms Reg had coaxed from Jeremy. He was sure he could have pleasured him more if they'd started earlier, but at four in the morning, after being worked over for hours, Jeremy's eyes drooped closed, and Reg decided to have pity on him rather than suck him awake. Not that Reg stayed up long after him. He'd had a long day and two orgasms himself. So he pulled Jeremy's lithe body into his arms, curled his chest around Jeremy's back, and kissed his nape before falling into a deep sleep.

The next day was a mad dash from beginning to end. They barely had time to shower before they left for Madison. They checked into their hotel and then walked right back out so Jeremy could field two interviews before heading to the concert arena and performing until after midnight. To make matters worse, paparazzi had been waiting for Jeremy outside the hotel and at the sites of both interviews, which predictably frustrated him and took an emotional toll.

By the time they got back to their room after the show, Jeremy was so exhausted Reg had to hold him up in the shower and carry him to bed afterward. Well, maybe he didn't *have* to do those things, but he wanted to. Reg loved the feeling of Jeremy in his arms, loved the way Jeremy leaned into him, trusted him, needed him. When they crawled under the comforter, Jeremy immediately scooted close, pressing his naked body against Reg and clinging tightly. Reg engulfed him in an embrace, kissed his head, and told him to rest. With a soft sigh, Jeremy did exactly that.

The first thing Reg noticed when he rose to consciousness the following morning was that Jeremy's slender legs weren't tangled with his. "JJ?" he said, his voice deep and rough with sleep. "JJ?" He patted the mattress with his eyes still closed but was forced to open them when he encountered nothing but a cool sheet.

Normally, Reg was up before Jeremy, and if they had something scheduled before eleven, he invariably had to wake Jeremy up. Usually, he succeeded with his passive-aggressive method—singing or whistling as he walked around the room wearing his heavy boots, opening and closing drawers and doors at random. But occasionally he'd have to haul the big guns out—jumping on the bed, tickling Jeremy, or, his favorite: straddling Jeremy's torso with both his elbows and knees planted on the bed and his face inches from Jeremy's. Staring at him from that position inevitably resulted in Jeremy waking with a shout.

Sitting up, he rubbed his palms over his eyes and then blinked rapidly to focus. Jeremy wasn't in bed. Actually, he wasn't in the room at all. A quick glance at the clock on the nightstand told Reg it was barely after nine. With a groan, he stretched his back and reached first one arm and then the other over his head.

"JJ?"

He slid out of bed and padded over to the bathroom. Also empty. Once there, he waited for his morning erection to fade, drained his bladder, and then splashed some water on his face and brushed his teeth.

"Where are you?" he muttered to himself as he walked back into the room. His phone was on the nightstand where it had been plugged in next to Jeremy's phone, which was gone. But both their wallets were still there.

"Damn it, Bill, I mean it this time!" The familiar sound of Jeremy yelling drifted in from behind the curtains leading to the balcony.

So that was where his fiery superstar had gone. Reg wouldn't have minded being woken up to support Jeremy while he talked to his manager; in fact, he would have preferred it to Jeremy being alone and having nobody to soothe his sure-to-be-ruffled feathers. But it was sweet that Jeremy had tried to let him sleep in. He'd have to thank him for that later. Maybe with a nice firm hand job. Because nothing says "I'm grateful" like a palm wrapped around your dick.

As he walked closer to the balcony, Reg could hear Jeremy more clearly. The fact that he was raising his voice helped too.

"How am I supposed to respond to them when they're in my face with a camera?" he shouted. "Great. Great. Well, next time give me a script, yeah? Because I'm not that clever."

Jeremy paused, and Reg could hear his footsteps. He pulled the curtain to the side and saw him pacing back and forth across the small stone-paved area. The space was gorgeous, with potted trees lining the entire perimeter. It was private enough that even a zoom lens wouldn't be able to capture Jeremy and high enough that nobody would be able to hear him. If Jeremy was going to let off steam, Reg wanted to make sure it was in a place where it wouldn't make headlines.

"Those are songs, Bill! Writing lyrics isn't the same as knowing what to say when they're taking pictures and yelling things at me. Hell, I'm still trying to come up with an appropriate response to the shithead who asked how I knew my father was really my father."

The rudeness and lack of consideration from the paparazzi never ceased to amaze Reg. It was as if they'd decided as a group that celebrities weren't human and therefore social norms and basic decency didn't apply to how they should be treated.

"I don't know," Jeremy said. He fingered his shirt collar and then bit down on it. "Five years ago, maybe. Don't you remember?"

He was holding the phone to his ear with one hand and dragging his shirt over his lips with the other. Then he threw his arm up in the air.

"Super. You can be pissed that I've been wasting my time trying to come up with a snappy response to a dumbass comment for five years, and I can be pissed that every single day I hear more dumbass comments because your dumbass staff can't figure out what 'undisclosed location' means!"

Reg grabbed the door handle and was about to walk out so he could share his theory of what was going on and also sit Jeremy on his lap and rub his shoulders while he talked, but Jeremy's next comment stopped him in his tracks.

"I already told you it isn't Reg." He paused. "Because I know him, that's how I know! He wouldn't do that to me. He cares about me, and he knows how much I hate all those photographers." Jeremy paused and then nodded. "Yes, he does. But other people also know my schedule. Other people who work for you! And maybe they're not as careful with it as they should be."

Jeremy collapsed into a chair and hunched down, looking worn out. Reg decided to count to one hundred and then, if Jeremy was still that upset, he was going out there, taking the phone away, and kissing him until he melted. He loved evoking that reaction in the powerful but vulnerable man, probably even more than he enjoyed the other reaction he could elicit with a kiss.

"Damn it, Bill, you're not listening to me. I know you vet your staff. I know they're good at what they do. But something is going on. The paparazzi are like fucking mosquitos swarming me everywhere I go." Jeremy looked up at the ceiling, and even from where he stood, Reg could see his jaw clenching. "I'm not being dramatic. It has never been this bad before. Never."

After another brief pause, he flew to his feet, shifting

from defeated to animated in a flash. "It isn't Reg!" Back to pacing, he tugged on his hair. "I don't know how I know, I just...wait." He stopped in his tracks. "I'll tell you how I know." Jeremy smirked, his posture straightening. "Where was I on Halloween?" He barely waited before continuing. "No. I meant what bars. But you know what? Doesn't matter, because you're wrong about that too. You don't know where I ate that night, where I drank, where I slept. You don't know what city I was in, let alone what state. And you know who else doesn't know?" He paused meaningfully. "Every fucking person in the world with access to the Internet, that's who! Because for the first time since I started this tour, there were no photographers!"

From the self-satisfied expression on Jeremy's face, Reg knew he had won. He slid the door open and stepped outside. Jeremy turned his head and smiled at him. Then the smile faded as he dragged his gaze down Reg's naked body. In response to the admiration, Reg's cock filled.

"Uh, what?" Jeremy shook his head. "Sorry, I didn't catch that."

Reg stepped closer.

"Yeah, of course he knew, Bill. He was with me the entire time."

Two more steps, and Reg was within touching distance. Jeremy closed the gap and leaned against him.

"For the millionth time, he's my boyfriend, that's why he was with me, and yes, I'm including that night in bed. I wasn't away from him. He knew when I got up to take a piss.

And we didn't see a single photographer until we got to the Madison hotel, which your people reserved."

Reg bent forward and licked Jeremy's neck. Immediately, Jeremy trembled and tilted his head, giving Reg better access.

"That's what I've been asking you," he said, no longer yelling. In fact, he sounded hoarse. "If I knew how they were finding me, I wouldn't have had to call you, yeah?"

"I think I know," Reg said, and then he parted his lips and latched onto Jeremy's skin.

"You're going to leave a mark," Jeremy rasped as he pushed up against Reg's mouth.

"That's the idea, superstar." Reg scraped his teeth over the reddened skin. "Fuckin' sick and tired of people acting like you're gonna play around on me."

Reg was close enough to the phone that he could hear Bill's reaction. "Very nice," Bill said. "I get the point, Jeremy. You can stop with the performance now."

Whether Jeremy was going to respond, Reg would never find out because he chose that moment to cup Jeremy's dick through his jeans and suck harder.

"Oh God, Reg." Jeremy bucked into his hand and gazed up at him, his green eyes wide, his skin flushed, and his lips dark red. "I wouldn't. I won't. There's nobody else." Reg squeezed his dick, and he gasped. "I promise."

"I trust you." He combed his free hand through the back of Jeremy's hair. "I know you're mine, and you do too, don't you?"

He flicked open the button on Jeremy's jeans and shoved his hand inside. Jeremy whimpered and panted.

"Charming," Bill said. "Piece of advice; if you're going to try to sell this nonsense, use a different kind of porn for a script. Having Jeremy Jameson act like a simpering maiden isn't going to—"

Reg grabbed the phone from Jeremy's hand and threw it onto the chair in the corner of the balcony. "You're not acting like a simpering anything," he said, looking Jeremy in the eyes so he could see Reg meant every word. "Feeling passion"—he rubbed his hand over Jeremy's glans—"letting go of everything and trusting someone else to hold you up"—he kept his palm over the top of Jeremy's dick and moved his fingers up and down the shaft slowly—"those things don't make you weak." He leaned down and swiped his tongue over the mark he'd left on Jeremy's neck. "Knowing who you are and letting yourself enjoy it"—he moved his fingers lower, across Jeremy's dick, across his balls, and all the way between his legs so that his fingers entered Jeremy's warm crease—"that's the strongest way to be."

"I know," Jeremy said breathlessly as he ran his hands over Reg's chest. "I've seen you. That's how you are." He spread his legs and rocked over Reg's hand. "I want that." He licked his lips. "I want to know who I am. I want to be who I am. I want...I want..."

"You want to feel." Reg tapped his fingertip over Jeremy's hole. "You want to connect." He gazed into Jeremy's eyes. "We have that together, JJ." He pushed the tip of his finger inside. "I'm here for you, with you." He dipped his face until his lips were almost touching Jeremy's and, hoping he wasn't pushing so hard he'd drive Jeremy away, said, "And I'll stay as long as you want me."

"I want that," Jeremy whispered. "All of it."

"Then it's yours, superstar." Reg brushed his lips over Jeremy's, enjoying their softness. "All yours."

Loving the way Jeremy leaned into him and followed his lead, Reg licked his way past Jeremy's lips, coaxed his tongue out of his mouth, and sucked on it. At the same time, he combed the fingers of one hand through Jeremy's hair and carefully, gently traced his other fingertips over the sensitive skin between Jeremy's firm globes, paying special attention to the wrinkled flesh he longed to breach.

"Let's go inside." Reg nipped Jeremy's ear. "I want to do things to you that would be much more comfortable in a bed."

"Okay, yeah." Jeremy nodded. "Want that too."

With a final, relatively chaste kiss, Reg stepped back, took Jeremy's hand in his, and led him into the hotel room.

"JJ?"

"Yeah?"

"Are you freaking out?"

Tilting his head to the side, Jeremy crinkled his brow, letting Reg know he was considering the question. "No, I'm not." His face brightened. "That's weird, yeah? I mean, we've been...and we're going to...and you're a guy, but..." He smiled and put his hand on Reg's bare chest. "You're you, so I want this."

"You're amazing." Reg cupped both sides of Jeremy's face and held him in place as he leaned down and kissed him. "Anyone else would be having an identity crisis or a meltdown, but not you."

"Yeah, I'm a real gem." Jeremy rolled his eyes and snorted. "Anyone else wouldn't have needed three decades to figure out something that should have been obvious."

"First off"—Reg pushed Jeremy's jeans down to his bare feet and took a moment to give his cock a squeeze— "that isn't true. Everyone figures themselves out at their own pace." He grasped Jeremy's shirt and pulled it over his head. "And I, for one, am glad it took you this long."

"Why?" Jeremy huddled against Reg, wrapping his arms around Reg's waist and resting his head against Reg's shoulder.

Reg cupped Jeremy's ass with both hands and started kneading. "Well, if you'd figured this out before we met, someone else would have snatched you up, and I would have missed out."

Jeremy was silent for several seconds, and then he tipped his head back and looked at Reg. "I don't think so. I was with lots of people before we met, and I never felt like any of them would be around for long, never wanted them to be." He licked his lips. "I mean, I know they were women, and I guess maybe that was part of the issue, but I don't think that was all of it."

"You saying I'm special, superstar?" Reg asked, tilting

one side of his mouth up.

A roll of Jeremy's eyes and a shake of his head was the only response he got.

"Admit it." Reg squeezed Jeremy's butt until he went on tiptoes and then tugged him closer, slotting their dicks side by side. "I'm the bomb."

Jeremy laughed.

Enjoying the game, Reg pulled him off his feet. "Say it."

Smiling, Jeremy shook his head.

Reg turned toward the bed, laid Jeremy down on it, and then blanketed him with his bigger body. "Here, I'll help." He pulled each of Jeremy's arms above his head. "Repeat after me: You're the bomb, Reg."

Jeremy pressed his lips together tightly and waggled his eyebrows.

Holding on to both of Jeremy's wrists with one hand, Reg used the other to tweak Jeremy's left nipple. "You're the bomb, Reg."

"Ungh," Jeremy moaned and arched his back, getting closer.

"You're the bomb, Reg." Reg moved his hand to the right nipple and twisted it slowly, waiting for Jeremy to gasp in pleasure before stopping.

"Please," Jeremy groaned.

"Please what?" Reg bent forward and latched onto a nipple, sucking it into his mouth.

"Don't stop. Oh God." Jeremy wiggled beneath him. "Please don't stop."

After another few minutes of attention to Jeremy's nipples, Reg slithered down his body, crouched over his groin, and gripped his hips. "Look at me, JJ," he said just before licking a long swath up Jeremy's cock. "Watch me while I suck you."

His nostrils flared and eyes wide, Jeremy focused on Reg's face as he licked around his crown and then dropped his mouth over his shaft.

"That feels so good."

Reg tightened his suction and pulled up, making Jeremy buck his lower body off the bed.

"Oh God." He flailed his arms. "Reg."

Tangy precum leaked from the hard shaft in Reg's mouth, arousing him further and making him ratchet up his efforts. He gripped the base of Jeremy's shaft and bobbed his head quickly, keeping the suction tight. At the same time, he took himself in hand and stroked hard and fast, chasing his own orgasm.

They moved in concert, both of them rocking their hips. Jeremy gasped and moaned, crying out Reg's name over and over again until he finally opened his mouth on a soundless wail and shot long and hard into Reg's mouth.

"Ungh," Reg moaned around the pulsing dick in his mouth. "Ungh. Ungh." He swallowed Jeremy's seed and stroked himself even faster. When Jeremy finished and lay limp on the bed, his body twitching, Reg threw his head back, yelled, "JJ!" and came, coating his fingers in ejaculate.

With his gaze glued to Jeremy's, Reg climbed to his

knees, raised his hand to his mouth, and licked.

"So hot," Jeremy said under his breath.

"You want a taste?" Reg planted his clean hand on the mattress by Jeremy's shoulder and leaned over him, offering his hand.

"Yeah." Jeremy reached up and grasped his wrist.

Reg was going to ask if he was sure, was going to tell him he didn't have to do it, but the look in Jeremy's eyes showed him without words how turned on the man was. The feeling of Jeremy's dick already reawakening against his thigh clued him in too. So he let Jeremy pull his hand to his mouth and watched him as he licked his palm and then sucked each of Reg's fingers into his mouth.

"Damn, superstar, look at you." Reg waited until he was done, and then he slammed his mouth onto Jeremy's, kissing him voraciously. "So gorgeous."

"Next time," Jeremy panted, "can I suck you?"

Reg shivered. "You can go down on me whenever you want." He kissed Jeremy again. "Even now." He smiled. "Now would be just fine."

"Okay." Jeremy chuckled and ran his fingers through the hair on Reg's chest. "And Reg?"

"Uh-huh?"

"You're the bomb."

CHAPTER 15

"JJ?" Reg whispered. "You awake?"

"Sort of." Jeremy turned around in Reg's embrace until they were chest to chest. He burrowed closer to Reg's warm body. "Is it time to go to the airport?"

"Not yet. We can nap a little longer." Reg caressed the back of Jeremy's head, his nape, his shoulders. "But I just remembered something I keep forgetting to tell you."

"You just remembered something you keep forgetting?" Jeremy chuckled and kissed Reg's chest, still amazed at how easy that was, how natural. "What's that?"

"I think I know who's leaking information about you to the press."

"Leaking?" Jeremy looked into his eyes. "What do you mean? Like the stuff about us faking it?"

"That too, probably." Reg leaned down and kissed the tip of Jeremy's nose. "And we are so totally not faking it."

"No, we're not." Deciding to see what else felt easy and natural, Jeremy slid his hand down Reg's thick chest, over his muscular belly, and onto his long, thick cock. He shivered at the feeling of it in his hand and kept stroking lightly.

"Cool." Reg smiled and dragged his fingers up and

down Jeremy's back in a delicious massage. "I like it when you touch me, JJ."

"Yeah? Am I—" He cleared his throat. "Am I doing it right?"

"Uh-huh. That feels nice." Reg lowered his face onto Jeremy's neck and nuzzled it. "My balls are really sensitive," he whispered.

Taking the hint, Jeremy cupped Reg's balls, immediately making the man tremble.

Though it was hard to focus on conversation, Jeremy forced himself to talk while he touched and rolled the sensitive orbs. "So you were saying? The leak?"

"Sorry, got distracted by how good that feels. And by your skin." Reg kissed Jeremy's shoulder. "You have the best skin." Grinning, Reg looked at Jeremy. "Maybe you should stop wearing clothes. It'll be, like, a public service."

"You're crazy."

"I'm crazy about you."

Embarrassed, though he wasn't sure why, Jeremy ducked his chin and avoided Reg's gaze.

"I mean it." Reg tangled his fingers in the back of Jeremy's hair and tugged. "You get that, right? I know it's a sappy thing to say, but—" He smiled widely. "I'm smitten with you, Mr. Jameson. Totally smitten."

"Smitten?"

"Uh-huh. Head over heels. Gone. Gaga."

Interrupting Reg's silly list, Jeremy said, "Usually people who spend a lot of time with me say I'm needy and temperamental."

"Yup." Reg smiled warmly. "I agree." He kissed Jeremy's cheek. "You're perfect."

"Um, I don't think they mean those things as compliments. Needy and temperamental generally fall under the category of imperfections."

"Well, I don't know who *they* are, and I can't speak for them, but I like being here for you, JJ. I like how much you enjoy being touched and held. I think it's adorable how you get all worked up. And I love taking care of you when you're ready to feel calm again."

"You do?"

"Uh-huh."

With a smile on his face, Jeremy snuggled closer and continued fondling Reg's package.

"It's Francis," Reg said after a minute. "He's up to something. I don't know what. But I think he's the one leaking your locations and all the other crap."

"Seriously?" Jeremy sat up. "I've never liked him, but why would he do that?"

"I don't know." Reg rolled onto his back and shrugged. "I don't understand half the shit I've seen the rich and famous do since I met you. But I'm telling you, it's him."

"I believe you." And he did. There was no doubt in Jeremy's mind. If Reg said Francis was responsible, that was exactly where he needed to focus. "Tell me what tipped you off. I'll need to fill Bill in when I tell him I want Francis off my account."

"Lots of little things. He's the one who sets up your interviews, so he knows where you're going to be. He acts really shifty when things are going down, like that time at the radio station when you'd had the annoying interview, and then all the paparazzi were outside. Instead of figuring out how to get you out of there, he got you worked up, practically put you in front of the cameras, and then stepped out of the frame."

Remembering that day and how angry he'd been before Reg stepped in, Jeremy nodded. "You really think he did that on purpose?"

"At the time, no. I thought he was acting weird, but it didn't stand out that much because I think half the people I've met on this tour act weird." Reg paused. "Maybe more like ninety percent. Anyway, that's not the biggest reason I know it's him. Remember that clown reporter on Halloween?"

"Yeah."

"Francis set him up. He told the paper to send a guy in a scary clown costume. When I heard that right after you said you've always been scared of clowns, I did a little online research."

"Research?"

"Yup. I googled your name and the word 'fear,' and I got a bunch of hits—articles, blog posts, all sorts of things—referencing an interview you did two years ago where you mentioned a fear of clowns."

"I think I remember that interview." Jeremy sighed. "They asked the most annoying questions. Biggest fear.

Favorite color." He paused. "Who has a favorite color?"

"Black," Reg said simply.

"What?"

"My favorite color. It's black."

"Oh." Jeremy blinked in surprise.

"You don't have a favorite color because you're too colorful to settle for just one." Reg kissed Jeremy's forehead. "But back to the clown. What do you want to bet Francis knew you were scared of them?"

"I'm sure he did," Jeremy confirmed. "It's not a secret."

"Good thing he hasn't ever seen you faced with a spider. Lord knows what he would have come up with."

Jeremy shuddered.

"Seriously, though. He knew about the clown thing, and he used that knowledge to catch you off guard and put you in a room with one. It was just like the radio-station situation."

Nodding, Jeremy said, "I'll call Bill. Tell him about this. I already pointed out to him that the only time I haven't had a camera in my face in months was when he didn't know where I was, so he has to realize the leak is someone on his team. It's just taking him a bit of time to admit it."

"I heard you say that to him. I was inside, listening," Reg confessed. "It means a lot that you trust me."

Feeling his chest tighten, Jeremy climbed onto Reg's bigger body and cupped his whiskery cheeks. "In my whole life, I've never trusted anybody like I do you." He dropped his forehead onto Reg's. "I can't tell you what that means to me, being able to just...be. Not having to think or be careful or pretend."

He kissed Reg, softly at first, but after the first few kisses, Reg tilted his head, and Jeremy found the perfect angle to slip his tongue inside. Reg slid his tongue over Jeremy's, the sensation unique and arousing, before sucking on Jeremy's tongue.

"Mmm, JJ." Reg tangled his fingers in the sides of Jeremy's hair. "I'll never take your trust for granted." Kissing his way across Jeremy's jaw, he whispered, "Won't take *you* for granted."

"I won't either," Jeremy promised. "Reg?"

"Uh-huh." Reg kept kissing and licking—his jaw, his neck, his ear.

"Don't let me, yeah?"

"Okay." He suckled on Jeremy's earlobe. "Wait." He pulled back and looked at Jeremy, his eyebrows drawn together. "What do you mean? What am I not letting you do?"

"Don't let me take you for granted. I know I'm high-maintenance and self-absorbed and..." He tried to think of all the descriptions his exes and staff had used over the years. "And spoiled, but you're important to me, really important, and—"

"Hey, cut it out." Reg smiled at him tenderly. "I won't let you talk about my boyfriend like that." He brushed Jeremy's hair off his forehead. "Besides, I like that you're high-maintenance; it gives me something to do. And spoiling you is fun, superstar."

Nobody else would put up with him, let alone

enjoy him. Nobody except the gorgeous, fun, smart man underneath him. Jeremy wasn't naïve; he knew relationships rarely lasted long in his world. But he also knew he'd never felt more whole, more safe, more at peace than he had since Reg had come into his life. And he knew how very rare and precious that was.

"Don't let me drive you away," he begged. "My parents weren't like yours." He swallowed down the thickness in his throat. "I haven't ever known anybody like that in real life. But I think, if you want to, maybe...but you have to help me because I don't know how." He looked at Reg beseechingly. "Will you help me keep you?"

"You break my heart sometimes," Reg whispered. "Kills me how alone you've been." He pulled Jeremy down, tucked Jeremy's head under his chin, and squeezed him close. "So glad I found you."

With Reg's muscular arms holding him, Jeremy felt safe, like nothing and nobody, himself included, could pry him away from this man.

"And don't worry," Reg said. "If you try to push me away, I'll remind you why you need to hold on tighter instead."

"Did you talk to Francis?" Jeremy asked Bill on the phone the next day. He and Reg were in Toronto for the final North American show. Then they were off to the UK. "Because

I swear to you, if he comes anywhere near me, I'll—"

"He won't," Bill assured him. "Francis is on his way back to LA, and I'm sending someone else to meet you after tonight's show. She'll work on your PR until I get things straightened out with Francis."

"You're not firing him?" Jeremy asked incredulously. "How could you not fire him after what he did? He—"

Reg squeezed his knee. "We're in a cab," he reminded Jeremy in a whisper.

Taking a deep breath, Jeremy nodded. "Anyway, he's off my file. Just make sure he doesn't have access to my schedule anymore."

"Jeremy, he's not going to spend his free time setting you up. In fact, I don't believe he was ever trying to set you up."

"Yeah, he did! That's exactly what he did. I told you about—"

"It felt that way, I realize, but what I'm saying is that I don't think it was his intent."

"And what do you think he intended when he told every asshole with a zoom lens where I sleep at night?"

"I think," Bill said calmly, "that he sincerely believed he was doing his job. You know the old saying, any press is good press? Well, he was getting you press."

"That is not my saying, Bill. It's your saying, but it's *so* not my saying."

Sighing, Bill said, "I understand, and I'm taking care of it. Calm down and focus on your show."

Being told to calm down tended to make Jeremy exponentially less calm, which Reg must have noticed because he plucked the phone from Jeremy's white-knuckled grip and brought it to his own ear.

"Hey, man. It's Reg. Anything we need to know before the show tonight?" He paused. "Cool. Have her call me instead of JJ, okay?"

Jeremy's tension started dissipating.

"Because he needs to get in his groove for the show, and I want to meet this new one and make sure she isn't a total schmuck like the last one."

Leaning against Reg, Jeremy could hear Bill's voice, but he ignored it and focused on the heat and strength at his side. Reg wrapped his arm around him and played with the back of his hair.

"Dude, he was a little shit who set Jeremy up to freak out. Seems to me he should have been able to do his job without that, but whatever. The point is, you need to tell... what'd you say the new person's name was?" A brief pause. "Okay, then tell Becky to call me with details about where JJ needs to be tonight and when. And also, let her know I'll want to meet with her when she has a break tonight before Jeremy gets off stage." Whatever Bill said next made Reg laugh. "Right on, man. Call me Yoko if you have to, because I'm stepping up my game."

Jeremy looked up at Reg, who smiled and stroked Jeremy's cheek.

"It means I'm playing intermediary between him and

anything I think stresses him out from here on out. You go ahead and tell everyone they're about to meet the new version of a rock-star wife if it makes you feel better. I don't give a shit. My only priority is JJ."

In that moment, Jeremy realized what it felt like to have someone care about him. He circled his arms around Reg's waist and hugged him.

"No. You work your ass off for *The Jeremy Jameson,* and hats off to you, dude, you do a great job. But I care about the man, not the rock star." He paused, and Jeremy could hear Bill ranting. "Think of it as a division of labor. You take care of the label, I'll take care of my boyfriend. Everyone's happy."

"What'd he say?" Jeremy asked when Reg hung up the phone.

"Do you really want to know?" Reg brushed his fingers through Jeremy's hair.

"No." He rubbed Reg's chest through his shirt. "All I want to do is sing and play my guitar. The rest of it can fall off a cliff for all I care." He sighed. "But if I want to do one, I'm stuck with the other."

"Not anymore."

It seemed almost too good to be true. But that was the case for so many things with Reg. The man himself was too good to be true, and yet here he was.

"Thank you." Jeremy kissed Reg's chin. "You'll tell me if it's important, yeah?"

"'Course I will."

"Okay." He flung one leg over Reg's thigh and closed his

eyes. "I'm beat."

"Sleep." Reg kissed his head. "I'll wake you up when we get there."

With a slow nod, Jeremy started drifting off, smiling at the image of big, burly Reggie Moore as barely over five feet, slender Yoko Ono. But then the thought shifted into something else Reg had said, something as exhilarating as it was terrifying: Reggie Moore as a rock star's wife, or in this case, husband. His husband.

"I can't even tell you how excited I am to meet you!" a diminutive woman with a blonde ponytail gushed as soon as Jeremy opened his dressing room door.

He knew this must be Becky Parks because Reg had prescreened her for evil. Those had been his exact words, and somehow, they'd made Jeremy laugh even though he was stuck waiting to do interviews at the end of yet another long day.

"Hey, Becky." Reg walked up from behind him, draped an arm over his shoulders, and kissed the side of his head. "Great show, right?"

"Oh my gosh, yes! I hope Bill lets me stay on your file so I can watch you perform for the last six weeks of your tour. Jeremy Jameson! I can't believe it!"

"See?" Reg said to Jeremy as he turned him around and

led him back into the room. "I told you she was a fan."

"You didn't tell me she was a teenager," Jeremy whispered under his breath.

"Hey, Becks," Reg said as he sat on the small love seat in the corner and pulled Jeremy onto his lap.

It figured Reg would already be on a nickname basis with the new publicist. Jeremy wasn't surprised. He'd never met someone easier to get along with than Reg. It was a testament to Francis's asshattery that Reg had never fully warmed up to him.

"Yes?" Her blue eyes got huge, and she rushed closer. "Do you need something?"

"Tell JJ a little about yourself." Reg stretched to the side and pulled a chair over. "Like, where you went to school and your work experience."

"Oh, sure thing." She sat in the chair and crossed her hands in her lap. "I went to Stanford for undergrad and Harvard for my graduate degree in marketing. Then I worked for a few different advertising firms in New York before moving to San Francisco and helping some dot-coms get off the ground. I had shares, and I did really well when we went public, so I took some time off, but I'm not really good with time off, and then I heard about this job and you're my favorite musician." She reached out and took Jeremy's hand in hers. "My favorite! And I couldn't turn it down."

The entire bio was given in what felt like thirty seconds. Jeremy's brain was reeling. "How old are you?" he asked, trying to assimilate all that life experience with the woman in front of him.

"I'm twenty-nine." Her ponytail swayed from side to side even though she was sitting perfectly still. "Why?"

"You look much younger."

"Oh! Aren't you sweet for saying that!" She cupped her cheeks. "I have great moisturizer. SPF 30." She leaned forward and whispered conspiratorially, "Do you want me to get you a bottle? It's pricey, but, oh my gosh, *so* worth it."

"I don't, uh." Jeremy looked at Reg, but all he got in return was a knowing smile. "Sure," he said to Becky. "That'd be great."

"Okay!" She bounced out of her seat. "So, listen, Francis already had three interviews scheduled for you tonight, which is crazy, right? I mean, after how hard you worked on stage." She shook her head. "But I didn't want to cancel because that'd be, like, totally rude."

Jeremy nodded, already knowing where the conversation was going. It'd be fine. He'd do the interviews and then go back to the hotel with Reg. Just the two of them. In a room with a bed. That thought alone was enough to have him firming up down below.

"So I came up with a great plan!" Becky was still talking. "I'll bring the three people doing interviews in here when you're ready. Each of them can ask two questions. That means they'll hear the answers to six questions total, which is good enough. Then they'll leave." She wiped her hands together. "Done and doner! What do you think?"

"Really? I just have to answer six questions?"

"Yuppers!"

"What about pictures?"

"Oh, I already handled those." She waved her hand dismissively. "I let them each have a few minutes up front while you were on stage. They were able to get great shots. And I promised to e-mail them some candid"—she raised her fingers in an air-quote gesture—"pics later. Bill said he has some that'll work."

"Okay," Jeremy said.

"Super! So are we good for me to bring them in?"

He nodded. Becky smiled, turned around, and bounced toward the door.

"Be back in a jiffy!"

"What the hell was that?" Jeremy said as he looked at Reg wide-eyed.

"I know. Isn't she awesome? I love her already. Seriously. If I dug chicks, we'd have to make room in our bed for—ow!" Reg rubbed his shoulder. "You punched me!"

"There is no more room in our bed!" Jeremy snapped.

Reg's eyes warmed. "Aww, my superstar's jealous."

"Talking to me like I'm two isn't helping, Mr. Room In Our Bed."

"It was a joke," Reg said with a chuckle. He tugged Jeremy closer. "Promise, JJ." He kissed the tip of Jeremey's nose and then nuzzled his neck. "Just a joke."

Jeremy huffed.

"In all seriousness, though. Becky was first in her class at Stanford and Harvard. Her time at the advertising firm is code for being the mastermind of those dancing-cat commercials. Remember them from, like, five years ago?"

"That was her?"

"Yup. And the dot-coms she's talking about blew up NASDAQ when they went public. Every single one of them."

"How do you know all this?"

"The google-fu is strong with me," Reg said in what Jeremy assumed was meant to be a *Star Wars* voice. It sounded like nothing of the sort.

"Wow. You're a dork, and she's brilliant." Jeremy looked at the door. "I wouldn't have thought it from the way she acts."

"I guess when you're that smart, you don't have to put on airs. She's confident enough to let her skill speak for itself."

They didn't get to talk more after that, because Becky returned with three reporters in tow. She had them in a single-file line, told them where to sit, monitored their questions, and, with a bob of her ponytail, politely yet firmly kicked them out of the room as soon as their six questions were up. It was amazing.

"You were right," Jeremy said, staring at the closed door Becky had just flounced out of after blowing them air kisses. "I think I'm in love. Ow!" He scowled at Reg. "You punched me!"

CHAPTER 16

"You were awesome tonight," Reg whispered into Jeremy's ear as he pressed him up against the bathroom wall in their London hotel.

"You always say that." Jeremy placed his hands on Reg's chest and leaned up, begging for a kiss.

"That's because it's always true." Reg slanted his mouth over Jeremy's and dipped his tongue inside as he tugged Jeremy's towel and dropped it onto the marble tiles.

"Mmm," Jeremy moaned and writhed against him, his cock hot and hard.

"Seriously. It was a perfect start to the UK leg of the tour."

"Thank you." Jeremy kissed his way across Reg's jaw. "I know I tease, but what you think means a lot to me."

"Is that right?" Reg traced Jeremy's earlobe with two fingers and shoved his knee between Jeremy's thighs.

"Yeah." Jeremy ground his dick and balls against Reg's leg, the feeling of it making Reg even harder than he had been in the shower with his finger deep in Jeremy's ass.

"In that case..." Reg gazed into Jeremy's gorgeous green eyes and slid their lips together again. "You might want to know that I think I'm in love with you."

They were close enough for Reg to feel Jeremy's heart start racing. "You *think*?" Jeremy said breathlessly as he dug his fingers into Reg's shoulders.

Nothing ventured, nothing gained. "I *know*," Reg said. He drew in a deep breath. "I love you, JJ." In a quick move, he circled his arms around Jeremy and tugged him off the floor into a hug. "Love you so much it scares me and amazes me all at the same time." Leaning forward, Reg lapped at Jeremy's lips. "But mostly, it makes me happy." He smiled. "So happy."

Jeremy didn't respond, at least not verbally. But he returned Reg's kisses, landed a few of his own, and clung to Reg—wrapped his arms and legs tightly around him.

"I'm taking you to bed," Reg said huskily. He walked out of the room, Jeremy in his arms. "I want to make love to you tonight." He skated his hand down Jeremy's back, over the rounded cheeks of his ass, and into his crease. "I want to be inside so bad." With his face buried in Jeremy's neck, Reg laid him on the bed and draped himself over his smaller body. "Will you let me?"

"I'd let you do anything." Jeremy kissed the base of his throat. "Everything."

Suddenly, it was too much. Reg crawled away from Jeremy's firm body and scooted off the bed.

"Where'd you go?" Jeremy gazed up at him and held his arm out. "Reg?"

Reg squeezed his hands into fists and released them over and over while he tried to regulate his breathing. "Want you so much it's nuts." He rubbed his hand over the back of his head and swallowed down the thickness in his throat. "You're beautiful, JJ. Inside and out." He started pacing across the small room. "Beautiful and sweet—damn, who'd have thought? Scowly Jeremy Jameson is sweet? But you are. And needy, never met anybody who needed to be held and seen and touched and loved more than you. And I know you think that's a bad thing, but it's not; it's the best thing."

He closed his eyes and took a deep breath. "All those months you were so close; I wanted to touch you, but I didn't know if I could, at least not the way I hoped, and now I can, but..." He sighed and rubbed his palms over his face. "We have, what? Barely more than a month left in the tour, a few months of traveling, and then—"

"And then I'm hoping you'll marry me," Jeremy said in a rush.

Reg jerked and shot his eyes open. Jeremy was sitting up at the edge of the bed, his legs crossed, his dick hard, and his arms open.

"What'd you say?" Reg stepped toward him.

"I want us to get married," Jeremy answered, his voice soft but sure. "My whole life, I thought it was something I'd never do. What was the point?" He shrugged. "I didn't need the press from it, didn't need the headache"—he licked his lips and looked Reg in the eyes—"didn't think being in love was a real thing, or at least not something I was capable of feeling."

"And now?" Reg rasped as he moved over to Jeremy,

instinctively brushing his hand through Jeremy's hair.

"Now I know it's real. I know I'm capable of feeling it." Jeremy dropped his forehead onto Reg's stomach and clung to him. "Because it's how I feel about you, how I've felt for a while now. I know I was slow to get it, and I know my life's a circus, and I know everything's always all about me, but…" Looking up, Jeremy gulped and then said, "I love you, Reg. I want what you told me your parents had, your brother. I want forever, and I want it with you." He kissed Reg's chest, his lips trembling. "When we get home to California, will you marry me?"

Smiling so wide his cheeks hurt, Reg said, "Yes."

"Yes?" Jeremy blinked up at him, his eyes noticeably wet.

"Yes, I love you. Yes, I want forever with you. Yes, I'll marry you."

"Okay." Jeremy sniffled and swiped at the sides of his eyes. "Good."

Tipping him onto the bed, Reg whispered, "Good," and then he slammed his mouth over Jeremy's. Licking, nibbling, and sucking, he tortured Jeremy's lips and reveled in the aroused moans and whimpers he received in response, in the slick tip of Jeremy's dick sliding against his belly, and in Jeremy scratching at his back with long fingers.

"I picked up some rubbers and lube." He nudged Jeremy's chin with his forehead, tilting it back, and then latched onto his neck. "At some point, if you want, we can get tested and go bare, but for now"—Reg rose to his knees and leaned over to the nightstand—"scoot to the head of the bed and let me get you ready."

It didn't take long to find what he needed, and then, with lube and a condom in his hand, Reg crawled over to the handsome man in his bed. The handsome, *anxious* man.

"Hey," he said, tenderly caressing Jeremy's cheek. "You went from hot for it to about to fall apart in two seconds. What's wrong?"

"Nothing." Jeremy shook his head too fast.

"Uh-huh." Reg dropped the supplies onto the mattress and lay down, his elbow folded, head resting on his hand, and pressed his body to Jeremy's. "Tell me anyway." He moved his hand down Jeremy's neck and across his chest, paying extra attention to his nipples.

"How's it work?"

Reg arched his eyebrows.

"Not that. I mean, I know how it works." Jeremy laughed nervously. "But it hurts a lot, yeah?"

"What?" Reg reared back in surprise. "No, of course not." He got onto his hands and knees and straddled Jeremy's lean frame, letting him feel his heat and presence. "I'm not looking to hurt you, JJ. Bottoming feels good. But if you're not up for trying it that way tonight, it's no big. You can top."

"No, I want to. I was just..." Jeremy's eyes widened as he seemed to register everything Reg had said. "You'd do that?"

"Do what?"

"You'd let me fuck you?"

Tilting his head to the side and wrinkling his brow in confusion, Reg said, "'Course. Why wouldn't I?"

"I don't know." Jeremy shrugged and ran his fingers down Reg's chest, focusing on his hand instead of looking Reg in the eyes. "You're bigger than me, and you're all tough guy, and isn't that how it works? One guy's the—"

"It's sex, JJ," Reg said with a chuckle. "It's not about some power play; there's no higher meaning about personality types or masculinity. It's about feeling good. That's all. And having a thick, hot cock stretch your hole and ram you hard feels fuckin' amazing. You'll see." He gripped Jeremy's chin and raised it until their gazes met. "We're getting married, right? So we have a lifetime to bend each other in every position imaginable. If you're not ready for me to top tonight, tell me. It's fine. We'll do it next time."

"It won't hurt?" Jeremy bit his lip nervously.

"It's not like I'm going to just shove it in there. I'll make sure you're relaxed, turned on, and ready. It'll probably feel a little strange because it's your first time, so it's new, but hurt?" Reg shook his head. "Nuh-uh."

After taking a deep breath, Jeremy said, "Okay. Let's try it."

"We don't have to—"

"I want to." Jeremy licked his lips and blushed. "It's something I've thought about a lot, and I really, really like it when you touch me there."

"You mean like this?" Reg slid his hand between Jeremy's legs and rubbed the smooth skin beneath his balls, exerting a bit of pressure. "Or this?" He moved his finger down into the heat of Jeremy's crease, and Jeremy immediately spread his legs. "Or maybe you mean when I touch you here." He tapped on the puckered skin around Jeremy's hole and then traced his finger over it.

"Oh!" Jeremy gasped and tilted his butt up.

"I think I figured it out." Reg leaned down and nibbled on Jeremy's ear. "So sexy, the noises you make." He sucked his way down Jeremy's neck. "Can't wait to hear you when I'm inside."

The reminder of what they were about to do made Jeremy whimper.

With kisses, nips, and licks, Reg made his way down Jeremy's body until he was crouched between his spread legs. Gripping his calves, he pushed both legs up so they were bent at the knees.

"Keep them like this, okay?"

Jeremy nodded.

"Thanks." Reg kissed the inside of his knee and then bent forward, rolled Jeremy's thighs up and pushed his legs out, and buried his face in Jeremy's groin.

"Reg," Jeremy gasped when Reg worked up a mark on his inner thigh.

"Reg," he moaned when Reg licked and sucked his balls.

"Reg!" he shouted when Reg spread his cheeks and licked a swath up his channel. "Oh my God. Oh my God. What are you...? Oh my God."

Smiling at Jeremy's reaction, Reg stayed focused on the sensitive ass in front of him. He dragged his fingers hard against the muscular glutes, massaging them, gently rubbed his whiskery cheeks against the silky skin, and then flicked his tongue against the opening over and over again.

"Ready for more?" he asked when he could feel the tense muscle relaxing. Without waiting for an answer, he pushed the tip of his tongue inside.

Jeremy's shoulders flew off the bed, but Reg held on to his thighs, keeping him in place. He moved the tip of his tongue around, letting Jeremy experience the feeling of being touched there, and then pushed in farther, not stopping until his mouth was pressed against hot skin.

With a deep, joyous groan, Jeremy went boneless. He flopped to the bed, gasped for air, and tossed his head from side to side as he muttered nonsense words interspersed with Reg's name. That was exactly what Reg wanted—for Jeremy to relax and enjoy the sensations that could come from having his butt played with. And he knew it would only get better.

Taking each of Jeremy's cheeks in his hands, he spread them wide and fucked his tongue in and out of the tight, hot hole. He wanted Jeremy turned on, needy, and slick, so he kept going as long as he could, licking and moving his tongue inside, blowing air on the sensitive skin outside, and starting all over again. When his tongue tired, he lubed his fingers and pressed first one and quickly a second into Jeremy's hole.

"Holy hell!" Jeremy yelled.

It sounded like pleasure, not pain, but Reg wanted to make sure. "Good?" he asked.

"Yeah," Jeremy gasped and started rocking his hips, riding Reg's fingers. "So good."

"Just wait," Reg said with a kiss to Jeremy's inner thigh. "It gets even better." He knelt between Jeremy's legs, working his ass with one hand, and dragged his free hand up Jeremy's shaft.

"You don't..." Jeremy panted. "If you touch my dick right now, I'm going to lose it."

"That close, huh?" Reg asked, loving that he'd been able to bring Jeremy to the brink so easily.

"Yeah." Jeremy grasped Reg's wrist and stilled his movements. "I don't think I've ever been this hard in my life."

"Okay." Reg let go of Jeremy's dick. "How about if I do this?" he asked as he curled his fingers and nudged Jeremy's gland.

"Oh! Reg!" Jeremy grabbed his shoulders tightly, spread his legs farther, and tilted his hips up. "Reggie?"

"I know." He pressed again and then moved his fingertips away, stimulating the area around Jeremy's prostate before returning to it.

"I'm gonna come," Jeremy warned. "You need to fuck me now." His eyes looked wild and desperate. "Please, now."

Reg slowly withdrew his fingers, petted them over Jeremy's pucker, and then quickly gloved up.

"C'mere," he said as he patted his thighs. "Get in front of me, your back to my chest."

Jeremy blinked, looking dazed, but eventually he rose to his knees and turned around, straddling Reg's lap and mirroring his position. "Like this?" he asked, looking over his shoulder at Reg.

"Uh-huh." Reg flattened his palm on Jeremy's back, encouraging him to bend forward. "Lube first, then me," he said as he flipped open the cap on the lube.

"'Kay," Jeremy said, his voice hoarse with arousal. He planted his hands on the bed.

Reg drizzled the slick into Jeremy's trench and then pushed it inside, swiping his fingers around to make sure everything was generously coated.

"Damn, that's amazing." Jeremy thrust back against Reg's fingers, working himself on them. "Never knew it'd feel like this to be touched there."

"Good." Leaning down, Reg kissed the small of Jeremy's back while he lubed his condom-covered cock. "Now me," he whispered, lining up with Jeremy's hole. He moved his cock around and around the puckered skin, increasing the pressure with every lap until he finally popped inside.

Jeremy gasped but didn't pull away.

"Still okay?"

"Better than okay," Jeremy assured him. "Don't stop."

With one hand on Jeremy's hip, anchoring him, and holding the base of his own erection with the other, Reg slid the rest of the way home. "You're so damn tight," he said once his balls were snuggled against Jeremy's ass. "Not sure how long I can last."

"Me too," Jeremy said, sounding strained. "Almost there."

Reg wrapped his arm around Jeremy's chest and tugged him up. Then, while keeping them pressed together, he rose to his knees and sat back on his heels, Jeremy in his lap. "I can touch you better this way," he explained as he kissed Jeremy's shoulder. Then he drew out until only his crown was inside before thrusting forward hard.

"Ah!" Jeremy shouted and started bouncing up and down, impaling himself on Reg's rigid shaft. "Ah! Ah! Ah!"

"JJ," Reg whispered reverently. "Love you." He reached around Jeremy's belly, grabbed his dick, and started stroking in time to his own plunges in and out of that tight, hot body. "Kiss me," he demanded as he tangled his free hand in Jeremy's hair and yanked his head back. "Kiss me."

Jeremy parted his lips readily, accepting the rough messy kiss.

"Ungh," Reg moaned into Jeremy's mouth, plunging his tongue in concert with the long strokes he made with his cock.

"Don't wanna finish, but I can't stop it," Jeremy said as he moved faster. He licked whatever part of Reg's face he could reach. "Oh, Reg. Oh God. Oh!" His mouth dropped open, and he wailed as hot ejaculate shot from his cock in long, thick streams.

Jeremy's orgasm seemed to go on forever, and the scent, along with the rippling muscles in Jeremy's passage, broke the last of Reg's control, bringing him to his own mind-shattering release.

"Yes," he moaned as he held himself deep inside and came into the condom.

Once they were both spent, Reg sat back on his heels, and Jeremy rested in his lap, both of them gasping for air and twitching with aftershocks.

"Holy hell," Jeremy said. "I can't feel my legs."

Reg chuckled, kissed his neck, and said, "You better lie down."

"'Kay." Jeremy nodded. With a hiss, he sat up, removing Reg's softening dick from his hole in the process. Then he rolled over onto his back.

Reg stripped the condom, tied it off, and dropped it next to the bed. He grabbed a bunch of tissues from the box on the nightstand, wiped off both of their bodies, and snuggled close to Jeremy.

"Mmm," Jeremy hummed and flipped onto his side so they were chest to chest. "You always make me feel so good, Reg." He kissed and nuzzled the base of Reg's throat.

"Does that mean you're not putting up with the sex just for the postcoital cuddling?" Reg asked as he draped his arm over Jeremy, holding him tightly.

With a groan, Jeremy raised his gaze. "You must have thought I was so stupid when I said that. You knew it was like this, and I..." He shook his head. "So stupid."

"No, you weren't," Reg assured him. "For the record, that was better than anything I've experienced too." He grinned. "And when you said sex wasn't a big deal, I just thought you needed someone to show you how great it could be and that I should be that someone."

Jeremy snickered. "No, you didn't."

"Oh, yes, I did." He gave Jeremy a light peck. "Superhot, superfun, supercute guy tells me nobody's ever really yanked his crank?" He waggled his eyebrows. "That right there is what I like to call a challenge, Mr. Jameson."

"And we all know how much you like to conquer a challenge." Jeremy snorted and shook his head.

"Yup." Reg dipped his chin in acknowledgement. "So, did I?"

"Consider me conquered." Jeremy rolled onto his back, flung his arms to the sides, and spread his legs. "Totally conquered."

"Yes!" Reg fisted his hand and threw his elbow back dramatically. "Mission accomplished."

"How do you have the energy to be goofy? I'm all melted over here."

"You're cute when you're melted." Reg kissed Jeremy's chest. "Hot too."

"Mmm, I might be hot, but this room isn't. Get your big body over here and serve as my personal heater."

"Pushy, pushy," Reg said, but he yanked the comforter out from under their bodies, draped himself over Jeremy, and then covered them with the blanket. "Better?" he asked.

"Mmm-hmm," Jeremy mumbled, his eyes already drooping closed.

Reg wrapped his arm around him and kissed his head.

Immediately, Jeremy turned into Reg's side and shoved his leg between Reg's knees. "I love you, Reg."

Reg watched him sleep, knowing for the first time that he wouldn't lose this, that it'd be his forever. With his heart full to bursting and a smile on his face, Reg finally closed his eyes. "I love you too, JJ."

CHAPTER 17

"HOLY crap!" Jeremy yelled when he woke up to Reg's face hovering inches from his. Reg was crouched over him, legs and arms on either side of him, staring. "You know it scares me when you do that!"

"I know." Reg smiled and kissed Jeremy's forehead. "But when you refuse to wake up, you leave me no other choice."

Jeremy grabbed the pillow, covered his face with it, and said, "I like it better when you wake me up with a blow job."

"I like that better too." Reg moved the pillow away from Jeremy's face and gave him a smoldering look that took his breath away. "You know how much I like it." Reg dragged his hard dick across Jeremy's thigh, reminding Jeremy of how turned on Reg got when he was going down on him. "But I think maybe you like doing it even more."

After a month and a half learning what he liked and what Reg liked in bed, Jeremy had figured out that he loved giving blow jobs. Loved it. Oftentimes, he'd come at the same time as Reg, humping his leg or the mattress. Other times it didn't even take that much stimulation, the taste of Reg's seed on his tongue enough to tip him over the edge.

"Unfortunately, that'll have to wait, because we have a flight to catch, and you've already overslept," Reg rumbled.

"I hate Bill," Jeremy whined as he thrust his hips up, looking for friction and coming up short. "The tour's done, and we're supposed to be on vacation, having adventures, and—" Jeremy gazed into Reg's eyes. "I think I might die if you don't touch me right now."

"How am I supposed to resist when you say things like that?" Reg grasped Jeremy's dick in his big hand and started stroking. "Love how hot you are for it all the time." He moved his fist up and down, rubbing his thumb over the crown on every upstroke. "Makes me fuckin' crazy knowing you had this in you all those years, but nobody else saw it."

"Only you." Jeremy gripped Reg's shoulders and whimpered. "Always you." He thrust his butt off the bed on the next stroke and came, moaning as Reg worked him through it, tugging and squeezing until his balls were drained and his body was trembling.

"Better?" Reg asked, his eyes twinkling.

"Yeah." Jeremy drew in a deep breath and sighed. His entire adult life he'd had a "take it or leave it" attitude about sex. A couple of months of getting sweaty with Reggie Moore, and he couldn't get enough. "Yeah, I feel better."

"Good." Reg wiped his hand on the sheet and then scooped Jeremy into his arms.

"What are you doing?" Jeremy asked, laughing as he threw his arms around Reg's impossibly broad shoulders.

"Carrying you into the shower so you don't get distracted. We are in serious danger of missing our flight."

Reg climbed off the bed, marched into the shower, and turned on the water. Once the spray was warm, he set Jeremy down.

"I don't care if we miss our flight," Jeremy said with a pout, which probably looked ridiculous, but he couldn't stop himself. "We're not supposed to be going back right now anyway."

Reg handed him the shampoo and started lathering his own hands with the soap. "If you want to record your next album with Frankie Z, then you have to go back now. You heard what Bill said. Frankie Z's retiring."

Jeremy rolled his eyes. "Nobody retires at forty, least of all the hottest producer in hip-hop. He'll be back within a year, two, max. Mark my words."

"Maybe so, but he says he's retiring, and you wanted to try something new and record with him. No reason to blow that chance." Reg tipped Jeremy's head under the water and dragged his fingers through it, pushing the suds out. "Besides, this way we can spend Christmas with our families, plan the wedding, and when you're done recording, we'll have our adventure in the form of a long honeymoon."

"I still don't like it." It made sense. Jeremy knew it made sense. But he resented anything and anyone that got in the way of his time with Reg. Even if that anything was studio time and that anyone was a producer he greatly admired. It was crazy and unexpected to enjoy being with a person more than he enjoyed playing music, but there it was. And it made him feel wonderful.

"Okay. All clean." Reg turned off the water. "Our bags are packed. I left clothes out for you to wear on the plane. Your hair stuff and toothbrush are on the counter." He tossed Jeremy a towel before stepping out of the tub and drying himself off. "Anything else you need?"

There were times Jeremy wanted to pinch himself to see if he was having an amazing dream. "Are you going to get sick of me?" He didn't realize he'd asked the question out loud until Reg responded.

"Hey," Reg said softly, dropping his towel to the ground before stepping back next to the tub. "What's going on in that head of yours?" He gripped Jeremy's elbow and helped him climb out, then he took the towel from Jeremy's hands and dried him off. "I adore you, JJ. You know that."

"I know." He did. He really did. There was no mistaking the way Reg's eyes got soft when he looked at him, the way his dick got hard, his voice gravelly. There was no missing the fact that Reg was constantly watching him, touching him, and smiling at something he said or did. "But look at what you put up with. You packed everything yourself, probably trying not to make noise so I wouldn't wake up. You had to think about what I'd want and leave it for me to use. You had to drag me out of bed and give me a hand job. You—"

"All right, that's enough." Reg put the towel over Jeremy's head and rubbed the wetness out. "Getting you off is one of life's greatest pleasures, superstar." He grasped

Jeremy's shoulders, walked him over to the sink, and readied his toothbrush. "And the rest of that stuff comes from being with the most talented musician of our generation. You're busy, you're tired, and you have a lot on your mind. If it's not concerts or albums or photographers, it's writing your next song." He kissed Jeremy's cheek. "Don't think I miss the little bars you hum during quiet moments or the way you text yourself lines for new songs." He tapped Jeremy's temple. "You have a lot happening here all the time. I get it."

All those things were true, but that didn't mean they weren't frustrating for other people. Jeremy had seen relationship after relationship fail because someone got tired of living in the shadows, of having the world revolve around their spouse. He'd heard people say those words to his mother, to acquaintances, to him. He could only imagine the same had been true for his father, though he doubted anyone who'd been with Beau Jameson would have expected anything different.

Jeremy didn't want that to happen with Reg. He wouldn't let it. "It won't bother you?" he said, biting his lip. "Because I can change. I can—"

"Don't you dare even think about it," Reg said firmly, his tone leaving no room for argument. He handed Jeremy his toothbrush, waited for him to start brushing, and then said, "I've already told you I love you just how you are. I don't want you to change."

Jeremy spit into the sink. "But taking care of me is like a full-time job. You'll feel ignored."

"Well, then, it's a good thing my boyfriend's loaded and I can do it full time." Reg gave him one of his sideways grins, and Jeremy melted.

"Fiancé," he corrected, touching Reg's chest.

Cupping his cheek, Reg smiled. "Fiancé." He pulled Jeremy into a hug, engulfing him in heat and strength. "And you never make me feel ignored, JJ. You make me feel like someone special."

"That's because you are," he whispered. "I love you so much, and I'm terrified of pushing you away."

"I won't let you."

Jeremy looked up, his heart in his throat. "Promise?"

"I do." Reg held Jeremy's face and gazed into his eyes. "This thing between us, it's forever."

Clutching Reg's forearms, Jeremy nodded and hoarsely said, "Yes." After a few seconds of silence with the air between them thick and electric, Jeremy said, "I want to get married soon. I don't want to put this off for months and months." He licked his lips. "I want a ring on your finger. I want legal papers. I want to call you husband. I want..." He didn't want to lose this man. He wanted to bind them together in every way he knew how. "Soon, yeah?"

Reg nodded. "Soon."

"Why is she calling me?" Jeremy stared at his phone

and tried to figure out what was happening.

"Only one way to find out," Reg said from the sofa where they'd been snuggling while looking at real-estate listings on the laptop.

Reg wanted to live close to the beach so they could learn to surf. Jeremy didn't care where he lived as long as it was with Reg, so he happily agreed. They'd been looking at listings for a few weeks but hadn't found the right place yet.

"I just talked to her a few weeks ago." Jeremy looked at the phone suspiciously. "There's no reason for her to call."

"It isn't a snake." Reg chuckled. "Answer the phone and talk to your mother."

As much as he'd resented being forced to come home instead of traveling the world with Reg, the previous couple of months had been wonderful. They'd celebrated Christmas with Reg's family, which had been slightly awkward at first, but once Reg's brother, sister-in-law, and mother had gotten past the star-struck stage, Jeremy had enjoyed spending time with them. And Reg had fit into Jeremy's life with his usual easygoing grace. Everyone who met him loved him, but he never took center stage, preferring to stand behind Jeremy, lending quiet support.

The only hitch so far had been wedding planning. Jeremy didn't have time to do it, and Reg hated it. They managed to fix that pretty quickly when Becky suggested a wedding planner. Reg asked for a small, simple ceremony. Jeremy's only request had been to make it happen quickly. It turned out late April was the best the planner could do.

They were two months out, and Jeremy was counting down the days.

And though Reg never said a word about it, Jeremy noticed things were easier in his life. Conflicts were resolved quickly and often without him getting involved. Arguments tended to deflate before they ever happened. Everyone who worked for him learned pretty quickly to go to Reg if they wanted to get something done, because if they went to Jeremy, he ignored them or yelled until Reg stepped in. So they left Jeremy alone, and he'd been able to focus on what he loved—his music and Reg.

His phone stopped ringing. "I guess she didn't need anything after all," he said as he started walking back toward the sofa. "So what were you saying about that one house? I know it's on the beach, but—"

His phone rang. He flinched, guessing it was his mother again and knowing what Reg would say.

"JJ, answer the phone right now." Reg set the laptop on the coffee table and sat up. "That's your mother calling."

Yeah, that. He knew Reg would say that.

"Hello?"

"Jeremy, thank goodness. I've been trying to reach you." For thirty seconds. She'd been trying for thirty seconds. "It seems there might be an issue, and I thought you'd want to know."

Without conscious thought, Jeremy hurried over to where Reg was sitting. Talking to his mother was stressful in and of itself. Having to deal with anything she was labeling an *issue* was sure to be worse.

"What issue?"

Whether in response to that question or Jeremy's expression he didn't know, but Reg suddenly looked concerned. He also looked inviting, one hand held out toward Jeremy and the other patting his muscular thighs. Jeremy climbed onto his lap.

"It seems Harold didn't take my decision not to star in his little project well."

That wasn't a surprise. The man had spent close to a year with Paula Radcliffe, and there had never been any doubt that he was in it for his career, not for his heart. Jeremy huddled close to Reg.

"What happened?" he asked.

"I'm afraid he became completely unglued. It was irrational for him to believe someone of my caliber would perform in a film without studio backing or a more prominent director. Unfortunately, there was no reasoning with him and listening to his constant demands became tedious, so I broke off the engagement."

"You were engaged?"

"Very briefly," his mother said. "Though the ring is lovely. I might have the stones set in a bracelet. Or perhaps a necklace. I'll speak with my jeweler soon and—"

"Mother," Jeremy said, trying to stay calm. "You said there's an issue?"

"Oh. Yes. Right. Harold claims to have a film."

"That's not a surprise, yeah? The man's a filmmaker."

"Yes. But this film stars you, darling. You and Reggie."

Jeremy's jaw dropped. "What are you talking about? Reggie and I never made any movies."

"That's what I've been trying to tell you. Harold procured footage of you in a compromising position."

"Compromising positi—what are you talking about?"

"A sex tape, dear. He has a sex tape of you and Reggie. He sent me a short clip, and he said he'd go public with the whole thing if I didn't agree to perform in his project. Of course I want to help you, but you know I can't. It's simply not possible for someone of my—"

"I know, Mother. Someone of your caliber can't be in a Harold West movie even though he's been sharing your bed for—"

"Jeremy, there is no reason to be crass. I didn't have to call you with this information. I would think you'd be grateful."

Yes. He was thrilled his mother had fucked over yet another up-and-comer with her version of the casting couch and he was the one taking the hit. After taking a deep breath, he said, "I apologize. Thanks for letting me know. I have to talk to Reg now."

"Of course, darling. Let's talk soon and schedule a lunch."

She hung up before he could say goodbye. Not that he cared.

"Damn it!" Jeremy shouted as he leapt from Reg's lap and threw his phone across the room. "Of all the stupid, selfish"—he kicked the coffee table—"things she could do, she had to fuck over a guy with a camera"—he walked over to the wall and started punching it—"and nothing to lo—"

"Stop." Reg circled his muscular arms around Jeremy's chest and yanked him back. "Tell me what happened," he said quietly.

"My mother!" Jeremy shouted. "That's what happened!"

"Okay." Reg pulled him to the couch, laid him on his back, and covered him with his bulky body. It was a little hard to breathe, but it made Jeremy feel better, safer, calmer. "What'd she do?"

"She pissed off that guy she was with—Harold West— by refusing to do his movie. I told you that's what would happen."

"Yup, you did." Reg buried his fingers in Jeremy's hair and massaged his scalp.

"Well, it turns out this guy has some balls but no common sense, and he thought he could blackmail Paula Radcliffe."

"How? Does he have dirt on her or something?"

Jeremy laughed, the sound high-pitched and bitter. "There is no dirt to be had on my mother. She is way too careful and way too...plastic for that. Nope. He did what he figured would be the next best thing—he got dirt on her son. Too bad he didn't realize that wouldn't do shit to help him because she doesn't care."

"What kind of dirt?" Reg growled, his expression stormy. It was hot and would have been arousing if the situation wasn't so horrible.

"A tape," Jeremy said. "A tape of us having sex."

Reg was quiet for a few seconds, and then he tilted his head to the side and said, "How is that possible? We've never recorded ourselves having sex."

It was a good question. "I don't know. I guess he could be lying, but I doubt it. My mother said he sent her a clip of it, and there's no way he would think she'd agree to make his movie without getting a copy of the whole thing." Jeremy bit his lip. "Maybe he filmed us."

"Where? I know we get carried away sometimes, but it's not like we've had sex in public, JJ. We're careful."

Careful was an understatement. Reg took Jeremy's privacy and security to level-red seriousness, always making sure Jeremy was protected and stepping between him and any paparazzi they encountered. That problem had thankfully improved significantly since Becky replaced Francis.

"I don't know," Jeremy said. He shook his head. "It doesn't make any sense."

"I'm calling the police." Reg got up. "This guy is trying to blackmail your mother. That's criminal. Plus, there's no way he could—"

"Reg, you can't." Jeremy grabbed his hand. "If you go to the police, my mother will be in the middle of it, and she'll be furious. You know how important her public image is to her."

"But it's her fault," Reg said in frustration. It was so rare for him to lose his cool that Jeremy was rendered speechless. "She acts like a...she doesn't handle things well, and you're stuck with the consequences, but you can't do anything to help yourself?"

Yeah. That was about right. "She's my mother." They weren't close and never would be. She wasn't a mother like Reg's mother. But she was the only family he had.

"Okay," Reg said, immediately calming down. "You're right. I'm sorry about that." He rubbed his palm over the back of his head and took a deep breath. "I'll call Bill and Becky. They'll know how to deal with this."

"Okay." Jeremy nodded. "What should I do?"

Reg flicked his gaze to the clock on the DVD player. "It's too late for anybody to fix this tonight. You go get in the shower, and I'll join you after I'm off the phone. Then we're going to bed."

"It's not even ten o'clock. You can't be tired."

"Who said anything about being tired? I said we're going to bed." He took both of Jeremy's hands in his and pulled him to his feet. "If we're starting a new porn career, I figure we better get some practice in." He winked. "We're going to be up for hours, superstar."

Jeremy snorted out a laugh. "Only you could find a way to make this funny." He rose to his tiptoes and kissed Reggie's cheek. "See you in the shower."

CHAPTER 18

"I HAVE a good handle on what happened, and I'm pretty sure I can contain it," Bill said the next morning in his office.

"So the tape is real?" Jeremy asked.

Reg reached for his hand and threaded their fingers together. He knew Jeremy had been holding out hope that Harold West had been lying.

"Oh, yes," Bill nodded. "I demanded a copy from Harold West. Told him I'd need to see it before I could determine what it was worth."

"And?"

"It's very real and very explicit. I watched it late last night, and I think I'll be ejaculating until fall."

"Dude!" Reg jerked his gaze toward Bill. "That's not cool."

"Maybe not, but it's true. Speaking of truths, I owe you two an apology for ever doubting the, uh, veracity of your relationship. I'm now intimately aware of how real it is."

Reg rolled his eyes. He was getting used to these people, but he'd never understand them. "So what happens now?"

"Don't worry. I'm working on negotiations," Bill said.

"I'm doing everything I can to hurry it along because I realize time is of the essence. By the end of the week, nobody but me should have a copy." He held his arms up. "I'll keep it in my bedroom safe, and I'm the only one with the combination."

"Is that a joke?" Reg asked. He looked at Jeremy for clarification. "Is he trying to be funny about that copy thing?"

Jeremy shook his head. "Bill isn't funny." He frowned. "Apparently he's a little pervy, but he's never funny."

"I've seen you two in bed," Bill reminded them. "I don't think I'm the only one in this room who can be described as pervy, and since I've already seen the video, several times, there's really no point in destroying my copy."

"Whatever." Reg shook his head and focused on bigger issues. "How'd they get a tape of us having sex? We're not out there going at it in public."

"They put a camera in your hotel room," Becky said.

Reg twisted around to see her walking into the office. "Hey," he said as he and Jeremy stood up. "I thought you said you were in New York."

"Oh, I was. But that was last night." She hurried over to them, kissed Reg's cheek, and gave Jeremy a hug. "I made sure to get the first flight out so I could make this meeting." She clapped her hands together. "And I have great news."

"Please have a seat," Bill said, pointing to Jeremy's chair. "I'm sure Jeremy wouldn't mind sharing with Reg."

"Dude!" Reg said again. "It's getting creepy now. Cut it out."

"What news?" Jeremy asked.

"The most important thing is that the copies are all gone." She flicked her gaze toward Bill and frowned. "Well, all but one."

"How?" Bill asked.

"After I got off the phone with Reg last night, I made some calls. Harold West got a visit from one of my friends who works for the FBI. He handed over his computer, and we were able to trace everywhere he'd sent the video. I got a call on my way here telling me the last one's been wiped, so you're good to go."

"You're sure?" Jeremy asked hopefully.

"Of course! I worked in the tech industry. I know how to follow trails. Harold West paid a bellhop to plant a camera in your room. The recording went straight to him, and he shared an abbreviated copy with your mother and a full copy with a friend of his who sent a copy to one person. Nobody else had it." She looked at Bill meaningfully. "Other than Bill."

"You're amazing," Jeremy said.

"Thanks, Becky." Reg smiled at her. "We're both grateful."

"Oh, please!" She waved the compliment away. "It wasn't a big deal. Besides, it's my job." Suddenly, the smile left her face and she looked at Bill. "Speaking of jobs, do you want to know how Harold West found out where Jeremy and Reg were staying so he could have the camera planted?"

"How?" Bill asked.

"From Francis Smith."

"But he doesn't do any work on Jeremy's file."

Becky crossed her arms over her chest and tapped her foot. "As long as he's working for you, he'll find a way to access the information."

"I want him gone," Reg said. "Enough is enough. I get giving a guy a chance. I even respect it. But this is—"

"I'll fire him today." Bill's look was murderous. "Jeremy, I'm truly sorry. I had no idea he'd do something like this."

There was a time when Reg was sure Jeremy would have yelled and thrown a fit, but he didn't do either. Instead he stepped closer to Reg, curling into his side, and said, "It's okay. We all make mistakes."

"Look at you," Reg whispered, pushing Jeremy's hair off his face.

"What?"

"You're not mad."

"Wouldn't change anything, right?"

Dipping his head down, Reg brushed his lips over Jeremy's. "That's right." He tugged Jeremy's bottom lip between both of his before slanting their mouths together and taking the kiss deeper. When Jeremy's heart was racing and his erection was pressing against Reg's thigh, he realized it was time to stop and go somewhere more private, so he pulled his mouth away.

"We're going to take off," he said to Bill and then looked around the room. "Where's Becky?"

"I told her we needed to talk about something confidential, so she left."

Reg hadn't heard that conversation, but then again,

he'd been distracted.

"Will it take long?" Jeremy asked, sounding annoyed.

Reg smiled, loving how eager Jeremy was to be alone with him.

"No," Bill said. "I just need you to sign a couple of papers."

"Oh, okay." Jeremy stepped over to Bill's desk, where he'd laid out the papers and a pen. "What are they?"

"A prenuptial agreement," Bill said.

Jeremy flinched and looked at Bill in horror. "I didn't ask you to have a prenup prepared."

"I realize that, but it's my job to think of these things."

"No." Jeremy shook his head. "I don't want that."

Bill sighed. "It's very standard language, Jeremy."

Jeremy ignored him and looked at Reg. "This wasn't my idea, and we're not going to sign it. Don't worry."

"I'm not worried." At least not about the document. Reg was, however, worried about how distraught Jeremy looked. He walked over to Jeremy and wrapped his arm around his shoulders. "What's wrong?"

"Reg already signed it," Bill said.

"What?" Jeremy shouted. "When?" He looked at Reg, pain in his eyes. "Why would you do that?"

Though he had no idea why Jeremy was so upset or what he'd done to cause it, Reg knew he had to make it better. "Yesterday, when you were in the studio and I was waiting in the lobby. Bill came by, talked to me, and I signed it. What's wrong?"

"And you didn't think to tell me?"

"You were excited to talk about your new song. Then we had dinner. I wanted to show you that house I found, and we were busy with that until your mother called and—" He took in a deep breath. "I'm sorry. I should have said something, but I didn't realize it was a big deal. I figured that's how things are done in your world."

"That is how things are done in his world," Bill confirmed. "Which is something you know very well, Jeremy. Your mother's entered into enough of these things to keep a lawyer employed full-time. There is no reason to get hysterical. Reggie is well provided for in the event of termination and—"

"No!" Jeremy shouted. "No. No. No." He lunged for the table, grabbed the papers, and started tearing them up.

"Jeremy!" Bill shouted. "Those were the originals with Reg's signature."

"Good." He kept tearing. "They're gone. It's over." He glared at Reg and held out a shaky finger. "You will not sign anything like this again."

"Okay. I won't." Reg nodded quickly. "JJ, come here." He opened his arms and whimpered in relief when Jeremy came to him. "I don't know what I did wrong, but I'm sorry. I didn't mean to hurt your feelings."

"I know." Jeremy buried his face in Reg's chest. "I shouldn't have freaked out like that, but do you know what a prenup is for?"

"It's to protect your assets when the marriage

dissolves," Bill supplied. "And like I've said repeatedly, it's very standard."

"When the marriage dissolves," Jeremy repeated, not looking away from Reg. "Our marriage will not dissolve."

"Of course it won't," Bill said, the sarcasm clear from his tone. "In which case the agreement is meaningless. But, in the very unlikely event things don't work out—"

"I am not signing a prenup," Jeremy growled as he rounded on Bill. "Reg is not signing a prenup. You work for me, and I am telling you to let it go."

"Fine, but if you change your mi—"

"I'm not going to change my mind." Looking at Reg, Jeremy lowered his voice. "Take me home. I don't want to be here anymore."

Reg nodded and led Jeremy out of Bill's office. His mind was reeling, trying to understand exactly what was going on in Jeremy's head. He'd figure it out later. They'd talk about it. But first, they needed to be alone. Jeremy was shaking apart, and Reg had a clawing need to hold him together.

"Do you want to talk about it?" Reg asked once they were in the house.

They hadn't talked on the way home, but Jeremy had held his hand the entire time, which eased his worry.

"I want to talk about everything with you." Jeremy

pulled off his shirt. "I never want secrets between us." He unbuttoned his jeans. "But right now, I want to go to bed. I want to feel you."

Nodding, Reg took hold of Jeremy's hand and led him to their bedroom. He removed his clothes slowly, watching Jeremy do the same. Once they were both naked, he came to Jeremy, curled around him—his chest to Jeremy's back—and caressed his shoulders before sliding his hands down his chest.

"I'm here, JJ." Reg ground his hardening dick against Jeremy's ass. "Tell me what you need." He kissed the sensitive spot behind Jeremy's ear and then trailed kisses all the way down his neck.

Shivering, Jeremy turned around and kissed Reg's chest. At first the touches were light, but when he reached Reg's nipple, he flicked his tongue over it and then drew it into his mouth, suckling.

"Mmm, feels good." Reg cupped the back of his head and held him in place. "Love when you do that."

Rocking his groin against Reg's leg, Jeremy made an aroused sound and sucked harder before swiping his tongue over the pebbled bud and working on the other side. Reg dragged his hands down Jeremy's back and cupped his ass, squeezing and massaging. They mapped each other's bodies, tasted each other's skin, luxuriating in the feeling of being together.

"Wanna suck you," Jeremy mumbled between nips and licks. He dropped his hand to Reg's dick and stroked. "Will you sit at the end of the bed?"

"Uh-huh." Reg stepped toward the bed, pulling Jeremy with him. When the mattress hit the backs of his legs, he sat down and spread his thighs. "All yours," he said, gazing up at Jeremy.

"Yeah, you are." Jeremy smiled down at him, the stress from earlier banked, and then he dropped to his knees and buried his face in Reg's groin. "Mmm, love how you smell." He licked each of Reg's balls. "Love how you taste too." He cupped the sensitive orbs with one hand and stroked Reg's erection with the other. "Love how you're hot and silky." He lapped at the drops forming at Reg's slit and moaned before opening his lips wide and pushing his mouth over Reg's flesh, taking him in.

"JJ!" Reg shouted, his hands going to Jeremy's head, touching, petting, but not pushing. "So good."

"Mmm-hmm," Jeremy moaned, sucking his way up voraciously before pushing his lips down again. "Mmm-hmm." His pace was fast and focused, bringing Reg to the brink quickly.

"Close already," Reg rasped. "Damn, you're amazing."

With a final suck, Jeremy popped off his dick. "Want you to come inside me." He kissed Reg's balls and then stood. "Stay there. I want to ride you."

"Okay." Reg grasped Jeremy's arm and tugged him down, kissing him gently before releasing him to get the lube. He was back in seconds, the bottle in his hand, and Reg leaned forward and licked the head of his rigid dick. "Let me get you slick?" he asked. "You know how much I love to put my fingers in your ass."

Trembling in response to the raw words, Jeremy nodded and drizzled lube into Reg's waiting hand. Reg curved his arms around Jeremy's back, pulling his cheek to the side with one hand and massaging the puckered skin with the other. At the same time, he nuzzled Jeremy's groin.

"Ah!" Jeremy shouted when Reg slid a finger inside. He spread his legs wider and grabbed Reg's shoulders for support. "So good."

Smiling, Reg moved his finger in and out, touching the silky skin and reminding the muscle of the pleasure he'd bring. Jeremy relaxed quickly, and Reg added a second finger, taking Jeremy's dick into his mouth at the same time.

"Reg!" Jeremy cried out. "Yes."

Reg twisted his hand as he sucked, making sure Jeremy felt him everywhere. "You're ready," he said when he felt Jeremy's legs shaking and tasted his pre-ejaculate. "You still want a ride, or do you want to finish like this?"

"Want you inside," Jeremy answered.

Reg kissed Jeremy's hip, reached for the lube, and slicked his swollen cock. "C'mere." He smiled. "Make us both feel good."

Nodding, Jeremy planted first one knee and then the other on the mattress, straddling Reg's lap. Reg grasped his dick, holding it steady while Jeremy slowly lowered himself, taking him in inch by inch until his ass was nestled on Reg's pubes.

"God, I love that." Jeremy buried his face in Reg's neck and huffed out hot breaths against his skin.

"Me too." Reg gently caressed Jeremy's flank. "Ready to move?"

"Yeah." Jeremy straightened his back, held onto Reg's shoulders, and slid up.

"Uh-huh," Reg groaned. "Just like that."

He held on to Jeremy's hips, helping him move up and down while at the same time bucking his own backside off the bed and thrusting his dick in and out of Jeremy's welcoming passage. With their gazes locked, they moved in concert, both of them panting and grunting, chasing their pleasure.

"Reg," Jeremy warned after a couple of minutes.

"Me too," Reg confirmed, wrapping his hand around Jeremy's cock and stroking quickly. "Me too."

Jeremy increased his pace, and his moans got louder, faster, until finally he threw his head back and cried Reg's name as he came.

"Yes," Reg hissed, bucking up once, twice more, before pulsing deep inside Jeremy's body.

He groaned at the pleasure, continuing to rock his hips, the movements gradually slowing until they were both spent. Jeremy stayed on his lap, kissing his neck and hugging him. Reg caressed Jeremy's back, massaged his scalp, and held him until he slipped out of his body.

"Let's get under the blanket," he suggested. "It's a little cold."

With a nod, Jeremy slid off his lap. They pulled the soft

comforter up and crawled underneath, Jeremy immediately finding his spot at Reg's side, his head pillowed on Reg's chest.

"Should we talk about earlier?" Jeremy asked.

Realizing how shaken up Jeremy had been and how important it was for him to know they could always—would always—be open with each other, Reg nodded. "Yes," he said. "I know you were upset that I forgot to tell you about signing that prenup, and you're right. I promise you, it wasn't intentional. It's just that it wasn't a big deal to me."

"It is to me." Jeremy combed his fingers through the hair on Reg's chest and sighed. "If things don't work out, it'll be my fault."

"Don't do that." Reg squeezed Jeremy tightly. "I hate when you run yourself down."

"I trust you, Reg. I trust you more than I trust myself. If I fuck up so badly that you want to leave me, then you should take half of everything. Maybe I'll remember that before fucking up. And if I'm in some crazy place where I even think about leaving you, then you can remind me what else I'll be losing. I'm not going into this marriage with me having all the power." He looked at Reg imploringly. "I don't want an easy out. I need you in my life. Hard or not, I want this to work."

With his heart full to bursting, Reg nodded. "It will work." He leaned down and pressed his forehead to Jeremy's. "I know you're scared of falling into the same patterns as your parents, but I love you, and I won't let that happen."

Jeremy relaxed in his arms. "And you know what else?"

"What?" Jeremy rasped.

"You won't let it happen either." Reg rubbed their noses together. "Because you love me just as much."

Jeremy beamed. "Yeah, I do."

THE END

(But wait…there's more—bonus scene ahead.)

BONUS SCENE

Denise from Shh Moms Reading asked for more of Reg and JJ so I wrote this short bonus scene shortly after the book's original release. I hope you enjoy it. — CC

"Hey, superstar. You're home early." Reg smiled at him, his entire face lighting up and his brown eyes warm and soft. "You been here long?"

He walked over to Jeremy as he rubbed a towel over his short brown hair.

"No. Only about ten minutes." Jeremy dragged his gaze from Reg's gorgeous face to his broad shoulders—one of which sported a black tattoo that Jeremy had mapped with his tongue more times than he could remember—over to a rippling set of six-pack abs, and down to a thick dick outlined in wet swim trunks.

"How was your day?" Reg looped his towel around Jeremy's neck and then stepped close as he tugged him forward and gazed down at him.

"Goo... Good." Even after two years, Jeremy still had trouble talking when faced with a partially undressed and, by the feel of the hard-on pressing into his hip, very aroused

Reggie Moore. "My day was good."

"The meeting with the new producer went well?" Reg wedged his leg between Jeremy's thighs and grazed his teeth over Jeremy's neck.

"Uh-huh." Jeremy trembled and grasped Reg's hips. "You were right. I like him and our styles will mesh well."

"Good." Using his nose, Reg tipped Jeremy's chin up and then began nibbling and sucking on his neck. "When will you start recording?"

"We're meeting at the studio on Monday and—" A well-placed shift of Reg's thigh had Jeremy losing his train of thought and gasping. "Do that again," he whispered.

"What? This?" Reg asked as he pinched one of Jeremy's nipples and rubbed against his balls.

"Yeah." Jeremy swallowed hard. "Yeah, that."

"How about we get your pants off and I do it with my mouth?"

Whimpering in response, Jeremy sought out Reg's lips and pressed their mouths together.

"Mmm, JJ," Reg moaned and slipped his tongue into Jeremy's mouth as he unbuttoned and unzipped his jeans. "Love you."

Reg was always generous with his affection, but Jeremy's heart rejoiced no matter how many times he heard the words or saw the fond expression on Reg's face when he looked at him. "I watched you surf," Jeremy said as Reg slipped his large hand inside Jeremy's jeans and palmed his package.

"I'm getting better at it," Reg said, giving him a sideways grin.

"You're amazing at it." Jeremy bucked into Reg's touch. "You're amazing at everything."

"It's fun." Reg glanced down and his eyes heated. "Damn, I love your cock." He dropped to his knees and, without delay, yanked Jeremy's jeans and briefs to his ankles and began licking him from root to crown. "Fucking love it." He cupped Jeremy's testicles and then lowered his lips to them. "And you have the best nuts." He buried his face in Jeremy's groin and inhaled deeply before sucking each of his balls into his mouth.

"Reg!" Jeremy shouted and grasped Reg's shoulders as his dick was engulfed in wet heat.

Bobbing his head and flicking his tongue over Jeremy's sensitive skin, Reg sucked him hard.

Unable to keep still, Jeremy rocked his hips and watched as his erection slid in and out of Reg's mouth. "I'm already close," Jeremy said, in awe and disappointment. It never ceased to amaze him how quickly and easily Reg could turn him on and he didn't want the pleasure to stop. Of course, who wouldn't be uncontrollably aroused by the sight of handsome, strong Reggie Moore on his knees?

"Don't come yet," Reg said. He rubbed Jeremy's cockhead over his lips and lapped at Jeremy's slit. "I want you to fuck me." With his gaze locked to Jeremy's, he opened his mouth and dropped it over Jeremy's dick again.

Knowing he needed to stop, but unable to keep himself

from pumping his hips, Jeremy begged for help. "Reg, feels too good. I can't hold it back if you—" He groaned. "Reggie, please."

With a huge grin, Reg popped off his cock and licked his lips. "Mmm, love that." He jumped to his feet, unlaced the ties on his board shorts, and then shoved them down, exposing his huge dick. "Love feeling it in my ass just as much."

Despite being so hard he was shaking, Jeremy laughed. Reg's happiness was infectious. He made everything fun—cooking, work interviews, sex, life. "Where are we doing this?" Jeremy asked as he toed off his shoes and stepped out of the clothing pooled around his ankles. "Please don't say the bedroom. It's too far." Their house wasn't big by his mother's standards or those of anybody else in his line of work—rock stars with Oscar winning parents were expected to live in ten thousand square foot mansions, not two thousand square foot beach houses—but the bedroom was on the second floor and Jeremy was too turned on for even that minor of a delay.

"Over the back of the couch," Reg rasped, his already deep voice scratchy. "We can watch the sunset at the same time." The large picture windows and ocean views were the reasons they'd bought the bungalow. Plus, the huge lot was right on the sand on a private beach.

"Why are you still dressed?" Reg asked as he took hold of Jeremy's T-shirt and yanked it up.

"You distracted me," Jeremy said.

"Who me?" Reg grinned, curved his arms around

Jeremy's waist, and squeezed his ass. "How'd I do that?"

Jeremy tipped his head up and fell into Reg's adoring gaze. "You were here," he whispered as he raised his hand to touch Reg's face. "That's all it takes."

"I'm always here, superstar." Reg turned his face and kissed Jeremy's palm. "Where you go, I go."

"I know." Jeremy swallowed thickly. "I love you."

"I love you too." Reg leaned down and suckled on Jeremy's earlobe. "And I want you."

Even without the words, Jeremy had known that. Reg's erection was pressed against him like a brand, his hands were everywhere—touching Jeremy's ass, his hips, his back, and he was crowding Jeremy toward the couch. Not a day went by that Reg didn't make him feel desired, not because of his money or his connections or his fame, but because of himself, just his needy, temperamental, socially-awkward self.

"Look at that sky," Reg whispered into his ear once he had them situated behind the couch, his chest pressed against Jeremy's back. "All those oranges and reds swirled together. Gorgeous, isn't it?"

It wasn't as gorgeous as the wall of muscle behind him, but Jeremy nodded. "Yeah." He leaned back against Reg and stroked his hip. "It is." He didn't remember ever watching a sunset or sunrise before Reg had come into his life, but since then, he'd seen them from all over the globe. Sometimes Reg would stop him on a street corner or pull him outside a hotel room onto a balcony and make him stop everything for ten minutes just to look at the sky. "It's my favorite one."

"This sunset?" Reg asked as he slid his hand around Jeremy's hip and took hold of his erection, smoothing slick liquid over him. "Why?"

Tipping his head back, Jeremy met Reg's gaze. "This one's ours," he explained, and he knew Reg would understand. Their home wasn't fancy or new. The walls were painted wood panels, the floors a scratched up pine, and the whole structure would fit in the living rooms of some of the houses he'd lived in growing up, but this place was their sanctuary, their space, their home. His and Reg's. It was the first home he'd ever had.

"I know," Reg said. He flipped Jeremy around and kissed him tenderly, keeping his hot, talented hand on Jeremy's cock. "I have a fun idea."

"Fun like Bill will need to up the dosage of his blood pressure medication again?" Jeremy asked, knowing Reg's idea of fun often had an element of 'Are you out of your ever-loving mind?' danger.

"What your manager doesn't know can't hurt him, but I don't mean that kind of fun anyway." Reg kissed his nose. "What do you say we pull out my old tent, set it up on the beach, and camp tonight?

"You want to camp outside in front of our own house?"

"Uh-huh. We can make a fire and roast marshmallows. What do you say?"

His heart full to bursting, Jeremy said, "I love s'mores."

"Awesome." Reg beamed. "But first"—he waggled

his eyebrows—"you need to do me before the sun goes all the way down." He reached his long arms out to the sides, grabbed the back of the couch, and then spread his thickly muscled legs and bent over.

"Look at you," Jeremy said. He shivered in anticipation. "You're gorgeous." He picked up the lube from where Reg had dropped it on the end table and drizzled a little into Reg's crease, wanting to make sure he was slick and ready. As usual, Reg was totally relaxed, letting him touch and explore, trusting him completely. "Ready for me?" Jeremy asked.

"Always," Reg said as he tilted his ass up, exposing himself further.

He leaned over Reg's back, pressed his cockhead against Reg's pucker, and slowly slid into tight heat.

"Ungh, that's good," Reg moaned. "Do me slow, superstar."

And Jeremy did. He draped himself over Reg's broad back, dragged his palms from Reg's shoulders, over his arms, and to his hands, and threaded his fingers with Reg's as he rocked his hips, thrusting in and out. Reg moved with him, his ass going forward and back, taking him in all the way and squeezing around his cock as he pulled out.

"You feel so good," Jeremy said. "Always so good with you."

"Mmm-hmm." Reg twisted his head back and landed a messy kiss on Jeremy's lips. "We're good together, JJ." He squeezed Jeremy's hand, their fingers wrapped tightly, and groaned when Jeremy altered his angle. "Right there." His eyes rolled back. "Keep hitting me there."

Jeremy's balls drew up close to his body and his cock throbbed in reaction to the pleasure on Reg's face. He loved that he did that, that he gave it to Reg. "Gonna," he said. "Soon."

Nodding, Reg pushed back against him harder and faster. He managed to spread his legs wider and take Jeremy in deeper, and when he squeezed his passage tightly over Jeremy's prick, the end was there.

"Reg!" Jeremy shouted and arched his back as he pounded hard for three strokes and then held himself deep inside Reg's welcoming body and came. "Reg," he whispered when he was spent, his entire body trembling.

After releasing one of Jeremy's hands, Reg shifted his arm down and then began moving rhythmically beneath him as he chased his own release.

"That's mine," Jeremy said. He gripped Reg's hip as he dropped to his knees. "Fuck my mouth."

In a flash, Reg turned around and shoved his cock between Jeremy's lips. The skin was tight and purple, Reg's need so intense. The veins in Reg's neck bulged as he grunted and pumped. "JJ," he moaned. "Damn, yes."

Holding onto Reg's thighs, Jeremy kept his mouth lax and his throat open, enjoying the taste of Reg's cock and need until, with a shout of joy, Reg threw his head back and shot long streams of ejaculate onto Jeremy's waiting tongue. Gently, Jeremy petted Reg's thigh and licked him clean as he came down and caught his breath.

"Hi," Reg said from above him, his eyes twinkling. "That was fun."

"Yeah," Jeremy agreed. "It was."

He took Reg's hands when they were offered and then Reg pulled him to his feet and enveloped him in a hug. "What do you say we take a shower and then I'll dig out my camping gear and you can get the graham crackers, chocolate, and marshmallows?" He kissed Jeremy's cheek and rubbed their noses together. "We have some steaks in the fridge so we can grill those up with a couple of potatoes."

"Sounds like a perfect plan." And a perfect night. And a perfect life.

THE END

REVIEWS

He Completes Me: When I'm in the mood for a romantic, highly entertaining story, time and time again I'll reach for a book written by Cardeno C.

— *Top2Bottom Reviews*

The One Who Saves Me: This author has a way of making every story unique, sexy, loving, emotional, and just plain wonderful.

— *Rainbow Book Reviews for*

Walk With Me: Whew. Cardeno C. knows how to write those sex scenes.

— *The Romance Reviews*

McFarland's Farm: The romance was fabulous, sexy and so hot.

— *The TBR Pile*

The Half of Us: Gah! If you want good MM Contemporary than Cardeno. C is your go to.

— *Live, Read, Breathe*

Jumping In: Loved, Loved, Loved this book! It was the perfect Valentine's week read and hit all my squishy feelings.

— *Guilty Indulgence*

ABOUT THE AUTHOR

Cardeno C.—CC to friends—is a hopeless romantic who wants to add a lot of happiness and a few *awwws* into a reader's day. Writing is a nice break from real life as a corporate type and volunteer work with gay rights organizations. Cardeno's stories range from sweet to intense, contemporary to paranormal, long to short, but they always include strong relationships and walks into the happily-ever-after sunset.

Email: cardenoc@gmail.com

Website: www.cardenoc.com

Twitter: https://twitter.com/cardenoc

Facebook: http://www.facebook.com/CardenoC

Pinterest: http://www.pinterest.com/cardenoC

Blog: http://caferisque.blogspot.com

OTHER BOOKS BY CARDENO C.

SIPHON
Johnnie

HOPE
McFarland's Farm
Jesse's Diner

PACK
Blue Mountain
Red River *(coming soon)*

HOME
He Completes Me
Home Again
Just What the Truth Is
Love at First Sight
The One Who Saves Me
Where He Ends and I Begin
Walk With Me

FAMILY
The Half of Us
Something in the Way He Needs
Strong Enough
More Than Everything

MATES
In Your Eyes
Until Forever Comes
Wake Me Up Inside

NOVELS
Strange Bedfellows
Perfect Imperfections
Control (with Mary Calmes)

NOVELLAS
A Shot at Forgiveness
All of Me
Places in Time
In Another Life & Eight Days
Jumping In

AVAILABLE NOW

Blue Mountain
(A Pack Story)

Exiled by his pack as a teen, Omega wolf Simon Moorehead learns to bury his gentle nature in the interest of survival. When a hulking, rough-faced Alpha catches Simon on pack territory, he tries to escape what he's sure will be imminent death. But instead of killing him, the Alpha takes Simon home.

A man of action, Mitch Grant uproots his life to support his brother in leading the Blue Mountain pack. Mitch lives on the periphery, quietly protecting everyone, but always alone. A mate is a dream come true for Mitch, and he won't let little things like Simon's rejections, attacks, and insults get in their way. With patience, seduction, and genuine care, Mitch will ride out the storm while Simon slays his own ghosts and Mitch's loneliness.

McFarland's Farm
(A Hope Story)

Wealthy, attractive Lucas Reika treats life like a party, moving from bar to bar and man to man. Thumbing his nose at his restaurateur father's demand that he earn his keep, Lucas instead seduces a valued employee in the kitchen of their flagship restaurant, earning himself an ultimatum: lose access to his father's money or stay in the middle of nowhere with a man he has secretly lusted over from afar.

Quiet, hard-working Jared McFarland loves his farm on the outskirts of Hope, Arizona, but he aches to have someone to come home to at the end of the day. Jared agrees to take in his longtime crush as a favor. But when Lucas invades his heart in addition to his space, Jared has to decide how much of himself he's willing to risk and figure out if he can offer Lucas enough to keep him after his father's punishment is over.

In Another Life
At age eighteen, Shiloh Raben is tired. He no longer has the energy to deal with mean classmates, inner doubt, and fear of familial rejection, so he takes a razor to his wrist. When he wakes up in the hospital, Shiloh meets Travis Kahn, the EMT who saved him and didn't leave his side.

Travis is handsome, smart, and funny—the type of guy Shiloh would never be brave enough to approach. But his near- death experience has an unusual side effect: the life that f lashed before his eyes wasn't the one he had already lived, but rather the one he could live. With visions of a future by Travis's side, Shiloh will find the strength to confront his fears and build a life worth fighting for.

Eight Days
Childhood family friends, Maccabe Fried and Josh Segal have always gotten along despite having nothing in common. Maccabe is an athlete with dreams of playing professional baseball. Josh is an aspiring architect with dreams of being with Maccabe. Despite all odds, both dreams come true.

Maccabe and Josh fall into a long-distance romance, which is everything Josh thought he wanted. But after years of hiding from the world, Josh wants to bring their relationship into the open. When Maccabe refuses, Josh is faced with a tough decision: stay with the man he loves or live the life he deserves. No matter the choice, somebody's bound to get hurt. Thankfully, in the season of miracles, there's always hope for a happy ending.

Walk With Me

(A Home Story)

When Eli Block steps into his parents' living room and sees his childhood crush sitting on the couch, he starts a shameless campaign to seduce the young rabbi. Unfortunately, Seth Cohen barely remembers Eli and he resolutely shuts down all his advances. As a tenuous and then binding friendship forms between the two men, Eli must find a way to move past his unrequited love while still keeping his best friend in his life. Not an easy feat when the same person occupies both roles.

Professional, proper Seth is shocked by Eli's brashness, overt sexuality, and easy defiance of societal norms. But he's also drawn to the happy, funny, light-filled man. As their friendship deepens over the years, Seth watches Eli mature into a man he admires and respects. When Seth finds himself longing for what Eli had so easily offered, he has to decide whether he's willing to veer from his safe life-plan to build a future with Eli.